PROVING COLTON'S INNOCENCE

Lara Lacombe

Special thanks and acknowledgment are given to
Lara Lacombe for her contribution to
The Coltons of Grave Gulch miniseries.

Recycling programs
for this product may
not exist in your area.

ISBN-13: 978-1-335-75954-2

Proving Colton's Innocence

This edition published by arrangement with Harlequin Books S.A.

For questions and comments about the quality of this book, please contact us at CustomerService@Harlequin.com.

Harlequin Enterprises ULC
22 Adelaide St. West, 40th Floor
Toronto, Ontario M5H 4E3, Canada
www.Harlequin.com

Printed in U.S.A.

Time to lay his cards on the table. "Randall is going to be furious you're out of jail. I think he's going to escalate his behavior and come after you."

The color drained from Jillian's face as she processed his words. "So you paid my bail to use me as bait?"

Her voice was low, but not from shock. As Baldwin watched, he could practically see her anger building.

"Yes, but it's not as bad as you think," he said.

The glare she sent across the table hit him like a dagger. "Enlighten me," she said through clenched teeth.

"You don't have to worry about Randall getting to you, because you won't be alone."

"How do you figure that?" she retorted. "Am I supposed to hire a bodyguard or something?"

Baldwin leaned back and offered what he hoped was a reassuring smile. "Nope. That's what I'm for."

* * *

The Coltons of Grave Gulch: Falling in love is the most dangerous thing of all...

* * *

Dear Reader,

Welcome back to Grave Gulch! I don't know about you, but I was so happy to see Jillian Colton get her story.

This book was a lot of fun to write. One of my favorite romance tropes is enemies to lovers, and while Baldwin and Jillian aren't exactly enemies, they definitely don't start out as friends. Baldwin is a quiet character, preferring to act rather than speak. He seems to operate without any trace of emotion, but as Jillian finds out, he feels very deeply. As for Jillian, she's used to doing everything on her own. She has a hard time adjusting to the idea of relying on anyone, much less someone like Baldwin.

I hope you enjoy getting to know these two and discovering how the events in Grave Gulch are resolved. As always, happy reading!

Lara

Lara Lacombe earned a PhD in microbiology and immunology and worked in several labs across the country before moving into the classroom. Her day job as a college science professor gives her time to pursue her other love—writing fast-paced romantic suspense with smart, nerdy heroines and dangerously attractive heroes. She loves to hear from readers! Find her on the web or contact her at laralacombewriter@gmail.com.

Books by Lara Lacombe

Harlequin Romantic Suspense

The Coltons of Grave Gulch

Guarding Colton's Child
Proving Colton's Innocence

The Rangers of Big Bend

Ranger's Justice
Ranger's Baby Rescue
The Ranger's Reunion Threat
Ranger's Family in Danger

The Coltons of Mustang Valley

Colton's Undercover Reunion

Deadly Contact
Fatal Fallout
Lethal Lies
Killer Exposure
Killer Season

Visit the Author Profile page at
Harlequin.com for more titles.

This one is for A and A. To be fair, they're all for you two, but let's make this one official.

Chapter 1

Jillian Colton had just stepped out of the shower when the doorbell rang.

She frowned as she reached for her towel. It was after ten at night—not exactly the usual time for a social call. Probably just a neighbor dropping off a misdelivered package, she decided, wrapping a second towel around her wet hair. Certainly nothing to get excited about.

But as she continued to dry off, the doorbell rang again, followed a few seconds later by a loud pounding on her door.

Maybe not a package after all, she mused.

"Coming!" she yelled as she slipped into her bedroom and hastily dressed in a pair of sweatpants and a long-sleeved T-shirt that had seen better days. She unwound the towel from her hair and finger-combed through the long strands. Then she grabbed the baseball bat that was leaning against the wall by her bed and headed down the hall.

The odds that someone hostile was standing outside her door were slim, but as a crime-scene investigator with the Grave Gulch Police Department, Jillian knew all too well what could happen to someone who let down their guard. And though her brother had recently killed Len Davison, the serial killer who had been terrorizing Grave Gulch over the last eleven months, there was still one man who had yet to be found: Randall Bowe.

Her former coworker had been on the run for months after the GGPD discovered he was tampering with evidence. His actions had led to wrongful convictions, while allowing guilty criminals to walk free. It was a mess the police were still trying to clean up, and likely would be for a while.

Still, Jillian had to admit that a small part of her was glad she no longer had to work with Randall. The man had been an insufferable know-it-all and deeply unpleasant. She'd like nothing more than to correct his sabotage and move on with her life and career. But it wasn't that simple; Bowe had been emailing and texting her lately, making it difficult for her to forget about him completely.

Which was why she now stood by her front door, gripping a baseball bat, as the pounding started up again. It was hard to imagine that Bowe was standing on her welcome mat, but she wasn't going to take any chances.

"Jillian? Are you there?"

Jillian relaxed as she recognized the voice—it was Grace Colton, one of her cousins, and a newer cop on the GGPD force.

She propped the baseball bat in the corner by the door and unlocked it. "Grace, what's going…?" The words died in her throat as she opened the door and caught sight of the number of people standing on the other side.

Grace gave her an apologetic look, but didn't speak. Jillian's eyes darted next to the acting police chief, Brett Shea, who was sporting a worried frown. Behind them stood two uniformed officers and a third man Jillian didn't recognize.

"Ah, what's all this?" she asked. Worry made her stomach feel tight, and she glanced from Grace to Brett, searching for a clue as to why they were at her home so late. Based on their expressions, something must be horribly wrong.

"We need to come inside, Jillian," Brett said. His voice was gentle, but firm. "We have a warrant to search your condo."

"What?!" Jillian stood rooted to the spot as an icy shock spread through her body, leaving numbness in its wake. "A warrant?" she repeated, certain she had misheard. "I don't understand."

"Step aside, Ms. Colton." The stranger standing behind Brett spoke up, his tone impatient. "You're already in serious trouble. You don't want to add obstructing an investigation to the list."

Brett turned and glared at the man. "That's enough," he said shortly. Then he faced Jillian again. "It's true," he said, pulling a folded piece of paper from his back pocket. Jillian took it from him, her eyes going wide as she recognized the legal document.

She shook her head as she stared at the text on the page, not really reading the words. "There must be some mistake. What's going on here?"

"Jillian." Grace stepped forward and placed her hands on Jillian's shoulders. Her green eyes were full of sympathy and worry, a combination that made Jillian's heart skip a beat. "You need to let us in. We have to do our jobs."

It finally sank in that she didn't have a choice. Grace, Brett and the others were here to search her place, and they would do it with or without her cooperation.

"Of course," she said dully, stepping aside as she opened the door wider.

Grace gave her shoulders a squeeze before releasing her. Brett nodded as he walked past, his lips pressed together in a thin line. The two uniformed officers slipped in without acknowledging her. Then the stranger walked inside, spearing her with a look of contempt as he entered her home.

Jillian tried to gather her thoughts as she shut the door. She turned around in time to see the two uniformed officers walk into her kitchen and heard the sounds of drawers opening as they began their search.

Brett stood in the middle of her living room, glancing around with an expression that was part misery, part embarrassment. Grace avoided her gaze, instead focusing on the bookshelves against the far wall. The stranger, whoever he was, had already started poking through her desk drawer. She narrowed her eyes as she watched his hands dig through her papers; even though there wasn't anything especially personal there, the fact that someone she didn't know was in her space was enough to jolt her out of her initial shock.

Jillian walked over to Brett. "What's this about?" She kept her voice low, hoping the stranger digging through her desk wouldn't overhear. He'd been quite eager to burst in, and she got the impression he was itching to arrest her.

Brett turned to face her, the corners of his mouth turned down. "I know it's all here," she said, lifting the warrant she still held. "But I'm not in the mood to read at the moment."

"There was a burglary early this morning," he said, his tone pained. "A rich widow living on the posh side of town."

Jillian nodded. "Ian mentioned it today," she said, referring to one of the forensic scientists she worked with. "What about it? Is there some connection to the other cases?"

Grave Gulch had seen a rash of robberies over the last few weeks, each one targeting homes in the richer, western part of the city. The thief liked jewelry, as that was the only thing missing from each home. Jillian had collected and processed evidence for all the other cases, but so far, there weren't any leads.

Brett rubbed the back of his head and frowned. "See, that's the thing, Jillian—" he began.

"I'd say there's definitely a connection."

She turned at the interruption to find the stranger standing behind her, a knowing smirk on his face.

"I'm sorry, who the hell are you?" Something about this man was rubbing her the wrong way, causing her usual good manners to fly out the window.

"Eric Wainwright. Grave Gulch IAB." He watched her closely, as though he expected her to react to his announcement that he worked for the internal affairs bureau of the police department.

Jillian wasn't about to give him the satisfaction. "Uh-huh," she said. "And you're here because?"

Wainwright stuck his hands in his pockets "The thing is, Ms. Colton, you're not only an employee of the Grave Gulch Police Department, but you're also related to several people on the force."

"I see," she said. "So you're here to insult my family members by insinuating they wouldn't follow all proper procedures while investigating someone named Colton?" On one level it made sense—she did have a lot of family members on the force. In fact, Grace herself had recently been the subject of an Internal Affairs investigation. But Camden, the IA officer in charge of that investigation and now Grace's serious boyfriend, hadn't been so rude about it.

From the corner of her eye, she saw Grace smile as she walked into Jillian's bedroom.

Eric frowned. "I wouldn't put it like that."

"Of course, you wouldn't." Jillian turned away from Brett, dismissing Eric. "What does the robbery from this morning have to do with me?"

"You'd know better than we would," Eric interrupted again.

Jillian glared at him. "What's that supposed to mean?"

Wainwright shrugged. "You tell us. Your prints were found all over the crime scene."

"What?" Jillian took a half step back as the bottom dropped out of her stomach. "That's not possible." She shook her head as she glanced at Brett's face, searching for clarification. This had to be a joke... right? There was no way Ian had found her prints at the scene of a robbery. Maybe this was some kind of ridiculous initiation for new forensic workers on the force. Even though she'd been working as a crime-scene investigator for over a year already, things had been busy. Now that Len Davison was no longer terrorizing the citizens of Grave Gulch, perhaps everyone had time to stage this practical joke.

Though, to be honest, it was going on a bit too long.

"This isn't funny," she said, hoping Brett would see the emotion in her eyes and call it off. He'd always seemed like a good guy, and she'd gotten to know him better recently now that he was with her cousin Annalise—surely he wouldn't let her suffer too much?

"I agree," Eric said. "But it does make a certain kind of sense. No wonder you didn't find any prints at the scenes of the other robberies. Since you worked those cases, I'm sure you were careful to erase any evidence of your presence there."

"I didn't rob anybody!" Panic was starting to set in, making her heart pound hard in her chest.

Brett held up a hand. "It's okay, Jillian," he said, his voice calm. "Let's just get through this and we'll figure out what to do next."

"It's got to be a mistake." Her head was spinning, her mind churning, as she tried to come up with some explanation that made sense. "Maybe the samples got switched, or cross-contaminated in the lab somehow." There had to be a reason her prints were at a robbery scene even though she'd never stolen a thing in her life!

"Like I said, let's just finish this and then we can talk." Brett ran a hand through his red hair and sighed. Jillian could tell by the lines of strain at the corners of his blue eyes that the acting police chief wasn't happy about this situation, but until the other officers had completed their search, there wasn't much he could do.

Jillian opened her mouth, but a quick glance at Eric made her close it again. The man was watching her intently, and she suddenly realized that he was filing away everything she said, likely with the intention of using it against her later.

Brett was right, she realized. Better to talk after the search was over. Once everyone concluded she didn't have any stolen jewelry in her possession, they could get down to the business of figuring out what kind of mistake had made them think she was guilty in the first place.

It shouldn't take long to wrap things up. Jillian's condo wasn't that large—it was a basic two-bedroom unit, and while she'd been in the living room with Brett and Wainwright, the other uniformed officers had gone through her kitchen and guest bedroom. She saw them walk down the hall now, headed for the bathroom.

Brett walked around her living room, checking out the contents of her bookshelves and the pictures on her walls. But he was careful not to touch anything, and she noticed he didn't open any table drawers or make any attempt to examine anything that wasn't in plain view. It was as if the interim police chief was trying to respect Jillian's privacy, despite the search warrant. It was a small kindness, but one she noticed and appreciated nonetheless.

Wainwright, on the other hand, had no such consideration. He finished up his examination of her desk and started poking through the drawers of the small tables next to her sofa. If anything, Eric seemed to relish the opportunity to invade Jillian's space, like he was excited to find a reason to arrest her. Jillian had to bite her tongue to keep from snapping at him, because she knew it would only make the situation worse.

Unable to watch Wainwright any longer, Jillian turned away in time to see Grace emerge from her bedroom. As soon as she saw her cousin's face, Jillian knew she'd found something.

But...it's not possible, she thought.

Things seemed to move in slow motion as Grace entered the living room, holding a brown paper bag in her left hand. Jillian shook her head, unable to speak as she watched Grace walk over to Brett and nod slightly. Brett turned to face Jillian, a look of disappointment flashing across his face.

"I knew it!" Eric crowed triumphantly. Brett and Grace both glared at him, but Eric merely grinned.

"Jillian," Grace said softly. "I found the jewelry in the back of your closet."

"I don't understand!" Her throat was so tight it hurt to speak. "I didn't steal anything!"

"All evidence to the contrary," Wainwright snorted.

"It's here, Jillian," Grace continued. "The pieces are exactly as Mrs. Evans described them."

"I didn't rob her," Jillian insisted. She glanced at Brett, hoping he might believe her. "Do you really think I'm some kind of jewel thief who robs by night and works for the police during the day?"

Brett didn't say anything, so she continued, her voice growing louder as her disbelief gave way to anger. "Let's assume for one minute I'm capable of leading that double life. Would I really be so stupid as to hide the stolen goods in my closet, where anyone could find them? And if I really am some kind of master burglar, where are the other pieces I've supposedly taken off with? Why did you only find these items and not any of the others?"

"Because you've already sold them," Eric said, sounding bored. "As fun as this little intellectual exercise is, I've seen enough." He glanced at Brett. "Are you going to arrest her, or should I do it?"

A muscle in Brett's jaw drew tight, and Jillian could swear she heard the man's teeth grind together. "I'll take care of it," he growled.

"This does seem awfully cut-and-dried," Grace said. But there was a note of doubt in her voice that gave Jillian a flicker of hope. "She has a point," Grace continued. "I mean, remember when she found that twenty-dollar bill on the stairs? She sent out a department-wide email asking if anyone was missing money. Who does that?"

Brett closed his eyes with a faint smile. "I know," he murmured.

"What if this is some kind of setup?"

Jillian seized the words like they were a lifeline. "It has to be!" She nodded vigorously, needing Brett and Grace to see the truth.

"Pretty elaborate setup," Brett said quietly.

Jillian's mind kicked into gear as she tried to figure out who might want to get her in trouble. More than that, who would have the access and ability to plant evidence and make her look guilty?

There was only one answer: Randall Bowe.

"It's Bowe," she declared. "It has to be him."

Brett nodded thoughtfully. "He does know how to manipulate evidence."

"And it's the kind of underhanded thing he'd do," Grace added.

"I can't believe what I'm hearing," Eric said. Jillian turned to find him shaking his head. "Are you two actually conspiring to let her off the hook despite the fact that her prints were found at the scene and the stolen jewelry was in her closet?" He leveled a stare at Brett. "It's a good thing I came with you tonight. I'd long suspected Coltons get special treatment, and this confirms it."

Brett put his hands on his hips. "You wait just a minute. No one is conspiring to do anything, and I don't appreciate your insinuation. We're merely having a conversation."

"What you should be doing is arresting the suspect." Eric reached for the cuffs on his belt. "But I suppose I'll have to do that for you."

"That's not necessary." Brett held up his hand and turned to Jillian. "Jillian Colton," he began, "you are under arrest for the robbery of Elsa Evans." He continued, reciting her rights as required. It was a surreal experience, one that left her feeling slightly disoriented. Even though Brett was standing next to her, his voice sounded tinny and small, and was almost drowned out by the rush of blood in her ears.

Is this really happening?

Something touched her arm, and she glanced over to see Grace's hand. "Come on," she said. "We need to go down to the station and finish the process."

Jillian nodded, too numb to speak.

She took a step forward but stopped suddenly as

someone grabbed her other arm. "Not so fast," Eric said. He pulled back her arm and she felt something cold close around one wrist, then the other.

Brett's cheeks reddened. "Was that really necessary?"

"Standard procedure," Eric replied smoothly. "Unless you think she warrants special treatment?"

"Are you serious?" Jillian's throat was so tight the words came out as barely more than a whisper. "I'm not fighting you. I'm not going to try to run."

"That's what they all say," Eric replied.

Jillian's eyes stung as tears began to well. Bad enough that her friends, family and colleagues had come into her home, suspecting her of a crime. She'd thought it couldn't get any worse when they'd discovered the evidence in her closet. But the handcuffs? That was a real low point.

"I'll escort her to the car," Grace said. She stepped forward to stand next to Jillian and stared at Eric until he released her arm. Jillian blinked back tears as her cousin placed her hand between her shoulder blades.

"Come on," Grace said softly. "Let's get you to the station. The sooner we get you processed, the sooner you can post bail and come home."

"I didn't steal that jewelry," Jillian said between sniffles. "I swear I'm not involved in those thefts."

"I know that." Grace led her out the door and into the hall. One of her neighbors was just arriving home from a night out, and she stood at her door, keys in hand, staring with wide eyes.

Great, Jillian thought. *Now everyone is going to think I'm a criminal.* She dropped her eyes as they passed the woman, too embarrassed to acknowledge her.

"Brett doesn't think you did this, either," Grace continued quietly as they approached the elevator. "We'll figure out what's going on. You just have to trust us."

Jillian nodded slightly. Her cousin's words meant a lot, as Grace had recently been through her own ordeal after being wrongfully accused of excessive use of force.

She stepped into the elevator, feeling subdued. Grace held the doors open to let Brett and Eric file in after them.

"The other officers are going to lock up your place," Brett told her. "You'll get your keys back once you post bail."

"Wow," Eric said dryly. "That's very considerate. Do you do that for all your arrests?"

No one replied. Jillian sneaked a look at Brett's face and could tell by the hard set of his jaw that he'd had just about enough of the man from Internal Affairs. At least she wasn't the only one…

Once outside, Grace helped her into the back seat of a patrol car. Her cousin climbed into the driver's seat, while Eric took the passenger seat. "Just to keep things aboveboard," he said, smirking back at Jillian. "Your last name isn't going to get you out of this."

Jillian turned away to stare out the window. It felt disorienting, seeing the world from the back of a police car. The view wasn't remarkably different; Grace didn't have the siren going or the lights flashing. If she hadn't been arrested, it would be easy to pretend this was just another night. But Jillian didn't have the energy to lie to herself.

She'd been set up. There was no other explanation. As much as Grace had assured her that she and Brett believed in her innocence, Jillian knew their faith wasn't going to get her very far. No judge would ignore the evidence that had been found in her apartment simply because her family and friends vouched for her character. No, she had to find some kind of proof, and soon.

Randall Bowe was smart, and he was devious. But he'd slipped up before. Jillian just had to figure out how he'd framed her.

Before it was too late.

Something was going on at the police station.

Baldwin Bowe decided to pause his workout and slowed his running pace to a walk as he watched a small crowd gather outside the main entrance of police headquarters. It was almost eleven at night; too late for the usual protesters to be out. Besides, now that the GGPD had caught serial killer Len Davison, the general mood of the city had improved a bit. There was still a die-hard crowd upset about the actions of Baldwin's brother, forensic scientist Randall Bowe. But for the most part, the reputation of the Grave Gulch Police Department was on the upswing.

So why was there a hum of anticipation in the air?

Trying to be unobtrusive, Baldwin made his way over to the periphery of the small group. "What's going on?" he asked when one man made eye contact with him.

The guy eyed him up and down, his gaze assessing. "News conference," he said shortly.

Baldwin scoffed. "This late?"

A woman glanced over and did a double take, her eyes glued to Baldwin's chest and the tight running shirt that fit him like a second skin. "They've arrested someone for the string of jewelry thefts." She finally looked up at his face, and in the glow of the nearby streetlight he saw her cheeks turn pink. "What's your name?" She offered her hand, and he gave it a half-hearted shake. "I haven't seen you around before. Are you new?"

"I'm Baldwin," he replied, deciding to leave his last name out of it. He was here to get information, and if these reporters knew he was related to Randall, they'd stop answering his questions and start asking their own. "And, yes, I'm new in town."

"I'm Shannon." She stepped closer, tucking a strand of blond hair behind her ear. "I'm a reporter for the *Grave Gulch Gazette*. Who do you write for?"

"I'm a freelancer," Baldwin said. It was the truth... sort of. As a ghost bounty hunter, he worked under the radar, taking on private clients who needed someone found. His job was to locate the target and deliver them to the client. He didn't ask questions about what happened next; that sort of thing didn't concern him.

The job had taken him all over the country and introduced him to people both wonderful and terrible. But despite everything he'd seen and experienced, he'd never expected that one day, he'd be hired to find his own brother.

There had always been friction between the two of them. Even though Randall was younger, he'd never looked up to Baldwin. Randall had been born with a chip on his shoulder, and his attitude meant he treated a lot of people badly. It hadn't surprised Baldwin to learn of his brother's crimes and the way he'd tampered with evidence to produce the results he had wanted. Most of his victims were understandably upset, but content to let the police handle the investigation, believing that the system would work the way it was supposed to and that Randall would eventually be brought to justice.

But Baldwin's client wasn't willing to wait that long.

Which was why Baldwin was here in Grave Gulch now, on the hunt for his fugitive brother.

Shannon edged closer. "I'd be happy to show you around," she offered. "Grave Gulch isn't a huge city, but there are some fun things to do. If you know where to look." Her voice dropped and she licked her lips suggestively.

Baldwin offered her a tight smile. "Thanks, but no thanks. I'm just here to work." Romance wasn't really his style, and he was too focused on the job to even indulge in a short-term fling, which was his usual MO. Besides, he'd grown up in Grave Gulch.

He'd only been back in town for a couple of weeks, and he was already itching to leave again.

Shannon shrugged. "Your loss," she said. She tossed her hair over her shoulder and turned away from him, facing the podium that had been set up on the steps of the police building.

Baldwin took a step back, ready to resume his run. The string of robberies didn't concern him. There was no point in wasting more time here.

But as he was starting to go, he overheard a conversation.

"Do you know who the suspect is?"

"Yeah, I heard it was Jillian Colton. She works for the department in the forensics lab and in CSI."

The word *lab* made Baldwin stop in his tracks, and he turned back to the podium, suddenly interested.

Had this woman, whoever she was, known his brother?

A few seconds later, the police commissioner and the mayor approached the podium. "I have a statement to read, regarding the recent string of jewelry thefts in Grave Gulch," the commissioner said. He cleared his throat and launched into his prepared remarks, confirming the arrest of Jillian Colton and assuring the reporters that Ms. Colton would not be given special treatment despite her family connections to many of the officers in the GGPD.

Baldwin listened carefully, sorting through the details the commissioner was providing. He couldn't care less about the robberies, or Jillian's family status. What he wanted to know was if she might be able to give him information that would help Baldwin find Randall.

The commissioner finished his speech and took a step back. Before he could leave, Baldwin shouted out a question.

"How long has Jillian Colton worked for the police lab?"

The older man frowned; it was clear he hadn't intended on answering questions. But he leaned closer to the microphone to reply. "Ms. Colton has worked for the department for the past eighteen months."

A few other reporters asked questions, but Baldwin wasn't listening. A year and a half. That meant she'd definitely worked with Randall. What could she tell him about his brother?

"There she is!" someone cried out.

Baldwin glanced at the street to see a police cruiser drive by. Amid the camera flashes, he caught sight of a woman in the back of the car. Her long hair hid most of her face, but she turned briefly, giving him a view of her expression.

She was terrified. Even from this distance, he could see the fear in her large eyes.

He watched as the cruiser turned right at the corner, taking her to the back of the building. Several of the reporters started jogging in that direction, evidently hoping to nab some photos of her perp walk as she was led into the station for processing. For a brief second, Baldwin considered following them. But, no, that wouldn't answer any of his questions.

Instead, he set off down the sidewalk, resuming his

run. He couldn't talk to Jillian Colton tonight, so he might as well finish his workout and get some sleep.

There would be time for introductions tomorrow.

Chapter 2

It was close to noon by the time Jillian was released from jail.

She'd passed a restless night tossing and turning on the thin, cold mattress in the holding cell. Her body had ached for sleep, but she hadn't been able to quiet her mind long enough to relax. Her thoughts had churned in a sickening mix of questions and half-baked theories. Not even a middle of the night visit from her brother had been enough to distract her. But through it all, she remained certain of one thing:

Randall Bowe had set her up.

Jillian didn't know why he'd targeted her, or what he hoped to gain by having her arrested and charged with the thefts. They'd worked together before his crimes had come to light, and while Jillian had never considered him a friend, she'd also not seen him as an enemy. Randall had been insufferable at times, and as the newest member of the team, she'd been his favorite scapegoat whenever something went wrong. He'd even gone so far as to blame her for the issues with the Everleigh Emerson case. Everyone knew the truth now, but at the time, her confidence had taken a dive. Still, Jillian had kept her chin up and soldiered on, determined to prove she was good at her job. There was no shortage of Coltons on the GGPD payroll, and while most people didn't bat an eye at her last name, there were a few who made it clear they thought Jillian had ridden her relatives' coattails in her career.

And wouldn't Bowe be thrilled by this turn of events?

The sun was high in the sky as she stepped outside, blinking against the brightness. What she wouldn't give for her sunglasses! She had half a mind to walk back inside and drop by her desk in the lab to grab her spare pair, but since she was suspended from her job, she thought it best to steer clear. IAB would have a field day if she walked into the lab, even on such an innocent errand.

"Ms. Colton, you are not to leave town, do you understand?" The judge's words echoed in her mind, the memory of his voice loud in her head.

She'd nodded, feeling humiliated anew at having to stand in open court as the charges against her were read aloud. The only saving grace was that her mother wasn't here to see it. Her sister, Madison, had kept their mom at home, but her brother, Bryce, had insisted on being there.

Her attorney had argued that since this was a first offense and the crimes hadn't been violent, she should be released on bail until her trial. The DA had countered that the stolen jewelry was worth a lot of money, giving her the means to flee. Apparently her cousin Troy's fiancée, Evangeline, a former ADA, had been unsuccessful at talking her old boss into taking it easy on Jillian. It had taken every ounce of Jillian's self-control to keep her mouth shut as the two lawyers sparred, but she'd remained silent.

In the end, the judge had split the baby. He'd agreed to set bail, but at a steep price. Jillian's heart had sunk when she'd heard the total; it was far out of the reach of her bank account. She'd blinked back tears as she'd been led away. Bryce had shouted that he'd figure something out, but Jillian expected to spend the foreseeable future in a jail cell.

The fact that she was standing outside now was nothing short of a miracle.

"Jillian Colton?"

The unfamiliar voice made her turn. A man was standing a few feet away, booted feet planted in a wide stance on the sidewalk. Black jeans outlined his long legs, and his dark gray T-shirt strained across his broad chest. The sleeves were tight on his muscular arms, which were presently crossed. His black hair was cropped close, reminding her of a military cut. She couldn't see his eyes behind the dark lenses of his sunglasses, but she could feel his gaze on her.

"Who's asking?" she said warily. He didn't look like a reporter and there weren't any protesters on this side of the building—they were all standing out front, on Grave Gulch Boulevard.

"A friend," he replied.

Jillian narrowed her eyes as she stared at him. "A friend, huh? Then why don't I recognize you?"

He shifted, dropping his arms to shove his hands into his pockets. "I paid your bail."

She took a half step back and narrowed her eyes. No wonder her brother wasn't waiting for her. "Why did you do that?" If he was even telling the truth. "Like I said, I don't know you."

"My name's Baldwin." He took off the sunglasses, revealing intense blue eyes the color of a summer sky. "I'd like to talk to you. Maybe over a burger? Are you hungry?"

Her stomach growled at the mention of food, but Jillian wasn't ready to wander off with this guy just yet. "You're not giving me a lot to work with here, Baldwin. What's your last name? And why do you think I'd have answers for you?"

He sighed and shook his head slightly, clearly reluctant to say more. The silence stretched for several seconds, until Jillian thought he might not answer at all. When he finally spoke, his tone was resigned.

"I'm Baldwin Bowe—" he began.

"Bowe?" she repeated, cutting him off. "Any relation to Randall Bowe?" Her lip curled up in disgust as she practically spat the name out of her mouth.

Baldwin nodded. "He's my brother."

"Then we're done here." Jillian spun on her heel and started walking, determined to put distance between them. She had no idea why Randall's brother had posted her bail, or what he could possibly want with her. But she wasn't going to stick around to find out.

"Jillian, wait!" Baldwin called out behind her, but she ignored him. Footsteps pounded against the sidewalk and his hand closed around her biceps, pulling her to a stop.

She glared at his hand, then up at him. He released her immediately, holding up his palms by his shoulders in a gesture of surrender. "I'm sorry," he said. "But I really need to talk to you."

Baldwin had seemed tall before, but now that he was standing so close, Jillian was acutely aware of how much bigger he was compared to her. Not just in height—Baldwin was muscular and toned, his body solid and imposing. She got the feeling that if he planted himself in front of her, she'd have better luck trying to run through a brick wall.

She took a deep breath to quell her nerves. The stress, lack of sleep and proximity to a large, potentially dangerous man had her feeling on edge. Right now, they were on a public street, with plenty of witnesses. She could hear him out and once he was gone, she'd duck into a store to borrow a phone and call a friend for a ride home.

"All right," she said, looking up at him. "What do you want to know?"

"Let's clear the air," he said. "I haven't spoken to

Randall in years. We're not friends, and I don't know where he is now."

Jillian searched his face, looking for any signs of deception. Baldwin didn't flinch from her gaze, but if he was anything like his brother, he was a practiced liar.

"I'm a fugitive-recovery agent," he continued. "I operate under the radar, and I'm good at what I do."

"Is that a fancy way of saying you're a bounty hunter?"

He nodded. "That's an older term for it. But, yeah, I find people who don't want to be found."

"Why are you in Grave Gulch?" Despite her misgivings, Jillian was curious to know more.

"I've been hired to find my brother."

She frowned. "I didn't realize the police had opted to bring in outside help." Jillian hadn't been informed of every development in the search for Randall, but she did try to keep up with the latest news.

"They didn't," Baldwin said flatly. "My client is not affiliated with the police department. But I've been working with Bryce. We've shared some leads with each other."

Interesting. She waited for him to say more, but he didn't elaborate.

It made sense that Randall had enemies. His actions had sent innocent people to jail and allowed those guilty of terrible crimes to walk free. Maybe one of his victims, or perhaps the family member of a victim, had lost faith that the GGPD could find Bowe and bring him to justice.

And now that she thought about it, she did recall Bryce mentioning that Randall's brother was helping him. It was easy enough to verify, so she doubted he was lying about that.

"So you'll...what? Find your brother and then just hand him over to your client?" That seemed awfully cold, even for a tough-looking guy like Baldwin. Surely he wouldn't leave his brother in the hands of someone who wanted revenge?

Another thought occurred to her, one that raised her already heightened suspicions. What if Baldwin wasn't really working for a client at all? Maybe he was on the search for his brother so he could warn Randall before the police closed in?

Baldwin shook his head. "As soon as I find Randall, I'm turning him over to the police."

"Uh-huh," she said skeptically.

He lifted one eyebrow. "You don't believe me." It wasn't a question; he was apparently smart enough to realize Jillian had serious doubts.

She shrugged. "For all I know, you're a double agent. You pretend to help the police on behalf of this mystery client, but really you're feeding Randall the information he needs to stay one step ahead of everyone."

Baldwin's lips twitched with a suppressed smile. "Do you question everyone's motives, or just mine?"

"I'm a crime-scene investigator," she replied. "Questioning comes with the territory."

"Nothing wrong with that," he murmured. He looked past her shoulder and nodded at something in the distance. "Look, I'm hungry. Can we continue this conversation at that diner down the street?"

Jillian didn't have to turn around to know he was talking about Mae's Diner. The place was a Grave Gulch institution, and in her opinion, home to the best pancakes in town.

She considered her options: she could leave Baldwin to his own devices, call up a ride home and scrounge around her half-empty fridge for something to eat. Or she could enjoy some decent food and hopefully get some information in return.

Baldwin said he had some questions for her. Maybe she could get him to answer a few of her own.

At the very least, she'd learn more about Baldwin's plans for his stay in Grave Gulch. Information like that might prove useful for Grace and the other cops assigned to Randall's case.

"Lunch sounds good," she said. "But I should warn you—I don't have my wallet."

"My treat," Baldwin said.

Jillian wasn't about to argue. Right now, her body needed sleep and food. If she couldn't have the former, at least she was going to get the latter.

Once she got some fuel in the tank, it would be easier to think about her next steps. She glanced over at Baldwin as they walked to the diner together. He was physically imposing, to be sure. Almost the complete opposite of his slender, fine-boned brother. And, on the surface, he seemed all business. Would he even answer her questions?

It was a good thing Jillian was used to solving puzzles. If she was lucky, Baldwin would turn out to be the missing piece she needed to prove her innocence.

Baldwin watched Jillian tuck into her second stack of pancakes with a combination of amazement and fascination. She wasn't a sloppy eater—far from it, as her table manners were impeccable. But after their food had arrived, she'd wasted no time digging in. He'd looked up from seasoning his meal to find she was halfway through her first stack of pancakes, with several pieces of her bacon already missing. By the time he'd eaten a few bites, she'd already ordered her second stack of the diner's all-day "limitless" special.

Where was she putting all that food? He discreetly ran his gaze over the top half of her body, verifying that she was, in fact, as slim as he'd thought when he'd met her on the street. Maybe she had a hollow leg?

"Did they forget to feed you last night?" he said, only half-joking.

She shook her head. "No," she said, between bites. "They offered. But I was too stressed to eat."

That made sense. Sympathy stirred in his chest as he imagined her pacing the confines of a cell, her mind buzzing as she tried to figure out what to do next.

"Why'd you pay my bail?"

The question interrupted his thoughts, and he refocused to find her watching him over the rim of her coffee mug.

"I told you, I have some questions for you about my brother."

"You could have visited me in jail," she pointed out. Amusement danced in her eyes. "Would have been a cheaper option."

"Maybe so, but I need more than just a conversation."

Her shoulders stiffened, and he mentally kicked himself. *Way to sound like a creep...*

"Listen," she said, narrowing her eyes as she set down her mug with a thump, "I appreciate you posting my bail. But if you think that somehow makes me beholden to you, or that you can manipulate me out of a sense of guilt—"

Baldwin held up a hand, shaking his head. "I'm not interested in sex."

It was true, despite the fact that she was pretty. Her light brown hair hung past her shoulders and was slightly tangled from her night in jail. Her face was long, her features delicate. The dark circles under her brown eyes made her look fragile, but he could already tell that was an illusion. Based on their conversation so far, Baldwin could tell Jillian was not a precious flower that needed to be coddled.

If the circumstances had been different, he might have pursued her. But, right now, he was too focused on the job at hand to think of anything else.

She leaned back against the cracked pleather of the booth, plainly still suspicious. "Do you think I did it?"

"Did what?" He popped some eggs into his mouth, puzzled by this sudden question.

Jillian arched one eyebrow as she stared him down. "Do you think I robbed those people?"

Baldwin took a sip of water and considered his response. Unless he missed his guess, his reply would determine Jillian's cooperation. If he answered correctly, she'd stay and hear him out. But if he said the wrong thing? There'd be a Jillian-shaped hole in the door.

"I'm undecided," he said finally. "I don't know you at all. Based on our limited interactions, you don't seem like the jewel-thief type. But I've misjudged people before."

"Does it bother you? The thought that you may have freed a guilty woman to rob again?"

He shrugged. "Nope. Even if you did steal that jewelry, you didn't hurt anyone. I don't really care if some rich people get their panties in a twist."

She tilted her head to the side. "I suppose that's fair." He watched as she took another bite of pancake. "For the record," she said after she swallowed, "I didn't steal from anyone."

"Okay." Baldwin had taken one look at her and known the truth, but he'd sensed Jillian wouldn't believe him if he'd said as much. She came across as a skeptical person; she didn't seem like the type to trust a gut instinct until there was evidence to back it up. Hopefully his own admission of doubt regarding her innocence would help convince her that he was also rational and measured.

Because what he wanted to ask of her? It was going to take a lot of trust on her part.

"All right," she said slowly. "Let's assume for a minute I believe you. That you really are searching for your brother and you'll immediately turn him in once you find him. What do you need me for?"

Baldwin took a deep breath as his nerves sprang to life, giving him a funny feeling in his stomach. It was an unfamiliar sensation. He normally had no problem asking for what he wanted or needed. But there was a hint of vulnerability in Jillian's brown eyes that touched him. She was putting up a good front, but under her tough, take-no-prisoners shell, he could tell she was frightened.

Randall had done that to her. Anger rose in Baldwin's chest as he imagined his brother's face. Randall didn't hurt people physically—he didn't have the strength for that. Physical wounds usually healed, though. The psychological injuries his brother preferred to inflict took much longer to repair.

"You have a history with my brother," he began. It was important that he led up to his proposal slowly, or she'd reject his idea outright.

Jillian frowned. "Yes. We worked together."

"And he probably wasn't nice to you."

Her short laugh held no humor. "That's an understatement. Randall found fault with everything I did. At first, it was just criticizing little things, like the way I held a pipette, or the way I labeled something. But then he started finding mistakes I'd made." Jillian shook her head. "He'd say I forgot to put a sample in the fridge, or that I had missed a step in a protocol." Her eyes narrowed at the memories. "But the thing is, I *knew* I hadn't messed up. I was always so careful, doubly so, since he seemed to be breathing down my neck at every turn. I double- and triple-checked every step, making sure I hadn't forgotten anything."

"Let me guess," Baldwin said. "He'd move things around when you weren't looking and accuse you?"

Jillian nodded. "Yeah. It would be hours, or sometimes days later, when he would confront me. By then, I'd moved on to something else. I'd insist I hadn't done anything wrong, but he'd show me a sample out of place, or a reagent that was spoiled and I'd look like an idiot trying to argue."

"He was gaslighting you," Baldwin said softly.

"I realize that now," Jillian said. "But at the time, I was a rookie. I was fresh out of school and didn't have a ton of experience. I began to doubt myself and wonder if maybe he was right. Maybe I was making a lot of mistakes. I was so mentally exhausted from hyperfocusing on every task, trying to make sure everything I did was perfect so Randall wouldn't find fault with my work."

She took a sip of coffee, clearly bothered by the memories. Baldwin didn't blame her—it sounded like Randall had tortured her for months.

"It didn't help that my last name was Colton," she continued. "There were already some whispers that the only reason I'd gotten the job was due to my family connections. I was determined to prove myself, and Randall used that against me."

"Did you ever suspect him of manipulating evidence before everything came out?"

She nodded. "Once he'd worn me down with his constant criticisms and fault-finding, things began to escalate. He'd suddenly find a piece of evidence he said I'd missed, or something that I had processed would mysteriously go missing and Randall would claim I had destroyed the sample with my careless handling. I was so twisted up inside and stressed that it never occurred to me to wonder why he didn't just fire me if I was so incompetent. But after his crimes came to light, I realized he needed to keep me around as a scapegoat."

"Did he ever target anyone else working in the lab?" Baldwin asked. He already suspected the answer, but he wanted her to confirm it.

"No." She shook her head. "There was a former assistant who'd worked in the lab a little before my time. He'd fired her for losing evidence, though now we know that wasn't true. Since she wasn't there anymore, I guess he picked me as his next target. He was so devious about it. He'd berate me for making a mistake, and then later that day he'd come back and apologize for losing his temper."

"That's what abusers do," Baldwin said. "He was trying to keep you close."

She smiled sadly. "I remember one day he was especially nice to me. My name had been leaked to the press in a story about evidence gone missing in a high-profile robbery case we were working. A group of protesters had shown up that next morning carrying big posters of my face, with a red *line* painted over it." She drummed her fingertips against the Formica tabletop. "I realize now that Randall must have been the one to release my name. But that morning, he seemed concerned for me and told me not to worry about it, that it would all blow over."

"He needed you to stick around," Baldwin said. It was a tactic his brother had deployed often when they were kids, but never to such an extent. Baldwin had learned early on that Randall was not to be trusted. Since Randall was never in a position of power over him, he hadn't been able to affect him that much. Nothing like the way he'd tried to wreck Jillian's career.

"Yeah," she said grimly. "When the truth came out about what Randall had been doing all along, I cried. It felt like a huge burden had been lifted and I could actually breathe again."

"I can understand that," Baldwin said. His heart did a little flip as he imagined Jillian's tear-streaked cheeks, and he was struck with the urge to pull her into his arms for a hug.

Not that she needed it. She was sitting tall and strong across from him in the booth, looking nothing like the stressed, nearly broken woman she'd once been. Jillian wasn't looking for comfort or protection.

So why did he want to provide it?

He shook off the errant desire and refocused on the conversation at hand. "Now that Randall is on the run, why do you think he's still focused on you?"

Jillian went still. "How did you know...?"

"The interim chief, Brett Shea," Baldwin said. "I stopped by a few weeks ago to officially introduce myself and let the GGPD know I'm in town, searching for my brother. Sort of a professional courtesy. The chief has given me what information he could, and he told me Randall has been calling and texting people to taunt them. Your name was on the list of targets."

Jillian relaxed. The waitress came by their table and offered to refill her coffee, but she declined politely. *Time to wrap it up*, Baldwin thought. Jillian would want to leave soon, so he'd better get to his point quickly.

"I don't know why he's still harassing me," she said. "But I'm convinced he's trying to frame me for these robberies."

Baldwin considered her theory. "That sounds like something he'd do."

"I just don't understand why he won't leave me alone," she said, sounding frustrated. "We don't work together anymore. We don't see each other. Why not leave without looking back?"

"Do you want to know what I think?" Baldwin asked. Jillian nodded, her brown eyes fixed on him. "I think Randall is obsessed with you. I think he's angry because after his crimes were revealed, you became the star of the department. That was formerly his place. It must eat him up inside to know that you, his former scapegoat, are now a big shot."

"Maybe..." She trailed off, sounding thoughtful. "He's certainly delusional enough to think that my reputation should suffer along with his."

"He must have broken into the lab to plant the new evidence," Baldwin said.

"Not necessarily," Jillian replied. "Before Randall took off, he stole a lot of files. My fingerprints and other personal information were probably part of the cache. I think he's the one behind the thefts, and he chose to plant my prints at this last scene to drag me through the mud again."

"Which is why I posted your bail," Baldwin said.

Confusion flickered across Jillian's face. "I'm not sure what one has to do with the other."

Time to lay his cards on the table. "Randall is going to be furious you're out of jail. I think he's going to escalate his behavior and come after you."

The color drained from Jillian's face as she processed his words. "So you paid my bail to use me as bait?"

Her voice was low, but not from shock. As Baldwin watched, he could practically see her anger building.

"Yes, but it's not as bad as you think," he said.

The glare she sent across the table hit him like a dagger. "Enlighten me," she said through clenched teeth.

"You don't have to worry about Randall getting to you, because you won't be alone."

"How do you figure that?" she retorted. "Am I supposed to hire a bodyguard or something?"

Baldwin leaned back and offered what he hoped was a reassuring smile. "Nope. That's what I'm for."

Chapter 3

Jillian stared at Baldwin, torn between the desires to scream and cry. "You?" she said incredulously. "Do you mean to tell me that you've appointed yourself my bodyguard?"

His smile slipped and he shifted in his seat. "I don't know if I'd call it bodyguard, per se," he said. "But I had no intention of springing you from jail and then leaving you at the mercy of my brother."

"How very chivalrous of you," she muttered. Baldwin's delusions aside, how was she going to protect herself? He was likely right, in that Randall would be angry when he discovered Jillian wasn't rotting away in a jail cell while she awaited trial. He'd have to know she would be working to prove her innocence, and it was improbable that he would sit idly by while she untangled the cocoon of lies he'd wrapped around her. But would he really come after her himself?

Randall had always been more of a behind-the-scenes kind of guy, preferring to manipulate others to his own ends. Still, he'd always had it in for her. Now that he was on the run, he didn't have access to his usual resources. It was possible he'd take the risk of a physical confrontation to ensure she went down in flames.

But she couldn't very well rely on Baldwin to keep her safe. She didn't even know him! He talked a good game about wanting to bring in his brother, but that didn't mean she trusted him. And she certainly wasn't ready to welcome him with open arms into her home! That space had already been invaded by strangers, and the memories from last night's search washed over her, making the pancakes in her stomach turn sour.

Maybe she could hire protection? She dismissed the thought almost immediately. She might be a Colton, but she wasn't rich. Her salary covered her expenses with enough left over each month to save, but nothing like this. Normally, she'd ask her brother, Bryce, for help. As an FBI agent, he might have connections in that area. He could at least perform a background check on Baldwin for her. But as for anything else, he was still recovering from the gunshot wound he'd sustained during the final confrontation with Len Davison. He was in no position to offer her protection, and Jillian wasn't about to crash with him and his new fiancée, Olivia.

And as for the rest of her relatives on the GGPD force? She couldn't go to them. They were already under scrutiny. If any of them were seen to be helping her try to clear her name, it would spell disaster for their careers.

It looked like the man sitting across from her might very well be her best option. But that didn't mean she was going to go along with his plan without doing a little research of her own.

Baldwin had been watching her, his expression guarded as she thought things through. At least he was smart enough to give her the space and silence to mull over her choices without interruption.

"I suppose you want to move in with me?"

He nodded carefully. "You're not the only one Randall hates. If he knows the two of us are living together, it will really bother him."

Jillian ground her back teeth together. "Next you're going to tell me we have to pretend to be romantically involved."

"Nope." Baldwin's blue eyes were cool as he looked at her. "I told you, I'm not interested in sex. I just want to get my brother so I can collect the second half of my paycheck."

Heat rose up her neck, and with it, her frustration. It was a good thing Baldwin wasn't angling for a personal connection! So why was part of her the tiniest bit disappointed?

"Although," he continued dryly, "it would help if we appeared to be on somewhat friendlier terms."

Her shoulders stiffened. "What's that supposed to mean?" she asked. "I'm friendly!"

Baldwin snorted. "Okay. 'Cause right now you're looking at me as though you're trying to decide if you want to stab me with your fork or strangle me with the waitress's apron strings."

Jillian rolled her eyes and fought back a smile. "Can you blame me?" she said. "This—" she gestured to him and the diner "—wasn't exactly how I thought my day was going to go."

"I can understand that." Baldwin leaned back, his expression softening a bit. He was still a big, strong, tough-looking man, but Jillian saw a glint of sympathy in his eyes.

"So what do you think?" he asked. "I know it's short notice and it's a lot to take in at once, but are you on board with my plan?"

Part of her wanted to say yes and get it over with, but Jillian's instincts wouldn't allow her to accept his proposal. "Not yet," she admitted.

Baldwin took her refusal in stride. "What's holding you back?"

"Well..." She wasn't sure how he was going to respond to this. "You, actually."

"Me?" He sounded surprised, but not angry.

"Look at you." She lifted her hand in his general direction. "You're tall and muscular. Physically imposing. And look at me." She pointed at herself. "I'm no match for your strength."

Baldwin leaned forward. "I don't hurt women," he said gruffly. "I swear to you, I will not touch you." His voice was quiet and serious, all traces of humor gone.

"I want to believe you," Jillian said. "But I'm not in the habit of inviting men I just met into my home."

"Fair enough." Baldwin reached for a clean paper napkin, then flagged down the waitress and asked for a pen. After she gave him one, he started writing on the napkin.

"What are you doing?" Jillian asked.

"I'm giving you my personal information," he said as he wrote. After a few seconds, he set down the pen and slid over the napkin. "That's all of it. Birth date, current address, social-security number, driver's-license info. The whole nine yards."

"Why are you giving me this?" She skimmed the information, noting with some surprise that Baldwin had been born in Grave Gulch.

"Your brother is an FBI agent, right?"

She glanced up. "Yes. I'm going to ask him to run a background check on you." If Baldwin came back clean, she'd let him stay with her. If not...well, she'd come up with another idea.

Baldwin smiled and gestured to the napkin. "That'll make it easier for him."

"What's this number labeled 'DOD'?" She tapped her finger on the writing.

"That's my Department of Defense ID number."

"You're in the service?" No wonder his haircut had made her think military.

"I was," he replied. "Retired, you could say."

"Moved on to bounty hunting, I see. More interesting work?"

He tilted his head to the side. "The pay is certainly better now."

Jillian nodded, her mind made up. "All right, Baldwin. I'd like you to take me home now, please. I'm going to call my brother and give him your information. If everything checks out, I'll go along with your plan."

"You're not worried about me knowing where you live?" Baldwin asked, a teasing note to his voice.

Jillian climbed out of the booth and shrugged. "You know my brother is a federal agent. You've been working with him. I'm betting you already have my address." What else did he know about her?

"That's true." Baldwin stood, and as she watched his body unfold from the booth, she was reminded again of their relative sizes.

"Just out of curiosity," she said as they headed for the door. "What will you do if I say no?"

He shrugged. "Follow you around and wait for Randall to strike."

"So I really am just bait to you?"

Baldwin nodded. "Like I told you before, I'm after Randall. I'll do whatever it takes to bring him in so I can get the second half of my fee."

For some strange reason, that stung a little. Jillian didn't expect a stranger like Baldwin to actually care about her, but she'd never before had such a blatantly transactional experience with someone. On one level, it was kind of nice to know the truth up front. Even if he was just using her.

Her thoughts must have shown on her face. Baldwin sighed as they walked out of the diner. "Look, it's nothing personal, okay? In my line of work, it's best not to make friends. I don't get involved with people and I don't stick around once the job is done."

"I see." Honestly, it was going to be better this way. Jillian wanted to close the book on the Randall Bowe chapter of her life—the sooner, the better.

Even if it meant working side by side with Randall's infuriating brother.

It didn't take long for Baldwin to drop off Jillian at her place.

"Call me when you're ready to talk." He nodded at the napkin she was holding in one hand. "You have my number."

"Something tells me you'll be close," she replied dryly.

Baldwin merely nodded. Jillian hopped down from the passenger seat of his truck, but before shutting the door, she turned back.

"Thanks for breakfast," she said. "And for bailing me out."

Surprise flashed in Baldwin's blue eyes. "You're welcome." Apparently, he hadn't expected her gratitude. But even though he'd only gotten her out of jail to serve his own purposes, she still appreciated it.

Inside, the hallway was blessedly empty as Jillian walked to her door. Although she knew she hadn't done anything wrong, the neighbors who had seen her getting arrested last night had probably made their own assumptions about her guilt. The building's gossip mill was likely already churning…

"One thing at a time," she muttered to herself as she unlocked the door to her condo. First, she had to clear her name of these false charges. Then she'd deal with her neighbors and whatever the co-op board might send her way.

It felt strange, walking into her own home after the events of last night. She half expected to find one of the uniformed officers still there, rummaging through the rooms in search of more planted evidence.

Her cell phone was sitting on the kitchen counter. Jillian hadn't bothered to grab it last night, knowing it would only be confiscated from her. She touched the screen now and it lit up, revealing a record of missed calls and unseen texts.

She walked over to the round table at the far end of the room and sat to scroll through everything. There were dozens of messages and voice mails, mostly from Bryce and their mother, Verity. But there were also a few from Madison and her father, Wes, who had recently come back into their lives. It seemed word of her arrest had traveled fast.

She typed out a group message to her family. Home safe. Going to rest. Will call later. Then she dialed Bryce.

He picked up on the first ring. "Jillian? What the hell? Are you okay?"

"I'm fine," she assured him. She gave him a quick

rundown of the situation, starting with her release from jail.

Bryce listened carefully as she spoke. When she got to the part about meeting Baldwin Bowe, he interrupted her.

"I've met him," Bryce said. "He's pretty intense."

Jillian laughed shortly. "Yeah, for sure. Here's the thing. He wants to use me as bait to draw out his brother."

Bryce sucked in a breath. "What?"

She filled him in on Baldwin's plan. "Are you actually considering this?" Bryce asked incredulously.

Jillian leaned back in the chair. "I don't have a lot of other options," she replied. "I've got to clear my name, and the only way to do that is to bring Randall in. He's been evading capture for the better part of a year. My case is going to go to trial before long, and I don't want to be sent to prison for a crime I didn't commit." Emotion welled in her chest, making her voice rise and her throat tighten. Just the thought of spending more time locked behind iron bars was enough to trigger a cold sweat.

"Okay, okay, I understand," Bryce said soothingly. "I know things look bad now, Jillian, but you have to know that everyone is working to clear your name."

"That's just it, Bryce. There's not much they can do." She reminded him of the internal-affairs case. "I don't want anyone to jeopardize their careers on my behalf. They shouldn't be punished for trying to help me."

"I'm not GGPD," Bryce said. "*I* can clear your name."

Jillian smiled and blinked back tears. "That's sweet of you. And I'll take all the help I can get. But you're still recovering from surgery. And the police might not be allowed to give you access to case files and evidence. The only way this is going to get resolved for good is to arrest Randall and get him to confess."

"I suppose you're right," Bryce said with a sigh. "But I'm not loving the idea of you putting yourself out there to draw him in. If what Baldwin says is true, and he's fixated on you, there's no telling what he might do to get back at you."

"I know," she said with a sigh. "But at this point, I'm willing to take the risk."

Bryce was quiet for a moment. She could practically feel his disapproval in the silence, but to his credit, he didn't try to lecture her.

"All right," he said finally. "But before you let this guy stay with you, I need to know more about him."

"I was hoping you'd say that." Jillian spread the napkin on the table and cleared her throat. "I have all his information so you can run a background check."

"Really?"

"Yep," she confirmed. "He wrote it all down for me."

"Huh." Bryce's tone was thoughtful. "I suppose that's a good sign. Hopefully that means he doesn't have anything to hide."

"Here's hoping," Jillian said. She rubbed her eyes,

which felt gritty from lack of sleep. "Listen, I was up all night, so I'm going to send you a picture of his info and then take a nap. Will you let me know when you're done with the background check?"

"Of course," Bryce said. "Do you need anything else?"

"Just a shower," she said.

Her brother laughed. "You're on your own for that one. But I'll call Mom and Madison and let them know you're fine. I got your text just before you called, but Mom is going to want to know you're really okay." He paused. "Do you want me to talk to Wes, as well?"

Jillian considered the question. Wes had missed much of her childhood, as he'd been in witness protection since she and her siblings were kids. Bryce had had some difficulty accepting Wes once he'd returned, but Jillian knew he was working on getting to know their dad better. They all were, truth be told.

"I appreciate it," Jillian said. "I think he'll probably be with Mom, though, so no need for a separate call."

"Good point."

"It's nice of you to be my secretary," she teased.

"Don't get used to it," Bryce replied. "Get some rest and I'll call you later."

"Sounds good." She ended the call and took a picture of the napkin, then texted it to Bryce. She didn't know how long it would take him to dig up information on Baldwin, but now that she'd gotten the ball rolling on the process it was time she took care of herself.

Exhaustion pulled at her, but she desperately wanted a shower first. The holding cell she'd stayed in last night hadn't been dirty, but there was something about being behind bars that made her feel gross.

The hot water streaming over her washed away the residue of fear and anger from last night. She stepped out of the steamy bathroom and headed straight for bed, not even bothering to put clothes on first. Her head hit the pillow and she had just enough energy left to draw the sheet over her body before sinking into sleep.

The ringing of her cell phone woke her.

Jillian blinked several times as she reached for the phone, fumbling to find it on her bedside table. She squinted at the bright display, trying to make sense of both the time and the name on the screen.

Bryce.

"Hello?" She rubbed her eyes, trying to shake off the grogginess that still clung to her mind.

"Sorry," Bryce said. "But I figured if I didn't wake you, you wouldn't be able to sleep tonight."

"No, it's okay," Jillian responded. According to the time on her phone, she'd gotten a few decent hours of rest. "Do you have the results from the background check?"

"I do," Bryce said. "This guy is legit."

"What does that mean?" She pushed herself up on the mattress and arranged a couple of pillows behind her.

"It means he's exactly what he says he is. Born and

raised in Grave Gulch. Joined the marines right after high school. Did a few tours overseas. He earned several medals for his conduct, including a Purple Heart, and a Navy and Marine Corps Achievement Medal and a Commendation Medal. He also earned several badges for marksmanship."

"Wow." That sounded impressive. She thought back to her meeting with Baldwin today; he'd given no indication of the extent of his military career or the fact that he'd been injured in combat. Talk about playing things close to the vest.

"Yeah," Bryce agreed. "He was basically a model marine. Honorably discharged, of course. Probably could have done any number of things for work, but decided to become a bounty hunter. From what I found, he started out with the conventional stuff and made a name for himself. He gradually started to go underground, and now he deals exclusively with select clients and high-profile targets."

"I figured that, based on what he told me about his current client," Jillian said. "What did you find out about his personal life?"

"Not much to find, to be honest," Bryce said. "He has excellent credit, owns his truck, rents a place. Never had as much as a parking ticket."

Jillian shifted on the bed. "What about girlfriends? Or boyfriends?" She held her breath, hoping her brother wouldn't read too much in to the question.

"He's been linked to a few women over the years, but nothing long-term," Bryce said. "Seems like the kind of guy who puts work above everything else."

"Gosh, who does that sound like?"

"Very funny," Bryce replied. "You know I'm not like that anymore."

"I do," Jillian acknowledged. "And I'm glad you have Olivia." It was true; both her siblings had found love in recent months, giving Jillian hope that her match might be out there, as well. But one thing was certain—she couldn't focus on her love life, or lack thereof, until Randall Bowe was behind bars and the charges against her had been dropped.

"Overall, I think Baldwin is a good guy," Bryce said, pulling her thoughts back to the matter at hand. "It's impossible to know everything about a person, but Bowe's records show a man who has a history of making good decisions and his military records are seriously impressive."

"So it's probably safe to have him stay with me," Jillian said.

"We definitely know more about him than some random guy you'd meet in a bar or find online," Bryce said.

"That's true." So why did the thought of Baldwin in her home make her heart pound?

"If you're determined to do this, I want you to check in with me frequently," Bryce continued. "At least once a day, so I know how things are going. Do you have any weapons in your house?"

The question sent a tingle of worry down her spine. "Just a baseball bat I keep next to my bed," Jillian replied.

"I suppose that'll have to do," Bryce said. "Just be sure to lock your bedroom door at night."

"O-o-kay..." she said slowly.

"I'm sure I'm overreacting," Bryce replied. "But Baldwin moving in with you is going to paint a very big target on your back. I just want you to be safe."

"I've been taking care of myself for years now," she pointed out. "I'm not going to suddenly become helpless just because some big, strong man has moved in with me."

"Big and strong, huh?" Bryce teased. "Do I need to get you some smelling salts?"

"Ha ha." Jillian couldn't help but roll her eyes at her brother. Even as she did, though, her stomach did a little flip at the memory of standing close to Baldwin earlier today.

"Thanks for doing the check," she said, determined to change the subject. The last person she would ever want to talk to about men was her older brother. There was only a year's difference between them, but Bryce didn't let that stop him from acting overprotective. Even their older sister was often subjected to Bryce's concerns, though Madison had confided to Jillian that Bryce had gotten better since she'd started dating Oren, a US Marshal.

"No problem," Bryce replied. "I might have to stop by later in the week, just to check on you."

Jillian sighed, knowing better than to argue. "Just call first, okay?"

"I can do that," Bryce said.

They ended the call, and Jillian climbed out of bed

and dressed. She retrieved the baseball bat from the corner by the door to her place, where it had been resting since last night. As she walked to her bedroom to put it away, she punched in Baldwin's number.

He answered on the second ring. "Are you calling to say yes?"

"How did you—?" Jillian stopped and shook her head. "Never mind." Of course, he had some kind of caller ID installed on his phone. He probably even knew exactly where she was standing in her home, for crying out loud.

"It's a nice program," he said, apparently reading her mind. "I can set it up on your phone, if you'd like."

"Maybe later," she replied. "I was calling to talk to you about your plan."

"Did your brother come through with the background check?"

"He did," she confirmed. "Apparently, you're quite the hero."

"I had a job to do," he replied flatly. "I did it."

Interesting, she thought. Baldwin apparently wasn't one for sentiment or looking back. "And now you just want to finish this job?"

"Pretty much," he confirmed. "So what's it going to be? Are you ready to work with me, or am I gonna do this alone?"

It was on the tip of her tongue to tell him to go pound sand, but Jillian swallowed the impulse. She had to clear her name, and cooperating with Baldwin would hopefully put her on the fast track to do it. And if a few days passed with no results? She'd figure out another approach.

"Let's just get this over with," she said, hearing her own lack of enthusiasm in her tone.

"With an attitude like that, I'm surprised you're still single," Baldwin drawled.

Jillian's temper spiked. "My love life is not your—"

"I'll be there in ten," Baldwin interrupted.

"Bring food," she retorted. "I didn't make it to the store today, and my fridge is empty."

He hung up without acknowledging her statement, making her wonder if he'd even heard it. Normally, she wouldn't ask a guy to buy her a meal twice in one day, but after that little crack about her personal life, she felt no remorse imposing on Baldwin or his wallet.

She glanced around, fighting the urge to do a quick clean of her place. Her condo wasn't dirty but a wipe-down wouldn't hurt.

No, she told herself. If she cleaned, Baldwin would know it and probably take it as a sign she was trying to impress him.

It was the same with her clothes. She'd pulled on another T-shirt and a pair of yoga pants when she'd gotten out of bed. It wasn't fancy, but the clothes were washed and the fabric didn't have holes. That would be good enough.

With a sigh, she walked into her living room and began to straighten some of the picture frames on the bookshelves. The officers who had conducted the search had been unusually thoughtful—they hadn't left a ransacked mess in their wake. But items were still out of place, enough that it would bother her to leave them.

"This is going to work," she muttered to herself as she moved around the room. "We're going to get Randall and then life will go back to normal."

It was the only option. The alternative was too terrifying to contemplate.

Chapter 4

Baldwin stood on Jillian's welcome mat, juggling several grocery bags while he waited for her to answer the door.

The sound of a lock echoed in the hall, and he glanced over to see Jillian's neighbor stepping out of her condo. She stopped in her tracks and stared at him, mouth agape, as though he was some kind of freak of nature.

"Evening," he said, jerking up his chin in acknowledgment.

The sound of his voice made her jump. She blinked at him, then turned and scurried away without a word.

Interesting, he thought. Apparently, Ms. Colton must not have too many visitors if the sight of him was enough to shock the neighbor.

She'd struck him as a bit of a workaholic. Nice to have his suspicions confirmed, even if only indirectly.

The door in front of him opened, Jillian on the other side.

"Hi," she said.

"Hey," he replied. He studied her face while he waited to be asked inside. Earlier in the day, she'd been tired but feisty, determined to find his brother and bring him down.

Now she looked subdued and a little resigned.

The change didn't suit her. He wanted to see that spark come back into her eyes.

Baldwin held up one of the grocery bags. "Can I—?"

"Yes, of course," she interrupted. She stepped back to allow him inside. "Sorry, let me help."

He handed her one of the bags and followed her down the short hall. The kitchen opened up off the left side, and straight ahead was a large living room. At the far end he saw another short hall, with two doors opening off it before it curved to the left. A half bath across from the kitchen completed the place.

Jillian led him into the kitchen and set the grocery bag on the counter. "What's this?"

"You said to bring food." He placed the other bags on the counter and slipped off his backpack. "I brought food."

"I didn't think you'd heard me," she said quietly. He started unpacking and she shook her head. "I thought you'd grab a pizza or something. I didn't mean for you to restock my fridge."

"Yeah, well…" He trailed off with a shrug. To be honest, he hadn't intended to stop at the grocery store. He'd meant to pick up some burgers. But then he'd realized his sarcastic remark about her love life had hurt her feelings, and he'd felt like an ass. So he'd decided to cook her dinner, as a sort of peace offering. They were going to be spending the foreseeable future together. Might as well get off on the right foot.

Jillian helped him unload. "Thank you," she said. "I didn't have a chance to stop at the store today, so I'm running a little low on supplies."

"It's not a problem," Baldwin said. "I figured I could make us something to eat and we could get to know each other a little better."

"Do you like to cook?" The surprise in her voice was evident.

Baldwin hid a smile. People were always shocked to discover he had talent in the kitchen. "I do, actually."

"Wow." Jillian didn't bother to hide her reaction. "I never would have guessed."

He turned and leaned against the counter, crossing his legs at the ankles. "Why's that? Don't I look like a guy who can make a roux or flambé some cherries jubilee?"

Jillian tilted her head. "I'm going to be honest with you, I only understood about half of what you just said. But to answer your question, no, you don't look like a chef." She eyed him up and down, her brown eyes lingering on his hips and his chest. Baldwin felt his skin prickle and warmth began to spread through his limbs. "You look like a tough guy, but I'm sure you already knew that."

"Even tough guys have to eat," he replied, willing his body's response to subside. A few minutes in, and he was already getting distracted. It was a clear sign that after he caught his brother, he needed to take some personal time before jumping into the next case. It had been a while since his last vacation; maybe he could call up one of his "friends with benefits" in Chicago or Dallas, spend a few days enjoying himself with some pleasant company. Baldwin didn't do relationships—lack of time was an issue, along with the fact that he didn't want to be tied down to any one location. His lady friends understood the score, and there were never any hard feelings. It was the perfect setup.

"Before you get started, let me show you your room," Jillian said. She nodded at his backpack on the floor. "You can get that out of your way."

"Sounds good." He bent and grabbed one of the straps of the bag and followed her out of the kitchen. He tried not to stare at her figure as she moved, but it was hard to notice anything else. She certainly wasn't dressed to impress, but even the T-shirt and stretched-out pants she wore did nothing to hide her long, lean lines. There was a grace to her walk, an intangible quality that made him wonder if she'd been a dancer at some point in her life. She seemed to carry herself with a physical awareness that he associated with athletes, like she was totally at ease in her own skin and knew exactly what her body could do. Baldwin was usually drawn to curvier women, but there was something about Jillian that made him want to touch her.

Not that he would.

He'd meant what he'd told her at the diner—he wasn't interested in sex. He was here to catch his brother and get paid.

Jillian led him into a bedroom next to the main bathroom. A glance down the hall gave him a peek into her room, but he didn't see much.

"Here you go," she said, stepping aside so he could enter.

It was on the small side, not that it mattered. A double bed was on the far wall, with a night table and lamp beside it. There was a dresser off to the side with a few books stacked on top. It was clear Jillian didn't use this space very often—there weren't any pictures or personal touches to be found. But it was clean, and he noticed a stack of folded towels on the end of the bed.

"Will this be okay?" She sounded a little uncertain, as though she was worried about his reaction.

"Oh, yeah," he assured her. "This is perfect." He set his backpack on the floor by the bed. "Is that your room down the hall?"

"Yes. The bathroom is just next door."

"Good." With the bedrooms so close, it would be easy to hear if she needed something. He glanced at the right wall. "Does your room have a window, as well?"

"Ah, yeah. Do you want to see?"

Baldwin nodded. It would be good to know the layout of her bedroom, for security purposes. And…he was curious to know what her personal space looked like.

"Okay. It's just this way."

He followed her down the short hall into her room. It was considerably larger, with space enough for a chair and small table set in the corner. He noticed a book on the table and figured she used the chair for reading.

There were a few framed photos on top of her dresser—he spotted Bryce in one of them and guessed they were of her family. A large window ran along the left wall. He walked over and glanced out, noting it was locked; they were three stories up, and there was no fire escape. If Randall wanted to come in, he was going to have to do it through the front door.

Baldwin turned, noticing a small bathroom set off to one side of the room, next to what he supposed was her closet. He spied some crumpled fabric on the floor by the door to the bath—something light pink and small. Jillian rushed over and grabbed it, her cheeks blazing.

Her panties, he realized. He turned away, a funny feeling bubbling in his chest. It was just another item of clothing, something most people wore every day. They weren't even particularly sexy, not red lace or a black thong. So why did a glimpse of Jillian's pink cotton underwear make him uncomfortably aware of her bed just a few feet away, with its slightly rumpled sheets?

He cleared his throat. "Looks like there's only one point of entry to your condo."

Jillian nodded, the flush fading from her face. "Some of the units have a balcony, but not this one."

"That's good." He smiled faintly. "If Randall tries to get in, he's only got one option."

"I—I hadn't thought of it like that." She frowned.

"That's why I'm here," he replied. "It's my job to think of these things." He nodded at the doorway that led to the hall. "Hungry?"

"Yes." She tossed her panties into the closet and walked past him. "What's on the menu?"

He followed her, heading toward the kitchen. "I thought I'd make salmon with a dill sauce and some lemon risotto."

Jillian stopped dead in her tracks; if he hadn't been paying attention, he'd have walked right into her. She slowly turned around. "Are you serious?"

"Yes. Why? Would you prefer something else?" He knew from the way she'd inhaled the bacon at the diner that she wasn't a vegetarian. But perhaps she had a food allergy?

Jillian shook her head. "No. That sounds amazing. I just wasn't expecting something so fancy."

Baldwin laughed. "Just wait. You'll see it's not that complicated."

As soon as they reached the kitchen he started to assemble the ingredients he'd picked up at the store. Jillian hung back, giving him space to work. "Is there anything I can do to help you?"

He could tell she wasn't used to standing around

while other people worked. So he told her how to make the dill sauce while he prepped the risotto. Soon, they were standing side by side, mixing and stirring together.

Baldwin felt himself relax as they worked. Normally, he cooked alone and only for himself. But having Jillian working beside him was...nice. They didn't speak other than to talk about the recipe, or for him to ask where something was located. Still, he enjoyed having her there. She wasn't one of those people who had to talk to fill a silence. She seemed just as content as he was to remain quiet and stay focused on the task at hand.

He showed her how to drizzle the sauce over the fish. After she popped it into the oven, she leaned against the counter and watched while he added broth to the risotto.

"How did you learn how to cook?"

Baldwin shrugged. "I spend a lot of time by myself when I'm working. I don't like eating fast food and dining out gets expensive. So I started watching cooking shows online in my downtime, and I decided to start practicing."

"That's impressive," Jillian said. "I take it you stay in places with a kitchen when you travel?"

He nodded. "Yeah, I always go for the extended-stay hotels. That way I don't have to haul pots and pans around." He didn't tell her that he enjoyed cooking, as it gave him something to focus on that wasn't work-related. He had a few close friends, but due to the nature of his job he moved around a lot, so it was difficult to make connections. The kitchen was a constant for him, a place he could go and forget about the world while he made a meal.

"Sounds like you think of everything," she said softly. She nodded at the pot on the stove. "It smells delicious."

"Hopefully it'll taste just as good." He stirred the broth into the rice, waiting until it was fully absorbed before adding a bit more. He could feel her gaze as she watched him work, but he refused to let it affect him.

In a matter of minutes, the meal was ready. Jillian gathered utensils and fixed drinks while he plated the food and brought it to the table.

She sat across from him and took a bite. "Wow," she said, her mouth full. "This is wonderful."

"I'm glad you like it," Baldwin said, pleased by her reaction. It was nice to know he'd impressed her, even if that hadn't been his main goal.

They ate in silence for a few minutes. If this had been a date, he would have tried to make conversation, asked about likes and dislikes, that kind of thing. But because it was just business, he didn't feel the need to be chatty.

Apparently, Jillian didn't feel the same way. She cleared her throat, then spoke. "Can I ask you a personal question?" She sounded hesitant.

Baldwin considered the request. He didn't blame her for being curious about him. It was smart of her to have run a background check before letting him into her home. But what more could she want to know?

"Sure," he said finally.

"Was your brother always so..." She trailed off, clearly searching for the right words. "So conniving?"

Baldwin nodded, relaxing a bit since he wasn't actually the focus of her question. "Oh, yeah. Even as a kid, he would hold a grudge forever. And he was always big on getting revenge if he felt like he'd been wronged somehow."

"Were you two close at all?"

"No. We're very different, so we didn't hang with the same crowds. He completely wrote me off when I joined the marines after high school."

Jillian's features twisted in disbelief. "Really? Why is that?"

The familiar feeling of resentment began to bubble up in Baldwin's chest as he recalled Randall's hateful words just before he'd shipped out for basic training: *You're going to make great cannon fodder.*

"Randall planned on going to college. He thought anyone who chose a different path lacked intelligence and wasn't worth his time."

"What about your parents? Did they share his opinion?"

Baldwin tilted his head to the side. "In a way, yeah. None of them understood why I chose to join the military instead of go to college."

Jillian finished the last bite of salmon and leaned back in her chair. "Still, they must have been proud of you, especially after you won all those medals and commendations."

"They were, kind of," Baldwin acknowledged.

"They still thought military service was beneath me, but at least I had distinguished myself, as they put it."

Jillian frowned. "Wow. I can kind of see where Randall got his attitude. How did he respond to your awards?"

Baldwin smiled. "It got under Randall's skin, to know I'd done well for myself. And when I got out and started my own business, it made him even angrier."

"So that's why you think he'll come," Jillian said.

"Exactly." Baldwin gathered Jillian's empty plate and placed it on top of his own. "He can't stand me, and he apparently has it out for you, as well. He won't be able to pass up the chance to go after us both."

He rose and took the plates to the kitchen sink, then gathered up the dishes they'd used to cook. "I'm thinking one or two days and he'll show his face. Maybe we could pose in front of the window in your bedroom—you know, make it look like we're a couple? That would really set him off."

He started the water and squirted some soap on a sponge. "Best-case scenario, he'll attack you and I can nab him while he's distracted."

Jillian appeared at his elbow. "I'll do this," she said shortly. She hip-checked him away from the sink, leaving him no choice but to step aside. He glanced down, surprised to find her face was tight with anger.

"Uh, what's going on?"

"Nothing." She practically spat the word as she attacked the risotto pot with the sponge.

Ri-i-ight. Baldwin was no expert where women

were concerned, but he recognized danger when he saw it. Jillian was now a ticking time bomb, and he had no desire to stick around and wait for her to detonate.

"Okay. Well… If you're cool here, I think I'll go unpack."

"Yep. Fine." She didn't look at him, just kept her head down as she focused on the dishes in the sink.

Baldwin took a step toward the door. "Ah, good night then." It was still early in the evening, but it was clear Jillian didn't want to see him anymore. Better to retreat to the guest bedroom and get some work done on his laptop.

"Good night."

He retreated through the living room into the guest bedroom and shut the door quietly. After toeing off his boots, he lay down on the bed and stared at the ceiling fan.

Jillian was clearly upset. But for the life of him, he couldn't figure out why. She'd seemed to like the food he'd made, and she'd been interested in helping him cook. Even their conversation had been going well, at least in his opinion. Apparently, she felt differently.

He sighed, hoping this wasn't a sign of things to come. They were going to be spending a lot of time together, and it would be much easier if she wasn't so moody about it.

His phone vibrated in his pocket. Baldwin removed it and glanced at the screen. It was a message from his client, asking if there were any updates on his brother's case.

Not yet, he thought, listening to Jillian's footsteps as she moved past his door and walked to her room. *But soon.*

What. An. Ass.

Jillian clenched her jaw as she scrubbed the dishes, her anger bubbling as she processed what Baldwin had said.

Best-case scenario, he'll attack you and I can nab him while he's distracted.

That was his plan? For her to be assaulted so Baldwin could step in like some kind of savior? She knew he'd intended to use her as bait to draw out his brother, but she'd had no idea of just how far he wanted to take things.

Even the thought of Randall touching her was enough to make Jillian's skin crawl. Randall wasn't physically imposing like Baldwin; he was about her height, and if anything, he was as thin as she was. But even slight men had a deceptive strength about them, and she didn't want Randall grabbing or groping her.

And what if he had a weapon? She might be able to fend him off for a few minutes if it was just him, but if he had a knife or a gun, she wouldn't have a chance.

Where the hell did Baldwin get off? Did he honestly think that she'd sit passively and wait for Randall to attack her, then just let him do it until Baldwin deemed the time was right to intervene?

"I don't think so," she muttered, jamming the last dish into the drying rack next to the sink.

But it wasn't just Baldwin's ridiculous plan that had her seeing red. It was the fact that she thought they'd been getting along. He'd seemed a little rough around the edges earlier today, and his comment about her personal life had stung. But then he'd shown up with groceries and cooked a lovely meal. He'd even taught her some tricks in the kitchen. She'd learned a little more about his family and his relationship with his brother, and he'd started to seem like a nice guy. A little on the gruff side, but still—a decent human being.

And then he'd gone and pulled the rug out from under her.

With one careless remark, he'd shown her what he really thought of her. And while Jillian understood she wasn't going to come out of this experience with a new best friend, she hadn't expected Baldwin to be so...detached. It was almost clinical, the way he'd talked about Randall attacking her. As if he truly didn't care if she got hurt. He'd said before that he was focused on apprehending his brother so he could get the rest of his fee, but Jillian had assumed he'd act within the limits of decency. That he didn't really intend for Randall to touch her, much less assault her.

Now she knew the truth. Baldwin saw her as nothing more than a pawn, an object he could manipulate to suit his purposes. He talked a good game about keeping her safe, but really, he *wanted* Randall to try to hurt her.

Jillian stalked through the living room and down the hall to her bedroom. She had half a mind to barge into the guest room and kick Baldwin out. But as she shut her door behind her, she knew that would be a mistake.

When Randall did strike—and Baldwin was acting as though it was a matter of *when* more than *if*—having Baldwin around would prove useful. The man might not give two figs about her, but no way was he going to let his brother escape. She had no doubt he'd move heaven and earth to get his hands on Randall so he could collect the rest of his money.

And while Baldwin's apparent lack of human emotion made him a world-class jerk, it also made him predictable. Jillian could count on him to make whatever choice would lead to him getting paid.

Which meant that even though Baldwin was staying just down the hall, in effect, she was alone. There was no need for her to worry about being a good hostess or to try to keep him entertained while he lived with her. She wasn't going to ignore him—that would be rude. But she wasn't going to initiate conversation or try to get to know him. What would be the point? He'd spelled it all out for her at the diner, making his motivations and intentions very clear. She had simply been too naive to take him at his word, choosing instead to think that no one could be that coldhearted.

Now, though, Jillian knew better.

In a way, it was a good thing that Baldwin had been so transparent tonight. If he hadn't just come out and said what he'd been thinking, Jillian probably would have made the mistake of trusting him. At least this way she knew to keep her guard up when he was around.

Hopefully, he wouldn't be here for long.

Chapter 5

She woke to the smell of coffee.

Jillian glanced at the clock on her nightstand: seven on the dot. It seemed Baldwin was an early riser, too. For a moment, she considered hiding in her room until he left. But, no, that was the coward's way out. Besides, she had no idea what his plans were for the day. He might very well intend to stay in her condo 24/7, until Randall decided to make his move.

While the idea of shutting herself off from the world held some appeal, Jillian didn't have that option. She had a midmorning meeting scheduled with her attorney. Hopefully he would have good news for her on the legal front.

Jillian took a quick shower and braided her hair. Then she slipped on a green sweater dress and a pair of dark brown knee-high boots. The first time she'd met her attorney had been in jail, when she'd been sporting sweatpants and an old T-shirt. Today, she was aiming for a more professional look.

As she stepped out of her room, she recognized the scent of hot syrup mingling with the aroma of coffee. Baldwin was standing by the stove, flipping pancakes with his back to her. He was dressed in a pair of flannel pants and a long-sleeved dark gray Henley that clung to his muscles. Jillian couldn't help but stare at his butt for a few seconds before reminding herself that no matter how good he looked, Baldwin might as well be a machine for all the emotion he displayed.

"Good morning," she said as she walked into the kitchen.

"Morning," he replied. "These are almost done."

She poured herself a cup of coffee and added a little sugar. "Not one for cereal?"

When he didn't respond right away, she turned to find him staring at her, the spatula held in midair as the pancakes sizzled in the skillet, apparently forgotten.

Baldwin blinked and turned back, but not before she spied a dark flush on his cheeks. "Uh, no. I prefer a hot meal in the morning." He scraped the last pancakes free and placed them to the side of the existing pile. "I'll eat those," he muttered. "They're a little burned."

Jillian hid a smile behind her cup. Had she actually caught Baldwin checking her out? The thought of it was almost enough to make her laugh.

The table was already set with plates and silverware, so she carried over her mug and took a seat as Baldwin brought the pancakes. "These look great," she remarked as he put down the plate.

He stepped away and returned with some sliced fruit. "Thanks," he said. "I know you had pancakes yesterday, but you don't have a waffle iron, so I couldn't make those."

"I'm not complaining," she replied. If Baldwin was going to cook every meal while he was here, she might be willing to overlook the more obnoxious facets of his jerkish demeanor.

"You look nice today," he commented. She saw his glance slide to the side, and realized he was staring at her boots.

"Thanks," she said, between bites of breakfast.

"Hot date?" His tone was deceptively casual, but she heard a note of genuine curiosity.

Why did he care? Because he was actually interested, or because he was concerned about acting like they were dating to draw Randall into the open? The latter, she decided quickly. Definitely the latter.

"Hardly," she said. "I'm meeting with my attorney to go over my case."

"Ah." His shoulders relaxed a bit, probably due to the relief of knowing she wasn't going to jeopardize this little farce. *Yes, I'm playing along*, she thought to herself. *You'll get your money soon enough.*

"What about you?" she asked between bites of pancake. Baldwin's cooking put Mae's efforts to shame, but she wasn't about to tell him that. "Any plans for the day?"

"A few errands," he said. "I have some friends in the region who are keeping an eye out for Randall. I'm going to check in with them, see if they've heard or seen anything."

Friends? Jillian nearly did a spit take with her coffee. Mr. Emotionless actually had friends?

The shock must have shown on her face because he lifted one eyebrow. "Yes, I know. Surprise, surprise, there are people out there who actually like me."

"Are they as repressed as you?"

The corners of Baldwin's mouth twitched. "You think I'm repressed?" He ran his gaze over her body, his blue eyes bright. Jillian felt a wave of heat wash over her at his frank appraisal, and she fought the urge to shiver.

He leaned forward, making her grateful for the table separating them. "Believe me," he said, his voice a low rumble, "I can be very expressive under the right circumstances."

Jillian wanted to look away, but she refused to give him the satisfaction of knowing he'd affected her. So she forced herself to shrug. "If you say so," she replied, bringing her mug to her lips to hide the flush she felt creeping up her neck.

Baldwin leaned back, the smug smile on his face making it clear he hadn't missed a thing.

"We should go out to dinner tonight."

Jillian choked on her coffee and began to cough.

Baldwin slowly got to his feet and stepped over to

crouch beside her. His big hand rubbed circles on her back while she sputtered and tried to catch her breath.

"I'm sorry, what?" she squeaked out. She blinked at him, eyes watering.

"You heard me," he said, handing her a napkin. Jillian glanced down, relieved to find that although she had coffee dripping off her chin her dress was still clean.

It was hard to breathe with him standing so close. The scent of his detergent filled her nose, along with a warm, slightly spicy note that she assumed was his skin.

"Are you tired of cooking already?" She dabbed at her chin, glancing down to avoid his gaze. His eyes were practically electric at this range, almost too intense to look at. "I'm not as skilled as you are, but I do okay in the kitchen."

"That's not the issue." His hand stilled on her back and she held her breath, torn between a desire for him to keep touching her and the need for him to stop before she made a fool of herself.

Baldwin got to his feet, his fingers trailing across her shoulders as he stood. Jillian's nipples stiffened in response. She hurriedly crossed her arms as Baldwin sat across from her once again.

"Then what's the problem?"

He lifted one shoulder in a casual shrug. "We need to be seen together."

"Oh." That's right—she'd forgotten about their little public charade. If they were going to draw out Randall, he had to think they were together first.

"Any suggestions?"

Jillian considered the question. Baldwin had said they didn't have to get physical in public, so that meant no overly romantic places. But they needed to look like more than just friends, or else no one would believe Baldwin had moved in with her.

"How about Grave Gulch Grill?" she suggested. Her uncle Geoff owned the place, and the food was consistently good. "It's nice, but not too fancy."

"Sounds perfect," Baldwin replied. "Does six work for you?"

"That's fine," Jillian replied. "I'll meet you here and we can go together." She stood and began to gather up the dishes.

"I've got this." Baldwin took the plates from her hands and walked to the sink.

"You cooked," she protested. "It's only fair that I clean."

He looked her up and down, his gaze hot. "Not dressed like that," he muttered.

A tingling sensation spread through her. It had been a long time since a man had shown any kind of interest, and she was out of practice. That was the only reason she had responded to Baldwin's touch. Her hormones didn't care that he was an ass who only wanted to use her to get to his brother. Her body had its own ideas about ways he could use her, and none of them was appropriate.

I've got to start dating, she thought. Between the stress of being Randall's favorite punching bag and the long hours she'd been pulling at work as they all tried to undo the damage Randall had done, there'd been little time for a personal life. Jillian generally wasn't aware of her loneliness but being around Baldwin emphasized how long it had been since she'd made a connection with someone.

"I have a key for you," she said, desperate to change the subject. "Let me grab it."

The junk drawer was next to the stove, so fortunately she didn't have to get close to him again. The spare key was buried under several layers of crap, but she found it soon enough.

"Here you go." Jillian set it on the counter, making sure to keep distance between them.

"Thanks," he said. He shot her a glance over his shoulder. "You have my number. Be sure to call me if you need anything today."

"Ah, okay." It felt strange, this sense of needing to check in with someone. Jillian was used to being on her own, doing stuff alone and on her schedule without thinking about someone else. Knowing that she was going to come home to Baldwin was a bit unsettling. "Same to you, I guess."

He turned around and leaned against the counter, drying his hands with a dish towel. "Oh, I'll keep track of you," he said, a sly grin spreading over his face that made her stomach do a little flip. "Trust me."

Baldwin breathed a sigh of relief as the door clicked shut behind Jillian.

He was used to seeing her dressed in shapeless

T-shirts and baggy pants. When she'd come into the kitchen dressed in normal clothes, he'd been stunned.

It turned out she did have curves. In all the right places.

The green dress wasn't at all revealing—it had a high neckline and long sleeves, and the hem came to her knees. But the sweater fabric clung to her breasts and hips, showing off her very feminine assets.

And those boots! There was something about knee-high leather that he found incredibly sexy. He'd had a hard time keeping his eyes off her legs, and he knew she'd caught him looking at least once.

Baldwin shook his head. Overall, it was a perfectly professional outfit, one she'd probably worn to work dozens of times.

Why, then, had it gotten to him so much?

And why was he irritated at the thought that his brother might have seen her dressed like that?

He had no claim on Jillian. She was her own woman, and they weren't involved in any way other than this temporary arrangement. It was ridiculous of him to be affected by her, or to even think about how other men might look at her.

Still, he couldn't deny that he'd felt the stirrings of attraction when they'd first met. Now that they were spending more time together, and now that he'd had a good look at what she'd been hiding under those glorified pajamas, his libido was definitely taking notice.

And unless he missed his guess, she was feeling something, too.

He'd seen the way her nipples stood at attention

when he'd touched her. Oh, she'd crossed her arms to hide her response, but not fast enough. It had taken all of his self-control not to react, but he didn't want to embarrass her. He knew she thought he was a jerk, but he saw no reason to validate that opinion. After all, he had assured her that he had no romantic interest in her; he wasn't about to go back on his word now.

Better to shake off any thoughts of Jillian Colton and focus on the job at hand. The sooner he found Randall and turned him in to the police, the sooner he'd get paid and could move on to the next job.

With that in mind, he headed for the bathroom and took a quick shower, then dressed and grabbed his phone and keys. Time to check in with his associates in the region and find out if they'd had any sight of Randall. He didn't think his brother had gone far, but it was good to cast a wide net.

He headed out the door—no nosy neighbors to scandalize today—and climbed into his truck. If his hunch was correct, and Randall was still around, then Baldwin needed to make himself visible in Grave Gulch.

"Tick tock, brother," he muttered to himself. "I'm coming for you."

Chapter 6

"I'm sorry, Ms. Colton. I wish I had better news."

Jillian sat in the office of Rodney Jones, attorney at law, and tried hard not to cry. Jones had just finished going over the evidence the police had against her, and it was even worse than she'd thought.

There were several full fingerprints at the scene of the most recent robbery, along with quite a few partials. People had been convicted on less evidence. But the true nail in her coffin was the discovery of the stolen jewelry in her closet.

"I know you probably hear this all the time, but I am innocent." How many times had she said that recently? But it was important that she kept saying it, kept pushing back against the narrative that she was a thief. People would always doubt, and her reputation might never recover from this. Still, she would never stop speaking the truth.

Rodney smiled kindly. "Believe it or not, I don't actually think you did this."

Jillian blinked in surprise. "You don't?"

Rodney shook his head. "I took this case as a favor to Evangeline," he said, referring to her cousin Troy's fiancée, the former Grave Gulch assistant district attorney. "She asked me to look after you, and I'm happy to represent you. But I have to say, as soon as I stepped in as your counsel, I heard from numerous people on the police force, everyone telling me you couldn't have committed these crimes. Not to mention, there's been a great number of people in Grave Gulch who have been framed in recent months. It's not farfetched to assume the same has happened to you."

"Really?" Her voice was barely a whisper as she struggled to contain her emotions. It meant a lot to know that the people she worked with didn't think she was a criminal, despite the forensic evidence against her.

"Yes," Jones continued. "I can call them as character witnesses if your case goes to trial. But I think the DA might be willing to cut a deal, and if so, you should consider it."

"No." Jillian started shaking her head before he'd even finished speaking. "I'm not going to jail for something I didn't do. I won't give Randall Bowe the satisfaction."

Rodney leaned back in his leather chair. "That

man has caused a lot of problems in Grave Gulch," he said. "But unless we can positively link him to these crimes, I don't see how we can prove your innocence."

"Isn't it enough to show he's always had it out for me? That we never got along and he was always picking on me?"

Rodney shook his head. "We can certainly try to create doubt and make it look like Bowe planted evidence. But that would be a tough sell for a jury, especially now that he's on the run."

"Did the police check the surveillance cameras in my building? I know there are cameras at the entrance. There's no other way for Randall to gain access to my condo, so he must be on tape!"

"They did pull the footage, and as soon as they release them I'll have my staff look over the recordings. But, Jillian, you have to know that some of the homes that were burglarized have security footage, as well. It shows a tall, slender figure dressed all in black and wearing a ski mask. Unfortunately, you match that general description."

"So does Randall," she said, a sense of desperation rising in her chest. Why couldn't anyone see? He'd planned all of this! He'd known exactly what to do to frame her, and now she was in real danger of going to prison. It was enough to drive her mad with worry!

"I know," Rodney replied. "That's a good thing—it means the surveillance footage doesn't definitively prove it was you committing the robberies."

"But that's not enough?"

"I'm afraid not," he replied. "Not at this point, anyway."

She was silent a moment, processing everything he'd told her. "So you're saying that unless I can find absolute proof that Randall Bowe is framing me, I'm going to jail?"

Rodney shifted in his chair, as though trying to dodge her question. "Nothing in life is certain," he hedged. Jillian lifted one eyebrow and he shrugged. "All right, yes. Based on how things look right at this moment, I'd say that's very possible."

Tears sprang to her eyes again and she blinked hard.

"Try not to get too discouraged," Rodney said. "We're still in the early stages of things. My team is going to examine all the evidence with a fine-tooth comb, and we'll do everything we can to exonerate you."

"I'm sure you will," Jillian said. "But I do a lot of my work in the lab. I know how powerful forensic evidence is, and how important it can be in getting a conviction. I'm sure the district attorney will have quite a lot to say about my fingerprints being found at the crime scene, and I can't imagine a jury is going to believe Randall Bowe would go to all this trouble just to frame me, despite the fact he tried to blame me for other things in the past, like the evidence he falsified in Everleigh Emerson's case. What's that saying? The simplest explanation is generally correct? Well, in this case, the simplest explanation must be that I'm guilty."

Jones nodded. "That's true. If this goes to trial, we will have a battle on our hands. But give me a little credit. I have my own rhetorical tricks, and I'm good at my job. I'm going to fight for you, Ms. Colton."

"I'm glad to hear it," she said. "I just hope it will be enough."

Jones got to his feet and extended his hand. "I'll be in touch as our investigation moves forward. Don't hesitate to call me if you have any questions, or if you find something that might help your case."

Jillian shook his hand. "I'll let you know." She debated telling him about Baldwin's plan to use her as bait to trigger an attack from his brother, but decided against it. If Baldwin's scheme worked, the case against her would disappear and Jones would be free to spend his time on his other clients. If it didn't work, well, she'd still be here, in need of an attorney.

Rodney's office was on an idyllic tree-lined street of shops, boutiques and cafés. Jillian set off down the sidewalk, feeling restless. The thought of going home held no appeal; she didn't feel like talking about the meeting with Baldwin. He'd listen to her talk all right, but he'd be about as sympathetic as a houseplant.

What she wanted was to talk about her situation with someone who cared. Grace's face popped into her mind, but no; she couldn't call her cousin, not with Internal Affairs watching her case so closely. Wainwright would assume any contact she had with her law-enforcement relatives was collusion, and she didn't want to get them in trouble.

Bryce was out, as well—he was still healing, and

besides, he'd done enough by running the background check on Baldwin. And as for Madison? Her sister had already gone through so much lately; she'd found Wes, and she'd nearly been killed by the son of a man seeking revenge for his own father's death. Jillian didn't want to add to the drama.

A few of her girlfriends had called, leaving messages of support. But Jillian didn't have the energy to rehash everything with someone who wasn't already in the loop. She was just so…tired. If only she could close her eyes and wake up to find this was all just a horrible nightmare!

She was settling in for a good sulk as she walked down the street, headed in the general direction of the parking garage and her car. There had to be some way to prove Randall had planted the evidence against her, but how? He'd gone to great lengths to put her fingerprints at the scene of the last robbery, and it had probably been child's play for him to break into her condo and hide the stolen jewelry. Too bad her building didn't have security cameras on each floor… And she doubted Randall would have been careless enough to leave his fingerprints at her place. How, then, could she prove her innocence?

"I need a better lock," she muttered to herself. The idea of Randall in her home, in her private space, was distressing. He probably didn't have a reason to come back—after all, she was on the hook for these robberies, and the evidence against her was pretty air-tight. But Jillian didn't want to take any chances. Randall was the kind of man who enjoyed gloating, and she didn't want to wake up one night to find him standing over her, terrorizing her in a sick celebration of his victory.

She stepped to the side, closer to the buildings to be a little sheltered from the chilly wind, and reached into her purse for her phone. A quick search yielded a couple of numbers for locksmith services, but five minutes and two calls later, she hung up in disappointment. Neither company could come out today; she'd made an appointment for the day after tomorrow, which would have to be good enough.

"Baldwin is there," she told herself. And while he might not care about her, he was fixed on getting his brother. If Randall did show up at her place again Baldwin would stop him, if for no other reason than his paycheck.

"Jillian?"

At the sound of her name, she turned to see another of her cousins, the former police chief, Melissa Colton, walking in her direction.

"I thought that was you!" Melissa said, smiling broadly as she approached. "It's good to see you!"

Jillian couldn't help but smile at the older woman. She'd always looked up to her cousin, who'd led the GGPD for years with the kind of grace under pressure Jillian envied.

"Hey!" she said, feeling a genuine burst of happiness break through the gray clouds of her mood. "How are you?"

They hugged briefly. "I'm fine," Melissa said. "Just doing a little shopping." She held up a small bag, embossed with the label of the baby boutique just down the street. "I couldn't resist," she said sheepishly.

"Are you feeling okay?" Jillian asked. Melissa was in her first trimester of pregnancy, and Jillian remembered their cousin Desiree having lots of morning sickness when she had been pregnant with her son, Danny.

"So far, so good," Melissa replied. "I get a little nauseated now and then, but nothing like what Dez experienced. Mostly I'm just tired."

"Then it's a good thing you turned the reins over to Brett," Jillian said.

Melissa nodded. "Yeah, he's the right guy for the job. I don't think I could have trusted anyone else. We're going to make it formal this evening. It's going to be a small ceremony, at my insistence."

Jillian touched Melissa's shoulder. "I know you don't want to make a big deal of it, but for what it's worth, I'm proud of you. You were a great chief."

Melissa smiled, but then a sudden gust of wind made them both wince. "Are you busy?" Melissa asked. "I've been craving hot chocolate, and I'd like to catch up with you."

Jillian considered her options. She could go home and wallow in self-pity, or she could spend some time chatting with her cousin.

It was a no-brainer.

"That sounds great," she said. "I could use something warm to drink."

They walked about half a block and ducked into

a small coffee shop. They ordered their drinks, then snagged a table by one of the storefront windows.

"So tell me," Melissa began, after a barista delivered two big mugs, steaming with hot chocolate. "How are you really doing?"

"I'm terrified," Jillian confessed. "I don't want to go to jail."

"Do you really think that will happen?" Melissa asked.

Jillian filled her in on the meeting she'd just had with her attorney, and the fact that all the evidence was currently stacked against her. Melissa was a good listener—she didn't interrupt or try to change the subject, and she only asked a few questions while Jillian told her everything.

"I just don't know if a jury would believe I'm innocent, given the evidence." She took a sip of her hot chocolate, feeling glum.

"It does seem like the deck is stacked against you," Melissa said. "But I think you're overlooking all of Randall's behavior."

Jillian frowned. "What do you mean?"

Melissa shrugged. "This is a guy who we know fabricated evidence to interfere with the convictions of several people. He's been on the run for months, but he hasn't disappeared quietly. How many people has he contacted to taunt while he's been in hiding? How many times has he texted or called or emailed, just to gloat or antagonize?"

"A lot," Jillian admitted. Randall had even contacted her a few times, telling her she was a bad scientist and that she should quit. He'd repeated his long-standing criticism that she wasn't cut out for her job and revealed that he'd messed with more of her cases than anyone knew.

"Based on what you've told me in the past, Randall was always hypercritical of you. I'm sure your coworkers would testify to that, as well."

"He certainly wasn't quiet about his thoughts," Jillian said, shuddering at the memory of some of his tirades against her.

"All of this paints a picture of a highly disturbed egomaniac," Melissa said. "It won't be hard for your attorney to argue that Randall is vindictive and sees you as a target. Given his forensic knowledge, and the fact that he's confessed to manipulating evidence in many other cases, it's not a stretch to assume he's planted some things against you."

"Maybe you're right," Jillian mused. What Melissa was saying made a lot of sense, and Jillian appreciated her positive take on the situation. For the first time since this all began, she started to feel a bit hopeful that maybe Randall wouldn't get away with framing her after all.

Melissa smiled. "I know it doesn't seem like it now, but don't give up yet. The truth will come out. It always does."

"I just hope it comes out in time to keep me from going to jail," Jillian sighed. "I don't mean to sound so negative, but I feel like I can't talk to anyone about this." She gestured to Melissa. "Present company excluded, of course."

"Why's that?" Melissa asked.

Jillian shrugged. "I just don't want anyone to get in trouble for talking to me. The guy from IAB who arrested me was practically salivating at the thought of implicating my family in a cover-up. I'm worried if I speak to anyone, he'll make a federal case out of it."

Melissa wrinkled her nose. "Yeah, both Grace and Brett mentioned that Wainwright got out of hand. He's new in the department. Camden wanted the case, but he was worried that given his connection to Grace, it might appear inappropriate for him to handle the investigation."

"I understand," Jillian said. "It would have been nicer to have him there the other night, but I get it."

Melissa leaned forward and lowered her voice. "Between you and me, Wainwright has been told to dial it back. A lot. Brett filed a complaint with his supervisor, so hopefully he'll calm down."

"Wow." Jillian was touched at the knowledge the police chief had stepped in like that. She had no doubt Brett would go to bat for his officers, the same way Melissa had when necessary, but as CSI, Jillian wasn't one of his direct reports. The fact that he'd stood up for her behind the scenes made her feel supported and gave her hope that the people she worked with didn't all view her as a criminal.

Melissa smiled. "We're all pulling for you, Jillian." She sipped the last of her hot chocolate. "You've been through a lot lately, what with your dad coming back into your life and the constant stress of Randall Bowe lurking over us all. Just know that a lot of people believe you're innocent and are working hard to find a way to prove it."

Jillian's eyes stung and she blinked hard to keep the tears from falling. "Thank you," she said, her voice shaking a little. "That means a lot."

"Call me if you need anything," Melissa said as she got to her feet. "My days are a lot freer now that I'm not the chief of police anymore. I'd love to meet for coffee or lunch sometime."

"That sounds nice," Jillian replied as they walked to the door. "I'll probably give you a ring soon."

Melissa pulled her in for a quick hug in front of the café. "I'm this way," she said, pointing up the street.

"And I'm this way," Jillian said, nodding in the opposite direction.

"It really was good to see you," Melissa said. She studied Jillian's face for a moment, and Jillian got the impression she was searching for something. She tried to look strong—maybe Jillian just needed to fake it until she truly felt that way?

"It's going to be all right," she said, holding Jillian's gaze intently. "I know it doesn't seem like it right now, but Randall is not going to win."

"I know," Jillian said, assuring both her cousin and herself. "I'm going to keep fighting. I'm not going to let him take me down."

Baldwin stopped at the door to Jillian's condo, taken aback by the thumping music he could hear coming from within her place. She hadn't struck him as the type to dial up the volume and disturb her neighbors. It was still daytime, though, so it wasn't like she was hosting a rave at two in the morning.

He unlocked the door and let himself in, expecting to find her relaxing on the couch or maybe working in the kitchen. As he moved into the living room, he caught a glimpse of what she was doing and it stopped him in his tracks.

She was dressed in a bright blue sports bra and black leggings, her hair pulled off her face in a braid that hung midway down her back. Sweat glistened on her skin, and in the late-afternoon light streaming in from the windows, she looked like she was practically glowing.

Baldwin swallowed hard as he tracked the movement of a droplet of sweat as it slid down her neck and into her cleavage. He tore his glance away to look at the TV screen, and realized she was watching some kind of exercise video. It looked like a combination of kickboxing and high-intensity dance. Jillian moved in time to the instructor, making him think she'd done this particular workout before.

She looked like some kind of graceful warrior, the way she planted one foot and lifted her other leg in a waist-high kick. Then she bounced on the balls of her feet, making her breasts move invitingly. Baldwin felt the stirrings of arousal and realized he needed to stop watching her or he'd wind up embarrassing himself.

Just then, Jillian pivoted to face him as she

punched out. She froze in midpunch, then completed the movement and turned back to continue with her workout.

Baldwin cleared his throat. "Sorry," he said loudly, so that she could hear him over the music. "I just got here. I didn't realize you'd be home yet."

"It's fine," she said, panting as she kicked, punched and twisted in her savage ballet. "I'll be done soon. The music won't be on much longer."

"Take your time," he muttered as he walked around her to get to the guest bedroom. He couldn't very well stand there and stare at her like some kind of creep.

He shut the door behind him and took several deep breaths, trying to subdue his libido. But the sight of Jillian Colton's long, lean body clad only in a few pieces of tight fabric was going to stay with him for a while. He'd seen the hint of her curves in that dress she'd worn this morning. Now, he'd gotten enough of an eyeful that he didn't have to rely on his imagination to fill in the blanks.

The sound of her panting breaths seemed to follow him into the room, making it hard to think. If he'd known she was going to be exercising, he could have mentally prepared himself for the encounter. But walking in and seeing her skin glistening with sweat and her figure on display was making his body respond in all kinds of annoying ways.

"Not gonna happen," he muttered. He was here to do a job, that was all. Jillian was nice to look at, but looking absolutely could not lead to touching.

It wasn't that Baldwin didn't enjoy sex; he was quite happy to sleep with a willing woman. But he never mixed business with pleasure. Sex would be a distraction that would keep him from doing his job. Not only did he have a reputation to uphold, but this case was also personal. If he let down his guard and succumbed to the temptation of seducing Jillian, Randall would have an advantage over him. And that was a thought that Baldwin simply could not tolerate.

The room seemed to vibrate with the thumping bass of her music, the walls pulsing in time to his heartbeat. He needed a distraction, and fast.

Shower. That would do it. He needed one before dinner, anyway. Might as well get it out of the way now. Perhaps the cold water would help cool his libido.

He grabbed a towel and his toiletries and opened his door. He deliberately kept his eyes focused on the floor, the wall, anything but the sight of Jillian only a few feet away, still kicking and bouncing in time to her video.

He ducked into the bathroom like a man evading enemy fire and closed the door behind him. The drone of the water soon helped muffle the lingering sounds of her workout, but he could still hear the echoes of her breathing in his head. That sexy, panting little gasp was going to haunt his dreams tonight—he just knew it.

Baldwin stepped under the cold spray of water, gritting his teeth against the chill. Focus on the job, he told himself. After he'd brought Randall into custody, he could indulge in some carnal pleasures.

Until then, he was going to embrace his inner monk.

No matter how tempting he found Jillian Colton.

Chapter 7

"This place is nice," Baldwin remarked as they walked into the Grave Gulch Grill.

Jillian nodded. "Definitely a step up from the diner. Nothing against Mae, but she's a little too practical for tablecloths and a fireplace."

Baldwin chuckled. "I imagine syrup and ketchup leave a lot of stains."

They approached the hostess station and Baldwin said, "We have a reservation under Bowe."

Jillian gaped at him. A reservation? When had that happened? She'd assumed they'd simply show up and grab a table. But it seemed he'd put more thought into this dinner.

She eyed him as the hostess led them to their table—a small spot right next to the large bay windows facing the street. As they took their seats, Jillian couldn't help but feel like they were on display.

"Did you ask for this spot?" she said softly after the woman had walked away. "We're very visible."

Baldwin winked at her as he opened his menu. "That's the plan, remember?"

Her stomach did a funny little flip. *Get a grip*, she told herself. *The man winked. That's all.*

Still, she'd felt a kind of nervous energy ever since he'd caught her working out. She hadn't planned on him seeing her like that; when she'd arrived home to find the place empty, she'd been so restless and frustrated that she'd figured a quick exercise session would help settle her mood. And it had worked, right up until the point she'd turned and seen Baldwin standing in the doorway, his icy gaze tracking her every movement.

He'd been dark and dangerous, the gleam in his eyes making him look like some kind of predator. Jillian's body had responded accordingly, her muscles locking as she froze in shock. For a brief, unhinged second she'd considered running, hoping he would chase her. Then her brain had taken control once more and she'd forced herself to continue exercising.

Knowing he was in the shower hadn't helped things. She'd walked past the bathroom door on the way to her room, pausing slightly as she'd entertained the ridiculous fantasy of letting herself in. It wasn't hard to imagine him naked, water running over his broad shoulders and down the valley of his spine. Did he have chest hair? Or was it all smooth skin and muscles? It was a question that was probably going to keep her up tonight…

"Jillian?"

She shook herself free of the memories and focused on the present once more. "Sorry, yes?"

A small smile crossed Baldwin's face. "Where'd you go?"

"Oh, just thinking about something that happened earlier today." Heat crept up her neck and she ducked behind the menu to hide the blush that was sure to follow.

"How did the meeting with your lawyer go?" he asked.

"About as well as could be expected," she said, risking a glance. He was reading his own menu, seemingly oblivious to her reaction. "Things don't look great for me right now."

Baldwin frowned and looked up to meet her eyes. "We'll get him," he said confidently. "Randall isn't going to get away with this."

"That's what my cousin Melissa said," she replied. "I ran into her and we had a drink together. She seemed convinced the truth would come out."

"It usually does," Baldwin said, studying his menu again. "Sooner or later."

Jillian envied his certainty. Both he and Melissa had a kind of breezy confidence that everything would work out in the end. It was an attitude she herself had once held, right up until she'd been framed for robbery and now faced the prospect of prison.

Since her circumstances had changed, she no longer had the luxury of embracing such platitudes.

A waitress stopped by their table and they ordered drinks. Jillian noticed the way the young woman subtly eyed Baldwin, her tongue darting out to moisten her lips when she spoke to him. Jillian couldn't exactly fault her response; he looked especially good tonight. This was the first time she'd seen him in anything other than a dark T-shirt and jeans, and the white dress shirt, slacks and sport coat gave him a classically handsome look. Not for the first time, she was glad she'd made an effort tonight, if for no other reason than to make their pairing more believable to anyone looking.

They made small talk until their drinks arrived, and then they ordered food. Once they were alone again, Jillian decided to ask a question that had been nagging her most of the day.

"You know, it's funny," she said, taking a sip of wine. "My attorney told me there's security footage from the last robbery, but the person on the tapes is dressed all in black and has a mask on. Since Randall and I have similar shapes, they can't prove it's not me."

Baldwin nodded. "But they can't prove it is you, either," he pointed out.

"I guess." She waved that way. "Don't you think it's a little odd that you and Randall look so different? I mean, he's about my height and thin, whereas you're..." She trailed off, gesturing up and down to encompass his body, which, to her eyes, was the exact opposite of his brother's.

Baldwin shrugged. "We've never resembled each other. He looks more like our father, whereas I've got our mom's coloring. For whatever reason, I put on muscle easily in high school. But then again, I worked at it. I played several sports, while Randall was more into studying. Then I joined the military, and fitness is a big part of being a marine. So while I can't help the fact that I'm taller than Randall, I think if he devoted any time to working out he'd probably bulk up a little more."

"That doesn't sound like something he'd be at all interested in doing," Jillian said with a laugh. "I got the impression he hated physical activity of any kind. Anytime we had to collect evidence from a scene, he'd complain if it involved more than simply walking into a room and getting started."

"Seems about right," Baldwin remarked with a smile. "He's always preferred to stay indoors, reading a book or watching television."

"Whereas you're the outdoorsy type?"

He tilted his head to the side. "Well, I can tell you that marines aren't known for being sedentary. And I was definitely roughing it for most of my deployments."

"I can only imagine." Jillian shook her head. "There's no way I could serve in the military."

"Why's that?" There was a note of genuine curiosity in his tone. "You're smart. You're active. You could do it."

"I like hot showers and flushing toilets and air-conditioning," Jillian retorted. "It's also nice to not have people shooting at me."

Baldwin chuckled, the low rumble sending a tingle down her spine. "Fair enough," he replied.

They chatted until their food arrived. Jillian had opted for chicken, while Baldwin had ordered a steak.

She took a bite and moaned slightly as the flavors hit her tongue. "This is fantastic," she mumbled around the food. Baldwin watched her chew, amusement in his eyes. She swallowed and wiped her mouth. "Sorry, I was really hungry."

"I'm glad you like it," he said, cutting into his steak.

They ate in silence for a few minutes until he spoke. "I've been meaning to ask, why crime-scene investigation? It's kind of an unusual field. What made you get into it?"

Jillian leaned back a bit, surprised by the question. Up until now, Baldwin hadn't seemed all that interested in her life, outside of how she could help him get his brother. But she had asked him questions about his family and time in the military. Perhaps he was simply trying to deflect?

"I've always enjoyed science," she began, taking a sip of wine. "I had thought about going to medical school and becoming a doctor, but I really enjoyed working in a lab and at crime scenes. A lot of my family is in law enforcement, as you know. And I guess through them, I became aware of CSI and realized that it would be a good fit for me. I get to help people and still be at the bench." She shrugged. "I have to say, I do love my job. It's a lot nicer now that your brother is gone."

"I imagine so," Baldwin said. "Based on what you've told me about how he treated you."

She studied him for a second, watching his Adam's apple move in his throat as he swallowed. "You're not like him at all, you know?" she mused. "Not just physically. Your personalities are polar opposites."

Randall was cool, aloof and vindictive. Baldwin was serious and focused. And while she'd initially thought he lacked emotion, she was beginning to realize her first impression had been too harsh. Baldwin *did* feel; he just tried not to show it. But she'd caught glimpses of him when he didn't know she was looking, and in those unguarded moments, she'd seen humor, desire and compassion. Certainly more humanity than she'd ever seen Randall display.

"Like I told you from the beginning," Baldwin said quietly. "I'm not my brother."

"I know that now," Jillian replied. "And I'm sorry I keep comparing you to him. You deserve better."

Surprise flashed across his face and he blinked at her. "I…" He trailed off. Then he shook his head. "Thank you," he said simply.

They finished their meals, and the waitress brought over dessert menus. Jillian began to demur, but Baldwin caught her gaze. "We're on a date, remember?" he said softly.

"Fair enough," she said. It was strange; this morning, when he'd suggested dinner, she'd figured it would be an awkward, torturous affair. In actuality, though, she'd enjoyed spending time with Baldwin and getting to know him a little better. Her trust in him was growing, that was certain.

As was her attraction.

She focused on the menu, pushing aside that annoying realization. "What looks good to you?" she asked. "I can't decide between the crème brûlée or the cheesecake."

"Why don't you order one and I'll get the other? We can share them both," he suggested.

Jillian arched an eyebrow. "You don't strike me as the sharing type," she said teasingly.

"Let's just say I'm willing to make some sacrifices." Baldwin grinned, and for the first time, Jillian noticed the dimple in his left cheek. For a moment, she forgot he was a single-minded bounty hunter and instead saw him as a charming, handsome man. One who made her skin tingle and her stomach quaver with nervous anticipation. Once again, she reminded herself that this was just an act.

But who said she couldn't enjoy herself a bit while it lasted?

It didn't take long for their desserts to arrive. Baldwin tasted the cheesecake and made a low sound in his throat. "This is really good."

Jillian couldn't help but smile at his reaction. Before she knew what was happening, Baldwin had scooped a bite of cheesecake onto his fork and leaned over the table, offering it to her.

"Here you go," he said softly, his blue eyes warm.

Jillian held his gaze as she leaned forward and took the bite. Her lips tingled with awareness as they touched the fork, the tines still warm from his mouth. It was a quintessential date move, one she knew he was playing up for their potential audience. So why did she see desire flash across his face as he watched her eat?

Warmth spread through her, along with a hunger for an entirely different kind of dessert. *It's the wine*, she decided. She'd only had one glass, but she didn't usually drink. It had to be affecting her—that was the only reason she was responding to Baldwin so strongly. She knew this was all an act, but her body seemed to have forgotten that point.

"Well?" he asked.

"It's really good," she said, swallowing the sweet bite. "Maybe we should trade?"

He laughed, genuinely laughed, for perhaps the first time since she'd met him. It was an infectious sound, one she wouldn't mind hearing again. "You haven't even tried yours yet," he pointed out.

"So I take it that's a *no*?"

Baldwin shook his head and pushed his plate to the center of the table. "It's fine," he said, smiling indulgently. "I like to watch you eat."

Jillian swapped the cheesecake for the crème brûlée, unsure of how to react to his statement. On one hand, she was flattered that he paid that much attention to her. But now that she knew he was looking, she felt self-conscious.

"You're going to give me a complex," she muttered. "I'm not used to having an audience."

"Don't worry about it," Baldwin replied as he used his spoon to break the caramelized crust of the dessert. "Mmm," he said after the first bite. "You do what you want with the cheesecake. I'm going to stay focused on this."

Jillian watched him from under her lashes, unable to look away as pleasure flitted across his face. He closed his eyes briefly, clearly enjoying himself. It was an expression she'd never seen him wear before, and her imagination ran with it.

A dark room, Baldwin moving over her, his eyes closed as he…

"Change your mind?"

She jumped at the question and realized she hadn't eaten again since he'd given her the cheesecake. "No," she said, forking off another bite. "Just pacing myself." *And having inappropriate fantasies about you*, she added silently.

They finished their desserts in companionable silence. The waitress dropped the check at their table. Jillian reached for it, but Baldwin placed a large hand on the small leather folder, preventing her from touching it.

"My treat," he said.

"Thank you," Jillian replied, knowing there was no point in arguing with him. They were supposed to be on a date, after all, so it made sense for him to pick up the tab.

An unexpected pang of reluctance hit her as they

stood to leave. This had been a surprisingly nice experience, one she didn't want to end quite yet. Even though she understood they were both playing a part, she'd enjoyed spending time with Baldwin and seeing a different side of him. Now that she knew a little more about him, it was hard to think of him as a laser-focused automaton.

They stepped out to the sidewalk just as a cold gust of wind blasted down the street. Jillian shivered, wishing she'd thought to bring a coat. She ducked her head and squared her shoulders against the wind, hoping Baldwin wouldn't mind if they double-timed it to the car.

But just as she'd taken a step, the intensity of the wind eased. A pair of shoes came into her view and she glanced up into Baldwin's eyes.

"Here," he said, shrugging out of his sports coat. "You're shivering."

"I—" She'd started to protest, knowing he'd likely now be cold. But as he draped the warm fabric around her shoulders, she sighed involuntarily. The jacket was far too big for her, but it enveloped her like a warm hug, and it smelled like Baldwin.

He leaned forward, arranging the fabric. The movement brought his face closer to hers, and she angled her head slightly to close the distance between them.

Baldwin sucked in a breath as their lips nearly touched. They stood there for a moment, breathing each other's air, hovering on the edge of a moment that could change everything between them.

Jillian felt a pull, almost as if Baldwin was tugging on the lapels of his jacket to bring her closer. She practically ached to kiss him, to feel the pressure of his mouth on hers. But she held back, unable to move that last half inch.

Time seemed to stop as they stood frozen, locked in this possibility. Baldwin's lips parted, his eyes warm as he looked down at her.

It would be so very easy to close the distance. To lift her head up, to brush her mouth across his. Her head spun with the thought of it.

She was tempted to blame her reaction on the wine, but any lingering effects from her drink had disappeared when the cold wind had hit her cheeks. No, she couldn't blame this on alcohol. She wanted Baldwin. Wanted to feel his strong body pressed against hers, wanted to run her hands along the solid warmth of his chest and arms. To know what it was like to have his arms around her.

But she just couldn't give in.

If she cast off her self-control and kissed him, she had no doubt he'd kiss her back. And kissing would lead to touching, and touching would lead straight to her bed. As tempting as that thought was, she was certain the morning after would prove awkward and uncomfortable. Who knew how much longer he'd have to live with her before Randall made his move? With everything in her life so unsettled right now, the last thing she wanted was to add more drama.

Baldwin let out a little sigh. He lifted one hand and gently brushed a strand of windswept hair off her cheek, pushing it behind her ear. "Let's go," he said softly. "Don't want you to freeze out here."

Jillian pushed down her rising disappointment and started walking alongside him. It was the right choice—she knew that. Still, a small part of her wished she'd thrown caution to the wind. At least she'd have had a nice memory to look back on later.

They made it to the end of the block when a loud bang split the air. Jillian jumped at the sound, startled. Before she could even turn her head to try to locate the source, Baldwin grabbed her arm and yanked her into the doorway of a nearby shop. He pressed her into the corner and stood in front of her, his back a solid wall shielding her from the sidewalk and the street. Her heart thumped hard in her chest as she craned her neck to see around him. She just managed to catch a glimpse of a car pulling out of a parking spot a few feet away. Its headlights passed over them as the driver took off down the road, apparently oblivious to the scene unfolding behind him.

She felt Baldwin relax as it became clear the sound they'd heard had been the vehicle backfiring. He stepped away, then turned and looked down at her. She couldn't see his face in the shadows of the alcove, but his voice was still tense.

"You okay?"

Jillian took a half step forward so her back was no longer pressed against the rough brick of the building. "Yeah," she said. Her nerves were starting to settle, now that she knew Randall wasn't shooting at them. "What about you?" He'd reacted so quickly to the noise—was that his training kicking in, or did loud noises in general bother him after his time in the military?

"I'm fine," he said shortly. "We should keep moving. I think we've been out long enough for tonight."

He took her hand, but there was nothing soft or romantic about the gesture. His grip wasn't painful, but it was the impersonal touch of someone doing a job.

Jillian walked quickly to keep up with the pace he set, each step taking them farther away from the restaurant and those enjoyable shared moments of conversation and food. Part of her was sad at the realization that their evening was at an end. She'd genuinely liked seeing Baldwin let down his hair, so to speak. It was unlikely he'd act that away around her again, not now that he was back in professional mode.

It's for the best, she told herself as Baldwin unlocked the doors to his truck and helped her climb inside. Far better to keep things the way they were now, rather than risk making a move she was guaranteed to regret later.

Her frustrated libido was just going to have to learn to live with disappointment.

Baldwin flipped his pillow over with a sigh, wishing his body would just relax already. But his mind was too active, thinking about this case and the woman down the hall.

Dinner with Jillian had been nice. He'd actually enjoyed himself, something he hadn't thought possible. Usually when he was working, he was totally focused on the job at hand. Anything he did was in service to finding his target. So when he'd suggested they go to a restaurant tonight to bait his brother into making a move, Baldwin had assumed it would be just another work function for him.

But it wasn't.

If he was being honest with himself, the trouble had started this morning, when Jillian had come into the kitchen wearing that sweater dress. Then, to add to his temptation, he'd seen her working out in a sports bra and leggings, with a lot more skin on display. She'd looked even better at dinner, with her hair worn down in loose waves framing her face. He could have stared at her all night and not gotten tired of the view.

Try as he might, Baldwin was finding it harder and harder to ignore Jillian.

And she wasn't as prickly as he'd first thought her to be. When they'd had breakfast together, she'd been a little sarcastic and even a bit defensive. She'd given off big leave-me-alone energy, which had been fine by him. Now, though, he realized her night in jail had rattled her more than she'd wanted to admit. His mistake had been assuming that once things calmed down, she'd keep those walls up.

But if tonight was any indication, she was warming to him. Quite a bit.

He'd seen that flash of desire in her eyes when he'd put his jacket around her shoulders. Heard her breath hitch as their mouths almost touched. She'd wanted him. If he had closed the distance and kissed her, she would have fallen into his arms, and probably into his bed.

So why hadn't he made a move?

It was the question his hormones had been asking ever since they'd arrived back at her condo and gone their separate ways for the night. It would have been so easy to lean forward and brush his lips against hers. She was beautiful—but more than that, she was smart and funny. He wanted her—he could no longer deny it. And she wanted him, too. Or at least, she had in that moment.

But something had kept him from taking the leap. He knew on a subconscious level that just one kiss with Jillian wouldn't be enough. And, as much as he enjoyed the thought of taking her to bed, sex would change things between them. So far, they'd found a kind of balance with each other. But if they slept together, the equilibrium would be destroyed. It wasn't a step he wanted to take, especially since he had no idea when Randall was going to make his move.

So as frustrating as it was, he'd made the right choice. Better to lie here alone and unsatisfied than give in to temptation and ruin the dynamic he had with Jillian.

Now if he could just scrub his memory of the images of her in that sports bra, or her dress, or somehow forget the sense of possession he'd felt as she'd worn his jacket…

He rolled onto his side, wishing his brain had an off switch. While he was in the marines, he'd had no problem dropping off to sleep whenever and wherever the opportunity presented itself. Now that he was back in the civilian world, he'd lost that particular skill.

Baldwin closed his eyes, determined to win this battle. But his attention immediately shifted as he heard a quiet scratching.

What was that?

He sat up in bed, listening hard. People generally thought the middle of the night was a time of silence, but he knew better. Was one of Jillian's neighbors doing something? Or was it the heater kicking on?

He heard the noise again, a little louder this time. Baldwin slipped out of bed and crept to the door. This wasn't one of the normal sounds Jillian's condo made at night. Something was going on in the living room, or maybe the kitchen.

Randall. It's got to be him.

It seemed their little ruse had worked.

Moving quietly, Baldwin opened the top dresser drawer and took out his gun. There was a chance Jillian was foraging for a midnight snack, but since he hadn't heard her walk past his bedroom door, he'd bet his last dollar that his brother had come to call.

Baldwin silently opened the door and slid into the hall, careful to stick to the shadows. As he moved out of the bedroom, the sounds grew louder.

Kitchen, he realized. A soft clinking of glass and the sound of drawers opening made him think whoever was in there was rummaging around.

A sense of eagerness began to rise in his chest, but he tamped down the feeling. Thanks to his time in the military, he knew how to channel his adrenaline, to keep it from interfering with his job. At least he'd retained *that* ability.

The wall that divided the kitchen from the living room was only waist-high. As Baldwin crept closer, he saw Randall, his back to the living room, reaching for something in one of the cupboards.

Taking advantage of his brother's position, Baldwin quickly crossed the living room and entered the kitchen near the small table at the far end.

"Looking for something?" he asked.

Randall jumped, dropping the glass he held. It hit the floor and shattered, shards flying everywhere.

"Let me guess," Baldwin said. "You're here for another source of prints. What are you going to frame Jillian for this time?"

Randall glared at him from across the room. "It's not her I'm after."

Realization dawned. "Oh," Baldwin said softly. "You're going to set *me* up now?" He waited to feel surprised, but the emotion didn't come. And why would it? He and Randall had never had a good relationship. Randall's attempt to frame him was just the latest in a long line of grievances between them.

He shook his head, torn between the desire to laugh and yell. "For what it's worth, you're not very good at this. I haven't touched those glasses."

Randall's eyes narrowed. "You're lying."

"Am I? It doesn't matter." Baldwin lifted his gun, pointing it at his brother. His heart squeezed a bit, but he quickly strangled any residual sense of sentimentality. Randall might be his brother, but he definitely wasn't a good guy. He'd brought this on himself.

"You're done," he said.

Randall eyed the gun distastefully. "Really? You're going to shoot me?"

"If I have to," Baldwin replied evenly. He didn't want to pull the trigger—hell, he never really wanted to shoot anybody, much less a family member. But he carried a weapon because he was prepared to use it if need be. Hopefully Randall wouldn't force the issue.

Randall leaned against the counter. "How do you think this is going to work? Do you imagine I'll just throw my hands up and surrender? That you'll shove me in the back of your truck and take me to the police station?"

"That would be the easy way," Baldwin agreed.

"Have I ever made things easy for you?" Randall taunted.

Baldwin's tightened his grip on the gun, certain his brother was going to try something. Randall had known breaking into Jillian's condo would be a risk, especially now that Baldwin was here. So he had to have some plan in place, to deal with the possibility of discovery. Baldwin just had to figure out what it was before Randall could get away.

"You're not as smart as you think you are," he said, hitting Randall where it knew it would hurt the most.

Anger flashed in his brother's eyes as the insult hit home. "And you're not as strong as you think you are," he spluttered.

"Maybe so, but at least I know when I'm beaten."

Baldwin took a half step forward, keeping the gun level as he moved.

Randall laughed. "You think that's what is happening here? That you've beaten me?"

The flicker of worry grew stronger as Baldwin watched his brother. It dawned on him then that Randall's right hand was down by his side, effectively hidden from view. Did Randall have something in his pocket? Some device or weapon he thought was going to protect him? "Show me your hand," he demanded.

Randall looked simultaneously amused and bored. "What?"

"Your right hand," Baldwin insisted. "Lift it up so I can see it. Do it slowly."

Randall narrowed his eyes. "When have I ever taken orders from you?"

Baldwin opened his mouth to respond, but before he could get the words out, the situation went from bad to worse.

Jillian walked into the living room, rubbing her eyes. "Baldwin, are you hungry?" she asked.

His heart leaped into his throat at the sight of her. She had to get out of here. He could *feel* that Randall was about to make his move, and he wanted Jillian as far away as possible when his brother acted.

She looked up and saw him, then glanced over and noticed Randall. She froze, her whole body going tense as she realized who was standing in her kitchen. *"You."* The word was laced with so much venom it was a wonder Randall didn't drop dead on the spot.

Randall gave her a wave. "Nice to see you again," he said cheerily.

"Jillian," Baldwin said sternly. "Go back to bed."

Either she didn't hear him or she ignored him, because she remained rooted to the spot, glaring at Randall. "What the hell are you doing here?" she demanded.

"Just popping in for a visit," Randall said. "But don't worry, I'm leaving now."

"No, you're not." Both Baldwin and Jillian spoke at the same time. He returned his focus to Randall, taking another step forward.

Something—was it jealousy?—flashed across Randall's face. "You two make quite the pair," he said quietly.

"Jillian, go get your phone and call the police," Baldwin commanded.

Randall rolled his eyes. "Really, brother? Could you be more predictable?"

Jillian didn't move, and Baldwin risked a glance in her direction. "Jillian?"

"My phone is on the counter," she said, sounding pained.

"Right next to me," Randall disclosed, nodding at the device near him. "You know, you really should be more careful about where you leave things," he continued. "You always were sloppy, Jillian. That's why you'll never make a good CSI tech."

It was a low blow, one Baldwin hoped she wouldn't internalize. He knew how hard she'd worked to overcome the insecurities Randall had cultivated while they worked together. Hopefully, she now realized he was simply trying to gain the upper hand.

"Go to my room," Baldwin instructed her. "My phone is on the dresser." He didn't want her anywhere near Randall. If she got close to his brother, there was no telling what Randall might try to do to her.

Before she took a step, Randall spoke again. "You know what? This has been fun, but I'm bored. Time for me to go." With that, he raised his right hand, and a sense of horror washed over Baldwin as he realized his brother had drawn a gun.

Time seemed to stop as Randall aimed at Jillian. Baldwin screamed at his body to move—he needed to get to her and push her out of harm's way. But he was too slow.

Randall fired, the sound booming through the room like a thunderclap. Jillian jerked back, her mouth open in surprise. Then she started to fall.

Baldwin glanced over and saw Randall's back as he left the condo. A clinical, detached part of him knew he should pursue his brother. They might not get another chance like this, and Randall was still so close…

But he couldn't do it. All his training went out the window as he looked over in time to see Jillian land on the floor.

The instant her body hit the carpet, it was as though someone had snapped their fingers. Time started again, and Baldwin's legs responded to his brain's commands. In two steps he was by her side, tucking his gun into the waistband at the small of his back as he kneeled down to assess the damage.

She stared up at him, her face contorted with pain and confusion. The fabric of her pajama top was quickly becoming saturated with blood, making it hard for him to see exactly where she was injured. He grasped at the neckline of the shirt and ripped it apart, exposing her left shoulder. A small, neat hole marred the skin there, her blood welling up to fill the space.

Cursing at the sight, Baldwin quickly stripped off his T-shirt and hastily folded it into something approximating a bandage. Then he pressed it over her wound, pushing down hard.

Jillian's eyes went wide and he felt, more than heard, her moan. His ears were still ringing from the gunshot, and he imagined hers were, too. "It's okay," he said loudly. "You're going to be fine. I've seen worse."

It was true, but part of him was still panicking. He knew how quickly a seemingly simple injury could go south, and turn into something life-threatening. If the bullet had nicked an artery, or if she went into shock from the experience… He had to call an ambulance. The sooner she got to the hospital, the better.

Baldwin grabbed her right hand and held it on top of his T-shirt. "I have to get the phone," he said.

Tears welled in Jillian's eyes and she shook her head. "No," she said, her voice laced with pain. "Please don't leave me."

"I'll be right back," he promised. "You won't even

know I was gone." Then he pulled away, before the look on her face trapped him there.

He grabbed his phone from the dresser and returned in a matter of seconds, resuming his spot by her side. His heart thumped hard in his chest as he pressed one hand over hers to hold the makeshift bandage in place and used his other hand to dial.

How had things gotten so bad so quickly? How had he let Randall get the upper hand? As soon as he'd seen the gun, he should have fired. He was a trained marksman, much more experienced than Randall. He could have gotten off a shot and incapacitated his brother before Randall had taken his next breath.

But he'd been distracted. He'd let his worry and fear for Jillian take over, and pushed his instincts to the side.

And Randall had taken advantage of his weakness.

"Nine-one-one, what's your emergency?"

Baldwin quickly relayed the situation, his calm voice at odds with his internal chaos. If Jillian died... He shook his head, casting away the errant thought. She wasn't going to die from his mistake. She couldn't.

The operator wanted him to remain on the line until the ambulance arrived. Baldwin put the phone on Speaker and set it on the floor so he could use both hands to apply pressure to Jillian's injury.

"Baldwin." Her voice was strained, the sound breaking his heart. Tears dripped from the corners of her eyes into her hair.

"I know it hurts," he said, trying to soothe her.

He'd been grazed by bullets before, but he'd never taken a direct hit. The pain had to be nearly unbearable.

Jillian slid her hand out from under his and gripped his forearm, and he realized she wanted him to lean down. He lowered his head, his gaze locked on her eyes as he got closer.

"Go after him," she said firmly. "Get that bastard."

He nearly laughed. He was supposed to be the one worried about his job, not her. But, in this moment, their roles were reversed.

Baldwin shook his head. "I'm not leaving you," he said. "Not until the paramedics arrive." At that point, he could reassess the situation. Randall was gone, but perhaps he'd left some kind of clue as to where he was hiding.

Surprise glimmered in Jillian's eyes, a mirror of his own feelings. Since when had he let his worry for someone outweigh his sense of duty? Jillian's injury might be painful, but he could see now it wasn't lethal—the bleeding was already under control. He could have easily left her there while he searched for Randall, and he might have even caught up to his brother if he'd left after dialing 911.

So why was he still here, holding her hand and trying to reassure himself that she was going to be okay?

He gradually became aware of the operator's voice calling to him from the phone. "Sir? Sir? Are you there?"

"Yes." He picked up the phone and brought it closer to his mouth. "I'm here. What do you need?"

"The EMTs are entering the building," the woman said. "Can you make sure the door to the condo is unlocked and unobstructed?"

Jillian nodded at him, returning her hand to the shirt so she could continue to apply pressure. "Yeah," Baldwin said. "I can do that."

He got to his feet, feeling a little off balance as he walked to the door to open it. The squawk of a radio floated in the air of the hallway outside her door, and he knew the EMTs were getting close.

That was good. Baldwin needed someone to take over Jillian's care, because he was feeling so flustered, he wasn't sure how much longer he could stay focused. After propping open her door, he walked back into the living room. The sight of her lying on the ground, blood staining her carpet and her shirt, hit him anew and he started to shake, a fine tremor running through his muscles.

Fortunately, the paramedics arrived. Two men nudged past him and kneeled to assess Jillian. Baldwin hung back, giving them space to work. But as they started tending to her, Jillian started looking around, clearly searching for something.

It's me, he realized with a start. *She's looking for me*. Even though it was his fault she'd been hurt tonight, she still wanted to see him.

"I'm here," he called out. He walked over to stand a few steps behind one of the medics, making it easy for Jillian to see him.

The instant their eyes connected, he saw her body relax. And the strange thing was, his did, too.

HARLEQUIN® Reader Service —Here's how it works:

Accepting your 2 free books and 2 free gifts (gifts valued at approximately $10.00 retail) places you under no obligation to buy anything. You may keep the books and gifts and return the shipping statement marked "cancel." If you do not cancel, approximately one month later we'll send you more books from the series you have chosen, and bill you at our low, subscribers-only discount price. Harlequin® Romantic Suspense books consist of 4 books each month and cost just $4.99 each in the U.S. or $5.74 each in Canada, a savings of at least 13% off the cover price. Harlequin Intrigue® Larger-Print books consist of 6 books each month and cost just $5.99 each for in the U.S. or $6.49 each in Canada, a savings of at least 14% off the cover price. It's quite a bargain! Shipping and handling is just 50¢ per book in the U.S. and $1.25 per book in Canada*. You may return any shipment at our expense and cancel at any time — or you may continue to receive monthly shipments at our low, subscribers-only discount price plus shipping and handling. *Terms and prices subject to change without notice. Prices do not include sales taxes which will be charged (if applicable) based on your state or country of residence. Canadian residents will be charged applicable taxes. Offer not valid in Quebec. Books received may not be as shown. All orders subject to approval. Credit or debit balances in a customer's account(s) may be offset by any other outstanding balance owed by or to the customer. Please allow 3 to 4 weeks for delivery. Offer available while quantities last. **Your Privacy** – Your information is being collected by Harlequin Enterprises ULC, operating as Harlequin Reader Service. For a complete summary of the information we collect, how we use this information and to whom it is disclosed, please visit our privacy notice located at https://corporate.harlequin.com/privacy-notice. From time to time we may also exchange your personal information with reputable third parties. If you wish to opt out of this sharing of your personal information, please visit www.readerservice.com/consumerschoice or call 1-800-873-8635. **Notice to California Residents** – Under California law, you have specific rights to control and access your data. For more information on these rights and how to exercise them, visit https://corporate.harlequin.com/california-privacy.

He wasn't sure how long he stood there, holding her gaze while the medics did their thing. The police arrived and he explained what had happened, but he never moved, never looked away from Jillian. Some irrational part of him was afraid that if he stopped watching her, the EMTs would whisk her away and he'd turn back to find her gone.

"You'll need to get your crime-scene people in here," he said. "Make sure they dust for prints in the kitchen and on the door handle." Randall hadn't been wearing gloves, which was a mistake on his part. One that would prove helpful to Jillian's case. Surely her attorney could use this break-in to lend weight to the idea that Randall was framing Jillian?

"Let's go," one of the medics said. They had rolled Jillian onto a gurney, which the two men lifted to waist height as they stood. They started wheeling her out of the room and Baldwin moved to follow.

"Hey," said one of the officers he'd been talking to. "You need to stay here and finish giving your statement."

"No," he said shortly.

"Sir—" the other officer began, but Baldwin cut her off with a wave of his hand.

"I go where she goes," he declared.

At that moment, Brett Shea arrived. He stopped at the gurney and murmured something to Jillian, then made his way toward Baldwin. "I just got the call," he said. "What happened?"

Baldwin shook his head. "Can't talk now. But it was Randall."

Brett's eyes widened in understanding as Baldwin moved past. "Keep this place secured, Chief," Baldwin called out. "He might try to come back."

"I hope so," Brett replied grimly.

Baldwin grabbed Jillian's purse from the kitchen counter and jogged after the gurney as the medics rolled Jillian down the hallway. As soon as they got into the ambulance, he was going to message a friend and ask him to watch over Jillian's condo. There was no way Randall would come back tonight, not with all the activity going on now. But the police had to leave eventually, and with Jillian in the hospital, he'd have the perfect opportunity to steal prints again for another setup.

Baldwin wasn't going to let his brother get away again. And as much as Chief Shea wanted to apprehend Randall, Baldwin wasn't going to let that happen either.

You're mine, he thought darkly, picturing Randall's face. *Now it's personal.*

Chapter 8

"When can I go home?"

The young doctor sighed behind his surgical mask as he finished stitching the hole in her shoulder. "Ms. Colton—" he began.

"Please?" Jillian interrupted. "I'd just really like to sleep in my own bed tonight. Or what's left of it."

The hemostat and scissors made a little clinking sound as the doctor placed them on a metal tray. "I know you do," he said, reaching for the gauze squares and medical tape. "But you were shot tonight. You lost quite a bit of blood at the scene, and since you'll be getting a transfusion, we have to keep you for observation for a few hours at least."

"So maybe by lunchtime?" she asked hopefully.

"We'll see," the doctor replied evasively.

"Just rest and enjoy the pain relievers," Baldwin suggested from his spot in the corner.

He'd been standing there since they'd brought her into the emergency room, a tall, silent form watching over everything. She hadn't expected him to accompany her to the hospital—she'd assumed he'd stay behind or try to go after his brother. But he'd hopped up into the ambulance bay with the gurney, and the EMT had taken one look at Baldwin's face and swallowed any objection he might have had. It had been the same story once they'd arrived at the ER—Baldwin had silently but firmly made it known that he was staying, and Jillian had given permission for him to do so. Since he wasn't getting in the way, the staff didn't seem to mind his presence.

"I'm not going to be able to rest," she grumbled. "Not knowing that Randall is out there, waiting to break back into my condo." Just the thought of Randall lurking in the shadows of her building made her stomach cramp.

"No, he won't." Baldwin explained he'd recruited one of his friends in the area to watch her place from afar, to stop Randall if he did try to come back.

"That does make me feel better," she admitted. "You seem to think of everything."

Baldwin shrugged one shoulder.

"You're all set here," the doctor said. He pulled off his gloves and eyed her bandage appraisingly. "You'll want to see your regular doctor in a few days to get the stitches out, and in the meantime, keep the area clean and dry. The nurses will teach you how and when to change the bandage."

"Does that mean I can go? I feel fine." She sat up eagerly, hoping maybe the doctor had changed his mind.

The man shook his head. "We've been over this," he said. "You feel good now because of the drugs we've given you. Once those start to wear off, you'll be singing a different tune. Besides, your lab work shows you need blood. If I were to release you now, you'd probably pass out on the way."

Jillian knew he was right, but it didn't change the fact that she was desperate to go home. "Okay," she said.

The doctor offered her a smile. "I'll go see if the blood bank has sent up your bag yet."

"Thank you," she said as he left the room.

Baldwin's gaze was steady on her. "Why are you so eager to leave? You're safe here, and I've got someone taking care of your place."

"I know." She looked away, searching for the words to explain how she felt. "I just… I need to reclaim my home. Does that make sense?"

He tilted his head to the side. "In a way."

"Your brother…" She trailed off, then shook her head. Baldwin and Randall might share genetic ties, but she needed to stop linking the two men together beyond that. Baldwin deserved better.

"Randall broke into my home," she continued. "He touched my things. And now I'm absolutely convinced it's not the first time he's done so. I feel like my safe space has been violated, and I need to scrub the place clean of any reminder of his presence. Not to mention, a CSI investigation leaves behind a bit of a mess."

Baldwin nodded. "I'll help you." He paused, then cleared his throat. "That is, if you'll let me...?" He looked almost shy, as though he was worried that she might take offense at his offer.

She blinked, surprised at the question. "I would appreciate it," she said. "But you don't have to indulge my weird quirk."

"It's not weird," Baldwin said. "Randall destroyed your peace of mind. If cleaning your place will help restore it, then I want to help you. Besides," he added, sauntering over to the side of the bed as the corner of his mouth turned up in a grin, "you're pretty much down to one hand now. You need me."

"That's true," she acknowledged. She *did* need him, and for more than just help with the housework. She'd been on the edge of panic when Randall had shot her—between the pain and fear and shock of it all, she'd felt herself slipping into hysteria. But Baldwin's presence had kept her grounded. There was something about him that made her feel safe and protected. Even though she'd been lying there, bleeding on her rug, Baldwin's touch and voice had made her believe that she was going to come through this. She didn't understand why or how, but in the short time she'd known him, she'd come to trust him.

Maybe it was because he didn't lie to her. He'd been honest from the beginning about what he wanted from her and what he was prepared to do. While she'd initially found his honesty off-putting, she'd come to realize it was a gift. Baldwin had always told her the truth, so when he'd kneeled over her and said she was going to be okay, she'd believed him without question.

He took her hand now, his touch gentle as he stroked his thumb across her knuckles. "Jillian, there's something I need to tell you." His voice was gruff, as though the words pained him.

She could tell by the look on his face that whatever Baldwin had to say, it was going to be serious. "All right," she replied. "What's going on?"

Baldwin took a deep breath, clearly bracing himself. "It's my fault you got hurt tonight. I didn't think Randall had a weapon, and when I realized he was pointing a gun at you, I should have taken my shot." He shook his head. "I hesitated, and I'm so very sorry." He looked positively miserable, and she could practically feel the guilt coming off him in waves.

Her first instinct was to laugh—surely he didn't really think he was responsible for her injury? Except…he did. His eyes were troubled, and his lips were pressed together in a thin line. His powerful shoulders slumped, and Jillian got the impression that if she told him to go away and never return, he would.

For a man who claimed not to care about anyone, Baldwin was doing a very good impression of a guy with feelings.

"Baldwin," she said. It was important she take this seriously; she didn't want him to think she was dismissing his concerns out of hand. "I don't blame you for what happened."

"I should have acted faster," he said, apparently determined to flog himself for his perceived mistake.

"And done what?" she challenged. "Shot your brother?" Talk about a huge, life-altering decision. He flinched at the question, so she pressed on. "Do you really think I'd blame you for not firing at your own family?"

Baldwin looked up, emotion swirling in his blue eyes. "I told you when we first met that I'd do anything to capture Randall. That I had no sense of obligation or loyalty to him."

"That doesn't mean you should be ready to shoot him," Jillian pointed out. "Even though your relationship is broken beyond repair, he's still your brother. You grew up with him. He's blood. Despite everything he's done, it's only natural you would hesitate when faced with the choice to kill him."

"I wouldn't have killed him," he grumbled.

Jillian nodded. "I know, I know. You're a marksman. I heard about your awards." She flipped her hand over so she could lace her fingers through his. "Look, I don't know anything about guns. I've never held one, much less fired one. But I imagine that shooting at someone is a big deal. And when you know the person you're aiming at, it's got to be even more complicated. I'm not going to blame you for what happened tonight. I hope you'll give yourself some grace and realize you're not at fault here."

She squeezed his hand, and after a few seconds, he squeezed back.

"Thank you," he said quietly. "I'm not sure I deserve that."

"Yes, you do," she replied confidently. "Between the two of us, I'm the one in the hospital bed. That means I'm in charge."

His eyes glinted with amusement. "Are you sure? Because I don't think that doctor got the memo."

Jillian shrugged, then gasped as the movement tested the strength of the pain relievers she'd been given soon after arrival. Baldwin winced in sympathy. "Sounds like your meds are starting to wear off," he remarked.

"Maybe so," she said, breathing carefully so as not to further aggravate the situation.

"I'll see if I can find a nurse," he said, his expression worried as he watched her. "Maybe it's time for another dose."

Before she could lie and tell him that she was fine, he was out the door, a man on a mission. Once more, she was struck by the disconnect between Baldwin's gruff outer shell and his inner softie. She wasn't sure how she'd managed to get past his tough, no-nonsense exterior, but she was equal parts honored and tickled to know she'd affected him.

Not that it was all one-sided. No, he'd definitely slipped past her defenses, as well. In some twisted way, she was almost glad Randall had shown up tonight. His appearance had served to reset their focus, an adjustment she'd needed as she'd started to spend too much time fantasizing about Baldwin. Getting shot was definitely not her idea of fun, but it was a potent reminder of just what was at stake for her. She had to stop letting her hormones run the show and devote her energy to clearing her name.

In a matter of minutes, Baldwin was back. "I spoke to your nurse," he said, running a hand through his hair. "She said you can have more medication if you need it."

"I think I do," Jillian said. The ache in her shoulder was growing steadily worse, and if she wanted any chance of sleep tonight, it would help if she felt more relaxed. "You should go home. Get some rest."

Baldwin stared at her, his features twisted with disbelief. "Are you kidding me? Do you really think I'm going to leave you here alone tonight?"

A warm feeling started in Jillian's stomach and spread up into her chest. "You don't have to stay." She was touched by his offer, but didn't want him to stick around out of a sense of guilt or obligation.

"You're not getting rid of me," Baldwin replied, sinking into the chair by her bed. "But I have to say, I hope they put you in a room upstairs. I heard the chairs up there extend out into a makeshift bed." He stretched out his long legs and crossed them at the ankles, then leaned back and folded his hands over his flat stomach.

For one brief, irrational instant, Jillian considered inviting him to share her hospital bed. It wasn't terribly comfortable, but it had to be better than that stiff chair. Although, if she had Baldwin stretched out beside her, her body would be incapable of relaxing.

There was a tap at the door and a nurse entered, pushing a small cart piled with supplies. “All right,” she said as she approached the bed. “Let’s get you set up with this transfusion.”

“If it’s all the same to you,” Jillian said, “I think I’ll close my eyes. I’d rather not watch all of this.”

“No problem, sweetie,” she replied. “You just rest and I’ll take care of everything.”

Jillian took a deep breath and closed her eyes, trying not to think about the fact that a stranger’s blood was about to be put into her veins. It was all for the best, she knew, but it was still an unsettling thought.

After a few seconds, she felt Baldwin’s hand slip over her own. She sighed softly as the heat of his touch soaked into the muscles of her hand and seemed to radiate up her arm. “It’s okay,” he said quietly, his voice a low note in her ear. “I’ve got you.”

“You okay, man?”

Baldwin cracked open one eye to see Bryce Colton standing in front of him, his brow furrowed.

Jillian’s family had arrived soon after the nurse had set up the blood transfusion. Her mother had barged into the room first, followed closely by her sister, Bryce and her father. Baldwin had quietly slipped out the door, both to give them some time alone with Jillian and because he figured he was persona non grata to her family.

He’d found a chair in the empty waiting room and

closed his eyes for lack of anything better to do. Now that Bryce was looking down on him, he wished he'd found a different spot. Like the cafeteria. Or another building.

Baldwin sat up and cleared his throat. "Yeah, I'm good." Bryce took the chair across from him, his arm in a sling. A hot sense of shame filled Baldwin as he realized that Jillian and her brother now had matching injuries, although for very different reasons.

"Look," Baldwin said, deciding to lay his cards on the table, "it's my fault Jillian was hurt tonight. I know that. I own it. I've apologized to her, and she says she doesn't blame me." He shook his head, still marveling over her quick forgiveness. "I think once the pain meds fully wear off she might come to her senses on that front."

Bryce looked a bit puzzled. "O-o-kay…" he said slowly.

Baldwin leaned forward and put his elbows on his knees. "I told Jillian I'd keep her safe, and I failed. I take that very seriously. But my brother is still on the loose, and I have to bring him in. Now more than ever."

Bryce nodded. "I think that's everyone's priority now."

Baldwin took a deep breath. "I understand that your family probably hates me right now. And I get it—I hate myself a little bit, too. But if you could just wait until I catch Randall, I'd appreciate it."

Bryce frowned. "Wait for what?"

Baldwin shrugged. "If you need to retaliate… If

you or Jillian want revenge…" He shook his head, seemingly at a loss for words.

Bryce stared at him, awareness slowly dawning on his face. "Oh," he said. "You think I want to hurt you because my sister was shot tonight? That I'm going to do an eye-for-an-eye thing? Is that it?"

Baldwin shifted in his chair. "I mean, I understand if you want to. Or need to."

Bryce threw back his head and laughed, the sound echoing in the empty room. "Oh, man." He wiped the corners of his eyes with his free hand. "Baldwin, you have been hanging out for far too long with some seriously shady people."

Embarrassment rose in Baldwin's chest, making him uncomfortable. "I'm only trying to say…"

"I know what you mean," Bryce said. "And while there are a lot of Coltons running around Grave Gulch, we're not the Mafia. That's not how normal people do things, buddy."

"I know that," Baldwin replied. "It's just…" He trailed off, gathering his thoughts. "My family is very different. Randall and I were never close growing up. If he thought I slighted him in some way, he always got revenge." He shook his head as his memories and past experiences floated to the top of his consciousness. "You know I work in the shadows. A lot of the people who contact me are seeking justice, but always with an edge."

"It wears on you after a while," Bryce said.

Baldwin glanced up, a little surprised at the other man's perception. "Yeah, it does," he said.

"I can relate." Bryce leaned back in his chair. "I catch killers for a living. Part of my job is to try to get inside their heads. It can be tough to shake that off."

"Exactly." Baldwin felt himself relax as Bryce spoke. It wasn't often he talked to someone who truly knew what he was dealing with. Even Jillian didn't fully understand—she thought him cold and unfeeling, but if she'd seen even half of the things he'd experienced… If he didn't shut down his emotions and put walls up to keep from getting close to people, he wasn't sure how he'd cope.

"How do you do it?" he asked curiously. He knew from his time in Grave Gulch that Bryce and Olivia Margulies were involved and had recently gotten engaged. How did Bryce let go and trust someone like that?

Bryce considered the question for a moment, seeming to sense Baldwin's true intent. "To be honest, it's taken me a while to learn how to trust." He nodded his head in the direction of Jillian's room. "Did you meet my dad on your way out the door?"

"No." Baldwin had been so intent on escape he hadn't stopped for introductions.

Bryce tilted his head to the side. "That's okay. The thing is, Wes has been out of our lives for twenty-five years. We grew up not knowing him, because he was in the witness-protection program. Before that, he was Richard Foster. That's the name I'd always associated with him. So when he showed up again with this new name, I had a really hard time trusting him. It's taken me a lot of soul-searching to accept the reasons why my father had to leave, and to make peace with the fact that he's now called Wes."

"I can imagine," Baldwin said. "That's a lot of changes to take in at once."

Bryce nodded. "I'm not saying everything is perfect between us. But I'm working on it. And Olivia has helped me so much with that process. That's part of what I love about her. She makes me better, or at least makes me want to be better. I eventually realized I'd be a fool to walk away from that kind of support."

"Yeah," Baldwin said weakly, his thoughts turning to Jillian. There was no doubt he cared about her, but did his feelings go beyond that? More importantly, could he *afford* to let them grow deeper?

"There you are," said a male voice. Baldwin glanced over to find Jillian and Bryce's father walking toward them. "I figured I'd give the girls a few minutes to say goodbye to each other and come find you."

Baldwin and Bryce both stood as Wes drew closer. He stuck out his hand to introduce himself. "I'm Baldwin Bowe, sir."

"Wes Windham," the older man replied. "You were the one with Jillian tonight. Is that right?"

Baldwin nodded, mentally bracing himself for the vitriol that was sure to come his way. Bryce might not want to pound him into the ground, but surely Jillian's father would have something to say…

Wes clapped him on the shoulder. "I'm so glad you were there," he said, staring hard into Baldwin's eyes. "I shudder to think what might have happened if Jillian had been alone when that man broke in."

"I… Yes, sir," Baldwin stammered. Jillian's family was so *nice*, the complete opposite of the kind of people he was used to dealing with. He kept waiting for the other shoe to drop, but was starting to get the feeling that maybe it wouldn't.

He saw Bryce hide a smile at his apparent confusion. At least he was keeping Jillian's brother entertained tonight.

"Jillian said you'd stay with her until her former coworker is brought into custody?" Wes asked. It was clear he didn't like the thought of Jillian being alone right now, and Baldwin definitely couldn't blame him.

"Yes, absolutely. I plan to stay with her as long as she'll let me," Baldwin replied. Then he realized what he'd said and mentally kicked himself. He would stay with Jillian until the job was done. After that, he was going to move on. It's what he always did.

So why did the thought of leaving Jillian behind give him a pang in his heart?

"Good, that's good," Wes said, interrupting his thoughts. "I know her mother will be relieved to hear she'll have someone with her. We've been so worried about her, and after Bryce's injury—" Wes indicated Bryce with his hand "—well, Verity nearly came out of her skin when she heard that she'd been shot."

"I can only imagine how hard it is to hear your child has been hurt," Baldwin said.

"Yes, well," Wes replied. "It was bad enough when Madison was targeted by a criminal. We thought the worst was over, but when Bryce was shot it was really difficult for Verity. And then to get the news about Jillian…" Wes shook his head.

Baldwin felt a surge of pity for the man. It was clear he cared deeply for his children, even though he hadn't been there for much of their lives. He seemed like a good guy, and he was glad Jillian had her father back.

"It's okay," Bryce said, clapping his free hand on his dad's shoulder. "Madison and I are fine, and Jillian is going to make a full recovery, as well. You and Mom can stop worrying."

Wes snorted. "Sure, son. Like that's possible."

"We are all adults," Bryce said. "You don't have to fret about us all the time."

Wes chuckled. "Just wait until you and Olivia start having your own babies. I'm going to remind you of that remark, and then you'll understand. It doesn't matter how old you or your sisters get. You'll always be my kids."

"Okay, okay," Bryce replied. From the tone of his voice, it was clear they'd had this discussion before. Baldwin couldn't help but smile at the interaction, while at the same time wishing he'd had that kind of relationship with his own father. There was a real sense of affection between Bryce and Wes, a connection that had perhaps been weakened but not extinguished by the years they'd spent apart. Baldwin's own dad had never been that way with him, certainly not in any sense that he could remember.

Jillian's mother and sister joined them, and Baldwin introduced himself. He extended his hand to Verity, but before he knew what she was about she'd wrapped her arms around him and buried her face in his chest.

"Thank you," she said, her voice laden with emotion. "You saved my baby girl."

Baldwin patted her shoulders, her gratitude making him feel awkward. "I didn't do much," he said quietly.

Verity leaned back, her eyes brimming with tears. "Don't try that with me," she warned. "Jillian told us how you stopped the bleeding and called the ambulance."

"Yes, ma'am." He had done those things, but he didn't feel they were deserving of praise. "She would have done the same for me," he added.

"That's true," Verity said, sniffing delicately. "But let's hope it doesn't come to that. I think one gunshot wound is more than enough." She looked meaningfully at Bryce, who held up his free hand.

"Don't look at me," he said jokingly. "It's not my fault Jillian tried to copy me."

Verity narrowed her eyes. "At least her injury doesn't require surgery."

Bryce lifted his uninjured shoulder in a shrug. "Maybe she should have tried harder."

Baldwin bit his lower lip to keep from smiling as Madison giggled and Verity shot Bryce a mock glare. "Very funny," she said archly. Then she turned back to Baldwin. "I'm not going to try to talk you into going home tonight—I like knowing that you'll be here with my girl. The nurse said they'll be moving her soon, and I made sure to ask for a few extra pillows for you."

"Thank you," said Baldwin, touched by her gesture. He'd basically accepted the fact that he was going to spend a mostly sleepless night by Jillian's side, but if he was able to stretch out with a pillow or two, he might actually get some rest.

Verity reached up to cup the side of his face in her hand. "You come see me later, after she gets out of the hospital. I'll make us some tea and we can get to know each other better."

"I..." It was on the tip of Baldwin's tongue to protest, to explain to Jillian's mother that it wasn't like that between them. To tell her they weren't dating, that he was simply using her as part of his job. But as he looked into Verity's eyes, so full of hope, he couldn't bear to tell her the truth.

"I'd like that," he said simply. And, for a second, he let himself imagine what it would be like to accompany Jillian to her mother's house. How nice it would be to sit with them and talk, and to learn more about Jillian and her family. Verity would grill him about his own family and intentions toward her daughter, and he'd reassure her about his feelings for Jillian.

It was the normal thing to do, and the way people all over the world met the parents of their partners.

But it would never happen for him.

Because Jillian wasn't his partner. Not in the romantic sense of the word, anyway.

And wasn't that a pity?

The ache in his chest intensified, as though his heart objected to classifying Jillian as "just" a professional acquaintance. She might have started out that way, but he was well beyond emotional detachment now.

"Come on, guys," Bryce said. "Let's get out of here so Baldwin can get some rest. I know Olivia is anxious for me to let her know how Jillian is doing."

Verity leaned in for another hug, squeezing tightly before releasing him. "I hope I see you again soon," she said, smiling up at him.

Baldwin smiled back. "I think you will."

"You take care, son," Wes said, shaking his hand again. "And thank you."

Madison and Bryce said goodbye, as well, and Baldwin watched as Jillian's family headed for the exit. They walked together, Wes with his arm around Verity's shoulder, Bryce and Madison following. The very picture of a close-knit group.

Watching them, Baldwin was struck by a sense of longing. He'd never had that kind of bond with his relatives. After a while, he'd stopped wishing for it, instead convincing himself that he was better off on his own. But listening to them tease each other with no trace of underlying malice, seeing the way they'd all rallied to visit Jillian in the hospital... It made him realize he'd been fooling himself. He did need people in his life. He wanted that connection with someone, that sense of belonging. His own family would never provide support and encouragement. But perhaps he could choose his own clan.

He turned and walked back toward Jillian's room, a new possibility dancing on the edges of his mind. What if he didn't have to leave when the job was done? Why couldn't he stay in Grave Gulch, maybe make a few friends? Would it be so bad if he let himself take a break?

The door swung open silently, and he stood there for a second looking at Jillian. Her eyes were closed, her face relaxed. She didn't appear to be in any pain, a fact for which he was grateful. The sight of her tugged at his heart, and he couldn't help but wonder—what would she think about this possible change of plans? Would she be happy to see him stay, or would she want him to leave so she could move on with her life without a reminder of Randall?

They were questions he couldn't answer, not yet. And…did he really want to know? The thought that she might tell him to go made his stomach twist into knots. Maybe it was better to just ride off into the sunset, the way he'd always done.

It was certainly the safer option. Given the risk to his heart, it was probably for the best.

After all, families were overrated.

Chapter 9

Jillian opened her eyes, blinking as she took in the unfamiliar surroundings. This room was…different, somehow. Not the same one she'd had in the ER. There was a quiet, steady beep coming from somewhere, and the faint scent of bleach in the air. They must have moved her at some point, though for the life of her, she couldn't remember when. Her last memories were of her mom and sister kissing her goodbye and walking out the door. Jillian had intended to rest for only a few minutes until the nurse came back in to check on the transfusion. Apparently, her body had decided to sleep instead.

Must have been the painkillers, she decided. They'd kicked in while her family had visited, giving her a dreamy, floaty sensation, making her feel like she was wrapped in a big cotton ball. It was a pleasant, if strange, state of being. Now her shoulder throbbed, making it clear the medication had worn off.

She shifted on the bed, debating whether she should call the nurse. What time was it? One might be coming soon, anyway, to do a check. She looked to the side, and that's when she saw him.

Baldwin was lying on the low couch against the wall, his large frame contorted into an awkward-looking position on the too-small cushions. It had to be terribly uncomfortable, but he'd managed to go to sleep. She watched the rise and fall of his broad shoulders with each breath, the way the fabric of his shirt pulled across his chest with each movement. His face was in the shadows so she had to imagine how his features must look when relaxed and peaceful. Something told her that even asleep, Baldwin probably still had a fierceness about him.

"You're awake." His voice rumbled in the otherwise quiet space, a raspy sound that made goose bumps break out along her arms.

How long had he been watching her stare at him? He must think she was some kind of weirdo. "Uh, yeah," she replied eloquently.

Baldwin sat up and stretched, unfolding his body to its normal length. He winced as he moved, confirming her suspicions about the comfort of the sofa. "I'm surprised you're still here," she said.

He tilted his head to the side. "I told you I wasn't going anywhere."

"I know. But when my family arrived, I thought maybe you figured I was okay. I saw you sneak out, but I must have been asleep when you came back."

"You were," he confirmed. "Out like a light and snoring like an asthmatic rhino."

Jillian's cheeks heated. "I don't snore!" she protested.

Baldwin leaned forward and she saw the grin on his face. "Yeah, you do," he said. "But not that bad. I've definitely heard worse."

She shifted in the bed, absorbing this new piece of information. Sleeping in the same room as Baldwin was a strange kind of intimacy, especially given these circumstances. They hadn't even kissed, so he really had no business knowing what kind of sounds she did or didn't make while unconscious.

"Are you hurting?"

"A little," she admitted. "How did you know?"

"Because you're tense," he replied. "And you're awake. If you weren't in any pain, you'd still be out."

"Maybe I'm just an early riser," Jillian said, feeling exposed. He was too damn observant, and it made her uncomfortable to be the focus of his attention while they were alone in the dark like this.

"Want me to find a nurse?" he asked.

"No," she said.

"There's no point to you staying in pain," he pointed out. "You're not going to get a prize for refusing medication."

"I know," Jillian replied. "But I'm sure they're busy. Someone will come check on me eventually.

Besides," she said, "I don't really like the side effects from the drugs."

"They make you feel loopy?" he asked.

"Yeah, something like that."

"Some people would say that's the best part," Baldwin teased. "But I understand. I don't like that feeling, either."

"You've had experience with hospital-grade pain relievers before?"

He nodded, and she remembered a snippet Bryce had told her about Baldwin's record. "That's right," she said slowly. "You have a Purple Heart, don't you?"

"I do," he confirmed. "It's buried somewhere in my closet, with my other medals."

"Not one for sentimental displays?"

Baldwin shook his head. "Not really. I suppose if I ever have kids, they'll want to see them someday, but I don't need to look at a few shiny bits of metal every day."

"Your mom didn't want to frame them for you?"

He laughed. "No. I told you, my parents are not happy with the choices I've made."

Jillian shook her head. "I don't get that. You're a good man. I don't understand why they aren't proud of you. My parents are over the moon when I have a good week at work. If I actually did something that warranted a military commendation, they'd probably burst."

Baldwin shrugged. "Your family is very different," he said. He scratched the side of his cheek. "Your mom is really sweet."

"You met her?" Jillian was surprised to hear that, given the way he'd left when they'd arrived earlier.

"Yeah," Baldwin said. "I was in the waiting room while your family was here. Bryce came and found me, and he and I chatted for a bit. Then your dad came out."

"You met him, too?" Jillian couldn't help but feel a little bittersweet over this news. She would have liked to have been there when Baldwin met her family. It would have been nice to see his face and watch how her parents responded to him.

"He's a good guy," Baldwin said. "Bryce told me it's a little awkward since he's been gone so long."

Jillian nodded, feeling a pang of sadness. "It's been tough," she said. "He left when we were very young."

"What happened?" Baldwin said. "If you don't mind my asking."

Jillian shook her head. "Of course not—it's fine." She filled him in on the story, about how her father witnessed a murder on the outskirts of Grave Gulch. He'd been put into the witness-protection program and her mother had been told he'd died in combat. "Mom never really moved on," she said. "He was the only man for her, and once she thought he'd died, that was it."

"It must have been quite a shock to find out he's alive."

"Oh, yeah," Jillian said. "We have my sister to thank for that. Madison is the one who saw him first and made the connection." She told him about her sister's realization, and all the danger that had followed. "Fortunately, that part of his life is over now."

"I'm sure he's thrilled to be back with all of you," Baldwin said.

"I think so," Jillian mused. When Wes had first returned, she'd had a few doubts. She'd questioned why he hadn't tried to find them before, even after the threat that had put him into witness protection was apparently gone. But she'd come to understand Wes had been afraid. He'd been gone from their lives for so long. They'd all thought him dead and had moved on, though her mother hadn't fallen for another man. If he had shown up out of the blue, there was no telling how they might have responded. "I wish things had played out differently, of course, but I think Wes has truly always tried to do the right thing. We're still getting to know each other again, but there's no doubt in my mind that he's good for my mother, and she's good for him."

"I can see that," Baldwin said. "He had his arm around her as they were leaving."

"They're like a couple of lovebirds," Jillian said, smiling. It made her happy to see her mother head over heels, especially after all the years she'd spent alone.

"That's nice," Baldwin remarked. "My family has never been affectionate like that. I can count on one hand the number of times I've seen my parents kiss each other."

"Really?" Jillian had a hard time imagining growing up in a home that was so…cold. Though it did help explain why Randall had turned out the way he had, and why Baldwin was so reserved.

"Yep," he confirmed. "They didn't talk much. Physical affection was in even shorter supply."

"Is that why you put up a wall?" she asked. "Because they never taught you to be open with people?"

Baldwin sucked in a breath. "I suppose that's part of it," he said, crossing his arms across his chest. "I also learned in the marines not to get too attached."

"Oh." Her heart ached for him. "You lost a lot of friends?"

"One. But that was more than enough." He cleared his throat. "Anyway, in my job I can't afford to trust too many people."

"Why do you do it?" It was a question she'd been wondering from the start. Why did Baldwin want to immerse himself in the underworld of crime, to surround himself with people he couldn't trust and didn't want to get to know?

Baldwin let out a weary sigh. "Because I want to help others."

Jillian leaned back against the pillow and studied him, grateful for the shadows in the room. It was easier to talk to him in the dark, when she couldn't fully see his face or those intense blue eyes. He was less intimidating this way, and it emboldened her to ask him things she wouldn't otherwise dare to say.

"But why bounty hunting? There are other ways to help people. You'd probably make an outstanding cop, or a firefighter. Even an EMT. Why not do something like that?"

Baldwin's foot started to tap, a sure sign she was annoying him. Well, that was just too bad. He didn't have to answer her questions. But she wasn't going to stop asking them.

"Because," he said, a slight edge to his voice, "when I got out of the service, I didn't want to go through a lot of training. I'd been there, done that. I didn't have the energy or the attitude to enroll in an academy and go back to the classroom. Becoming a bounty hunter was a much simpler process."

"Do you enjoy it?"

He shifted, crossing his legs at the ankles. "It pays well. At least, the work that I do. And it's fine."

"Money isn't everything," Jillian said softly. Growing up as one of three kids with a single mother, she'd had to do without much. But she'd never lacked for the necessities or been poor in the things that really mattered. Still, the experience had taught her that she couldn't find happiness in possessions—it was the people in life that made it worthwhile.

"No, it's not," Baldwin agreed. "But money makes life a lot easier."

"Has that been true for you?" she pressed.

Baldwin went very still. "What do you mean?"

Jillian shrugged, then moaned softly as the gesture aggravated her shoulder. "I mean," she said, grinding her back teeth together as the pain subsided, "you work all the time. You talk about getting paid well for what you do, but when do you actually sit back and enjoy the benefits of having that money? Do you ever go on vacation?"

He didn't reply, so she continued to speak. "Bryce told me you rent a place and own your truck. There's nothing wrong with either of those things, but you don't act like a man who knows how to relax. Do you ever think about finding someone to share your life with? Having financial security is great, but it's not a substitute for real connection."

"I didn't realize my personal life was of such interest to you," Baldwin said. His tone was icy enough to make her shiver, but Jillian wasn't deterred. Maybe it was the residual painkillers in her system, or maybe getting shot tonight had made her realize there were things in her own life she was lacking. Either way, she felt reckless and unfiltered, and since Baldwin was here, he was the most logical target for her mood.

"You're a good guy. You deserve some happiness. I know you got into bounty hunting to help people, but at what cost to yourself? You have trouble trusting people, you don't want to put down roots, you work all the time." She shook her head. "I just don't want you to miss out."

He pushed to his feet and her heart jumped into her throat as he loomed over her. *Too far*, she thought to herself. *I said too much.*

"Baldwin, I—" she stammered. She wasn't afraid of him—she knew he would never hurt her—but she hadn't intended to make him angry or bruise his ego.

"I'm going to go find some coffee," he practically growled. "You should try to go back to sleep. It's still about an hour before the nurses change shifts."

He stalked from the room before she could respond, leaving her aching and alone in the dark.

"I'm hungry."

Baldwin glanced across the back seat of Bryce's car and tried not to smile. "You're always hungry," he pointed out.

Jillian shot him a mock glare. "Yeah, but this time it's for real. Breakfast was a long time ago." She'd finally been released from the hospital around noon, and her brother had volunteered to drive them home.

Bryce let out a long-suffering sigh. "What do you want?" He spoke like a man who was used to catering to his sister's culinary demands.

She thought for a moment, then said, "A spinach knish, some matzo-ball soup and some of Olivia's raspberry rugelach."

Baldwin's own stomach growled in appreciation. Bryce chuckled. "Fair enough. I'll swing by the deli on the way home. But I think we should get it to go."

"Agreed," Baldwin said. "It's been a long night and I'd really like to take a shower." The nurses had given him a scrub top and he'd washed up as best as he could in the bathroom sink, but parts of his skin were still sticky with the residue of Jillian's blood.

Something flashed in Jillian's eyes, there and gone before he could identify the emotion. "I could use a nap," she said, stifling a yawn. "I didn't sleep very well in the hospital." She glanced away, avoiding his gaze.

Baldwin didn't respond. When he'd finally returned to her room, her eyes had been closed. Maybe she'd been asleep, or maybe she'd been bluffing so she didn't have to talk to him. Either way, he hadn't tried to rouse her. Instead, he'd curled up on the fold-out sofa again and managed to doze a bit until a nurse had come in for shift change.

They'd fed Jillian around seven thirty, and the doctor had visited around eight. She'd done a quick exam and checked Jillian's stitches, then told her she could go home today. But it had taken a while to dot all the i's and cross all the t's, so she hadn't been released until around noon. Fortunately, Bryce had come to pick them up, since Baldwin's truck was still parked at Jillian's condo.

Bryce pulled into a parking spot in front of Bubbe's Deli. "Stay here," he instructed as he climbed out of the car. "If you come in with me, Olivia might never let us leave." With that, he shut the door, sealing them in together.

For a moment, neither spoke. The silence stretched between them, taking on an awkward, strained quality. Then Jillian sighed softly.

"I'm sorry."

He turned to look at her, certain he'd misheard. "What?"

She glanced at him, biting her bottom lip. "I'm sorry. I said some things last night that I probably shouldn't have. I didn't mean to pry in to your life, or to act like I know what's best for you."

Baldwin blinked slowly, trying to process this turn of events. "It's okay," he said. "You were tired, in pain and probably still feeling the effects of stress. People say funny things when they're upset."

Jillian nodded, relief in her eyes. "Yeah. I was feeling…unsettled from everything. Being shot kind of made me realize all the things that are missing from my life, and I lashed out at you because you were there. I shouldn't have used you as my punching bag."

Her words made his stomach do a funny little flip. Truth be told, she *had* upset him last night. But not so much because of what she'd said—he'd had the same conversation with himself countless times. No, it was the fact that she'd said anything at all. She was the only person in his life who talked to him like that. His friends occasionally made reference to his single status or joked that he should take some time off. But no one had ever come out and blasted him with the truth the way she had or interrogated him on what his actions actually meant. He'd never been asked if he was happy, never been pushed to answer for his choices.

Jillian might have been projecting a bit last night, but her words had made one thing clear: she cared.

And that scared the hell out of him.

He could handle the physical attraction. That was the easy part; sex could be a transactional affair. He touched her here, she touched him there, they both had fun and no emotions had to be involved.

But that conversation last night? It had been nothing *but* emotions; raw, unfiltered and directed at him.

The fact that she cared about him enough to say something? That made her dangerous.

Because the truth of the matter was, he was catching feelings for her, too.

And he didn't know what to do about it.

He cleared his throat, knowing he needed to say something. "Uh, what do you think is missing from your life?" Maybe if he flipped the conversation to focus on her he could get his thoughts straightened out.

Jillian ducked her head. "I…" She trailed off, her cheeks turning a faint pink. "I don't have a lot of friends," she continued. "Once I got the job at GGPD, I threw myself into work. I wanted to prove myself, to make it clear to all the naysayers that I belonged there because I'm good at what I do, not because of my last name. But then Randall put a target on my back, and things started to fall apart."

"It's hard to make connections with people when you're under constant pressure." In the marines, the shared experiences of boot camp and training and finally deployment had served to forge bonds between Baldwin and the others in his battery. In fact, some of the training exercises had been designed to be terrible, to give everyone a common enemy to unite against and help the group overcome their individual differences. But Jillian had been alone, without the benefit of any kind of support from most of her coworkers.

Jillian nodded. "Exactly. I was so stressed all the time I didn't have the emotional bandwidth to make friends or even think about dating."

He swallowed hard as he imagined Jillian with another man. Kissing him, touching him, moving over him… A possessive surge of jealousy rose in his chest and he clenched his jaw.

Don't be ridiculous, he told himself. Where did he get off being so upset over the thought of Jillian with another man? He had no claim to her. No right to expect anything from her. A sense of unease started to build as he realized what was going on. Wanting her was one thing. The troubling part was that he was moving beyond that—he wanted her all to himself.

"Anyway," she continued, apparently oblivious to the emotional storm swirling inside him. "I guess now that things are getting so complicated, I'm aware of the fact that I don't really have people in my life to share with, or to lean on. I can turn to my family, of course, but it would be nice to have more than my relatives, you know?"

"Mmm," he said in acknowledgment. Baldwin didn't trust himself to speak at the moment. He wasn't used to feeling so agitated, so internally unmoored. He was normally calm and rock-steady; even when in a tense situation, he didn't emotionally engage, but instead held himself above it all so his mind could function without distraction.

Why didn't that approach work with Jillian? What was it about this woman that kept pulling at him, making him want to break his own rules?

"Baldwin?" He looked over to find her watching him, a concerned expression on her face. "Are you okay?"

"Yeah." The word came out as a croak, so he

cleared his throat and tried again. "I'm good. Just thinking."

She offered him a small smile. "I've been doing a lot of that lately. No hard feelings?"

He shook his head. "Of course not." He was quiet a moment, then added, "I appreciate your honesty. Maybe not in the heat of the moment, but I get it now. And it's okay."

Jillian nodded. "Feel free to return the favor," she said, her tone half joking. "I owe you after last night."

"No, you don't." She blinked and he realized how harsh he had sounded. "You don't owe me anything," he said, more gently this time. "I'm not a hero, Jillian. You don't need to lift me up on a pedestal because I put pressure on your shoulder and called an ambulance."

She opened her mouth, but before she could respond the driver's door opened and Bryce climbed inside. He placed two large bags onto the front passenger seat, and the air filled with the scents of warm bread, chicken and a mix of savory spices. "I hope you're hungry," Bryce muttered as he clicked his seat belt into place. "I told Olivia you just wanted a few things, but she loaded me up with challah, some fresh latkes, chicken soup and about a dozen hamantaschen." He shook his head. "She wanted me to stay until the potato kugel came out of the oven, but I told her I had to get you home."

"Oh, man," Jillian said. "Is it too late to go back inside?"

Bryce glared at her over his shoulder. "Trust me, you have enough food here to feed an army."

"Did you get the raspberry rugelach?" Jillian asked hopefully.

"Yes," Bryce confirmed. "And she threw in some chocolate ones, as well."

Jillian leaned back against the seat, humming happily to herself. Baldwin had never tried rugelach, but he could tell by the smells coming from the front of the car that he was going to enjoy this lunch very much.

Bryce pulled into the parking lot of Jillian's building a few minutes later. "Why don't you join us?" she asked.

He shook his head. "I appreciate it, but I've got to get back to work. Someone's got to pay the bills, since Olivia insists on giving away mountains of food to my mooching relatives."

Jillian stuck her tongue out at her brother. "You're just mad because she likes me better than she likes you."

Bryce laughed. Baldwin gathered the bags of food from the front seat and took a step toward the door, giving the siblings a chance to speak privately. He saw Jillian lean down and heard the murmur of voices. Then she straightened and smiled, reaching through the window to pat Bryce's shoulder. "Get out of here," she said playfully.

Bryce turned to look at Baldwin. "Thanks, man," Baldwin called out. Bryce nodded and gave him a little wave as he drove away. Together, Jillian and Baldwin walked inside.

"My friend kept an eye on your place all night," Baldwin told her. "He said Randall never came back."

"That's good," Jillian replied. They arrived at her door and she stopped, staring at the handle as though she'd never seen it before. A strip of crime scene tape stretched across the doorway, but Bryce had passed along the message that they were okay to enter.

"Everything okay?" He figured she was mentally preparing herself to go inside, to start reclaiming her space from the memory of his brother.

She glanced up at him. "I'm glad you grabbed my purse. I never would have thought to bring my keys." She fished them out and unlocked the door but made no move to enter.

Baldwin stepped forward. "I'll go first," he said. "But like I said, no one's been here except for the evidence team. My friend Carter watched over the place for me. He's a good guy—we were in the marines together, and now he runs a security company. He's a stickler for details. He would have noticed any activity after the police left."

Baldwin walked down the entry hallway, noting the police had left the kitchen lights on. There was a faint dusting of fingerprint powder on the counters, and he noticed the larger fragments of broken glass had been collected from the floor. He set the bags of food on a small table and stepped into the living room.

The furniture had all been pushed to the side to

make room for the medics and their gurney. He didn't remember doing that, so the EMTs must have moved things when he wasn't looking.

Jillian's blood stained the carpet, a dark, visceral reminder of what had happened here. Baldwin stood in place, staring at the rust-colored splotch as the sounds and scents came flooding back. The acrid stench of gunpowder. The thud of Jillian's body as she hit the ground. The metallic tang in the air. The slick warmth as he touched her shoulder, trying to assess her injury.

He felt her presence next to him and glanced over to see her staring at the same spot. "That's not gonna come out," she muttered. "Guess it's new carpet for me."

Baldwin blinked and then laughed out loud, tickled by her practical response to seeing her own blood on the floor. Most people would have been repulsed or gotten emotional at the reminder of being shot. Not Jillian. Rather than dwelling on the past, she shifted to plan for the future. It was an admirable quality—one he appreciated.

She looked up at him with a puzzled smile. He shook his head and put his arm around her shoulder, being careful not to touch her wound. "Come on," he said, leading her back to the kitchen table. "Let's eat while it's still hot."

Chapter 10

The food was delicious—it always was. Olivia had a real gift in the kitchen. It was one of the many reasons why Jillian was glad Bryce hadn't scared her away.

Baldwin seemed to enjoy their meal, as well. "This knish is fantastic," he said around a mouthful of food. "I'm going to have to ask Olivia for her recipes."

Jillian laughed. "Good luck. She's very protective of them. A lot of them have been passed down in her family for generations. She's always happy to share what she makes, but she's quite stingy when it comes to telling others how to replicate her dishes. Except to Bryce, of course, and Chef Hernando."

Baldwin nodded. "That's only fair. I'll just have to earn her trust. Maybe I can talk her into showing me how she does it someday."

Jillian's ears caught on his last word. *Someday* implied that Baldwin might stick around after catching Randall. Was he actually considering staying in town? Did he see a future for himself here?

And if so, she thought to herself, *am I a part of it?*

It was a far-fetched idea, she knew. Baldwin had made no secret of the fact that he intended to leave Grave Gulch just as soon as this job was done. The fact that she'd developed a crush on him during their time together wasn't going to change his mind. His little comment about earning Olivia's trust and watching her make knish was simply him thinking out loud; it didn't represent an about-face in his plans for the future. As much as she might wish otherwise, she couldn't read too much into his statement. If she dared to hope, she was going to wind up disappointed.

They finished eating and Baldwin helped her wrap up the leftovers and tidy up the dishes. Jillian stood in the middle of the kitchen and looked around, making a mental list of chores she'd need to do to put things back to rights.

Baldwin stood next to her, his arms crossed. "I know you want to clean," he said. "I get why you need to erase all traces of Randall from your home. But I am desperate for a shower. So if you can wait a few minutes, I'm going to clean myself and then I'll help you tackle the bigger job."

Jillian nodded. "That sounds great. I want to wash up myself."

A wicked voice in her head urged her to suggest

they save water and shower together, but Jillian refused to even jokingly mention it.

"Okay. Meet you back here in a few."

She watched him walk away, the ill-fitting scrub top the nurses had given him at the hospital doing nothing to dampen his physical appeal. It simply wasn't fair—she'd spent a stressful night in the hospital and it showed, whereas he'd been by her side the whole time and looked like he could step onto a runway in some avant-garde European fashion show.

With a small sigh, she headed for her room and stripped off her clothes. She showered quickly, moaning slightly as the hot water washed away the blood and iodine residue and general griminess she'd accumulated overnight. It would have been so nice to linger under the spray, but Baldwin was waiting. Besides, she wouldn't be able to truly relax until she'd cleaned her place.

Jillian toweled off and replaced the bandage over her stitches, then fished out a couple of ibuprofens from the medicine cabinet and swallowed them with a handful of water from the faucet. Her shoulder ached a bit, and she knew it would only hurt worse as she used it.

She cast a longing look at her bed as she got dressed. "Soon," she muttered to herself. With Baldwin's help, it wouldn't take long to scrub her condo. Then she could collapse into bed and sleep for a week. Or at least a few hours.

The guest bathroom was quiet as she walked down the hall. Either Baldwin was getting dressed, or he was already done. As she stepped into the kitchen, she got her answer.

Baldwin was on all fours investigating the contents of the cabinet under the kitchen sink.

Jillian stopped in her tracks, unable to take her eyes off his perfect butt, so nicely displayed in the flannel pants he was currently sporting. It was rude to stare—she knew that, just as she knew that she herself hated being objectified by men. But logic and common sense were no match for her hormones. Awareness flickered to life low in her belly, and her palms itched to reach out and touch him. He would be hard and warm and, oh, God…

"Found it!"

Baldwin extracted his head and shoulders from the cabinet and sat up, holding a spray bottle of cleanser triumphantly. "I knew it had to be around here somewhere."

Jillian cleared her throat to make her presence known. "Uh, what's that?"

He glanced over his shoulder and showed her the bottle. "Most people keep cleaning supplies under the sink. You're no exception. I think this'll work for the countertops in here, but what do you want me to use to mop the floor?"

He was going to mop the floor for her? Hubba-hubba. "I, uh, I usually use a vinegar and water mix for the mop," she stammered, trying to reconcile her physical attraction for Baldwin with her growing mental attraction, as well. She'd assumed that she would have to ask him to do specific chores for her as they cleaned, but it seemed Baldwin was perfectly happy to take the initiative and get to work without making her assume command of Project Restoration.

Baldwin nodded. "All right. Here's what I'm planning. I'm going to wipe everything down in the kitchen, then sweep and mop the floors. I'm going to wipe off the door handles, the cabinet pulls and anything else Randall may have touched. Then I'm going to dust and vacuum the living room and wipe down the guest bathroom."

"Wait a minute," Jillian protested. "You can't do everything! What am I supposed to do—just sit on my hands and watch you work?"

Baldwin shrugged. "Why not? Maybe you can find something to watch on television."

"Absolutely not," Jillian said. She was touched that he was so willing to take on all the jobs, but it simply wasn't fair. She couldn't stand back and do nothing while he worked, especially since she knew he was doing it all as a favor to her.

"Of the two of us, I'm not the one who got shot last night." A shadow crossed his face at the memory, and unless she missed her guess, Jillian thought he might be feeling some residual guilt. Even though she'd made it clear he wasn't to blame, she knew he still felt at least partially responsible for her injuries. Scrubbing her condo was likely his way of trying to make amends.

"I'm fine," she said. "I just took some ibuprofen."

"You need to rest and let your body heal. If you do too much now, it'll make things worse."

Jillian sighed, recognizing that all-too familiar stubborn note in his voice. Not only had she been hearing it from Baldwin lately, but Bryce also had an identical tone he often deployed. "I'm going to try to clean the carpet in the living room," she said. "And I'll keep going until I get tired."

Baldwin opened his mouth, but wisely shut it again without argument. "Promise me you won't overdo it?" There was real concern in his voice, and she couldn't help but smile.

"I promise."

About an hour and a half later, Jillian sank her aching body onto the couch.

As it turned out, falling to the floor after being shot last night had left her with some bruises. And lying in an uncomfortable hospital bed hadn't helped the situation.

Neither had her determination to keep up with Baldwin.

She'd spent some time on all fours, scrubbing at the bloodstains on the carpet with hydrogen peroxide and dish soap. It looked much better, though the area was still discolored. But more in a people-live-here kind of way as opposed to a haunted-house-murder-scene vibe.

Satisfied that she'd done all she could do for the carpet, she'd set out to dust everything. Her desk against the far wall, the bookshelves, the end tables—everything. Even though Randall hadn't made it as far as her closet on his last visit, she was more convinced than ever he'd planted the evidence there. Which meant at some point, he had gone through her entire condo to invade her most personal space. Just the thought of him standing in her closet, possibly touching her clothes, was enough to turn her stomach.

She tackled her bedroom next, dusting and wiping and vacuuming until she felt like she'd erased his presence from every surface in her bedroom, closet and bathroom. Then she'd gathered up most of her clothes and sorted them into piles for laundry. The logical part of her knew this was bordering on overkill, but her peace of mind demanded she continue. She was determined to reclaim her space and take back her feeling of security.

Eventually, though, her shoulder insisted she take a break. Her spirit was all too willing to continue sanitizing, but her flesh was weak. So she allowed herself to rest, with the understanding that she was going to start up again after a few minutes. Right after she rested her eyes for a spell…

Jillian opened her eyes to discover she was lying flat on her stomach, her head turned to the side. She was warm and secure, and as she gradually woke, she realized the cushions she was pressed against were slowly moving up and down in a soothing rhythm.

No, scratch that. *Not* the cushions. Baldwin's chest was moving under her.

She sucked in a breath as she appreciated the full magnitude of her situation. Jillian was stretched out on top of Baldwin, her torso pressed flat against his chest, her cheek on his breastbone, their legs tangled. His muscular arms encircled her, with one of his big hands splayed on her back to anchor her in place while the other cupped her butt in a gesture of masculine possession. He was warm under her, and though his body was hard and solid, he made a surprisingly comfortable mattress.

Her head spun as she tried to figure out how, exactly, this had happened. The last thing she remembered was sitting down on the couch—alone—to rest for a few minutes. She'd clearly fallen asleep, and Baldwin had apparently joined her at some point. But surely he hadn't pulled her on top of him? She dismissed the thought almost immediately. That kind of move wasn't his style, and besides, Jillian would have wokcn up if she'd felt herself being repositioned like that.

The only conclusion was that *she* had moved in her sleep. But had she curled up to him after he'd drifted off, or had he been aware of her somnolent activities?

Her face warmed at the thought that Baldwin had been awake when she'd flung herself on top of him. If that was the case, the poor man must have felt trapped. He acted like a tough guy, but she knew that a soft heart lurked underneath that hard shell. If he'd seen her moving, he would have tolerated her embrace so as not to disturb her rest. Especially since she'd been shot and he blamed himself.

If she had any luck at all, they'd both fallen asleep and moved together afterward. That meant she could extract herself, and Baldwin would wake up none the wiser about the fact that she now knew exactly how good it felt to be pressed up against him.

It was going to be tricky, though. If they were in a bed… Her mind started to drift at the possibility, conjuring up fantasies about all the *other* things they could do in a bed.

Focus, she told herself sternly. Now was not the time to get distracted!

She returned her attention to the dilemma at hand. Since they were on the couch, she couldn't simply roll off him, because she'd land on the floor. Their legs were entwined, which meant it was going to be difficult to plant a foot on the floor. And she couldn't very well slide up his body or she'd wind up crawling over his face, which was a surefire way to wake him up.

No, it seemed her best bet would be to shimmy toward his feet. The problem was, Baldwin's big frame covered up all of the seat cushions, leaving her no place to put her hands to support herself while she tried to move. She was just going to have to slide against him until she got to his hips, where there should be space for her to plant her hands and take her weight off him.

She slowly drew in a breath, closing her eyes briefly to enjoy her last few seconds pressed against Baldwin's muscular form. It had been a long time since she'd had full-body contact with a man, and she knew that any future guy was unlikely to live up to Baldwin's build.

Still, she couldn't stay like this forever. It was time to get off him.

Slowly, carefully, she started to shift down. His hands slid along her back as she moved, triggering a wave of goose bumps along her skin. The fabric of her shirt remained trapped between their bodies, exposing a growing strip of her skin as she continued her journey south. This was turning out to be more complicated than she'd thought, but she couldn't stop now.

Her shoulders were even with his hips when Baldwin shifted under her. She froze in place, holding her breath and silently pleading with the universe for him to stay asleep. If he woke up and found her like this, her breasts lined up with his crotch, her cheek at the level of his belly button…well, she'd have a lot of explaining to do.

Fortunately, his eyes remained closed. She exhaled quietly and braced herself to move again.

"I can tell you have a plan," he drawled, his voice deep and slightly rough from sleep. "Mind filling me in on it?"

Startled, Jillian let out an undignified squeak and nearly jumped out of her skin. Before she knew what was happening, Baldwin's large hands wrapped around her biceps and he carefully pulled her up his body as he sat up. She wound up facing him, nearly plastered to his chest as they shifted to untangle their legs.

"I will admit," he continued as Jillian leaned back to sit on her bottom, "I didn't mind the direction you were headed, but I could tell you didn't have seduction in mind."

Jillian's eyes locked onto his mouth, which was

presently turned up at the corners in a faint smile. "Uh, no," she admitted. "No, I was trying to move without waking you."

Baldwin snorted. "Let me give you a little tip for next time. If you want a man to stay asleep, don't drag your breasts across his chest and down his stomach."

Her cheeks burned so hot she imagined she looked like a tomato. "Good to know," she muttered. "Sorry about that."

"Don't be," he replied. "I'm not."

Jillian glanced up and discovered his eyes were locked on her face, the blue of his irises practically electric at this distance. A shiver ran down the valley of her spine and she realized he was still holding on to her arms.

His gaze dropped to her mouth. Reflexively, her tongue darted out to swipe across her bottom lip. Baldwin made a low noise that was more vibration than sound as he stared at her. Jillian's tenuous grip on her arousal began to slip. Her nipples hardened, as though begging for his attention. The expression on his face was captivating; he was normally so cool and composed, but right now he was staring at her with such blatant desire that it made her a little dizzy. It was a heady thing, knowing Baldwin wanted her.

She leaned forward, wanting to get closer, needing to see how much she affected his self-control. Would he draw back and deny this pull between them? Or would he accept it and give in to the temptation that had been plaguing them both?

The muscles of his jaw tightened as she moved.

"Jillian," he said, his voice deadly calm. "I'm going to count to three and then I'm going to kiss you. If you have any misgivings, now is the time to stop me."

Jillian bit her bottom lip to hide a smile. Baldwin made a strained noise. "One," he said, sounding like a man on the edge. "Two."

Before he could say another word, she closed the distance between them and pressed her mouth to his.

He moved like a striking snake. Between one breath and the next, his arms banded around her, pulling her flush against his chest. There was a hunger to his kiss, a hint of desperation in the way he gripped her. It was almost as if he couldn't believe this was happening and he didn't want to risk letting her go.

Jillian felt her own sense of urgency as their lips and tongues connected. Kissing Baldwin was like trying to bottle the wind; he was thrilling and unpredictable and intoxicating. But despite the intensity of their embrace, she could tell he was holding himself back. Even as his hands roamed over her he was careful to avoid her injured shoulder. He broke free from her mouth to trail his lips down her neck, but he made sure to hold her so she didn't fall against the arm of the sofa. Even now, Baldwin was still fully in control of himself. Jillian was touched by his consideration, but part of her wanted to see him let go, to give in and just *feel*. She wanted to be the one to drive him wild, to cause Mr. Professional to totally lose it. She wanted to watch that composure melt, to see his powerful body respond to her touch.

So much of this year had been about things happening to her. Randall targeting her at work. Protesters going after her because they thought she'd played a part in guilty people going free. Randall framing her for the robberies. Hell, even Randall breaking into her home and shooting her. She'd been at the mercy of other people's actions for long enough, and she was tired of it. She wasn't about to simply lie back and let Baldwin have his way with her. It was her turn to be in charge, her turn to call the shots.

He just didn't know it yet.

One of his hands cupped her breast, his thumb stroking over her nipple as his licked his way down her neck. Jillian leaned her head back, giving him full access to her skin. For a few seconds she reveled in the sensation of his breath on her, his hands on her curves. The scent of him filled her nose, her entire awareness shrinking down until all she saw, all she knew, was the man in front of her.

More. She needed to see more of him, feel more of him. The couch was too small; it was time to graduate.

Jillian stood and tugged Baldwin to his feet. He gave her a questioning look, his hands on her hips as he leaned in for another kiss. "My room," she murmured against his lips.

He made a sound of agreement as she started to lead him down the hall. When they stepped into her room, she turned around and rose to her tiptoes to kiss him. She joined her hands at the back of his neck and gently guided him until the back of his thighs hit her mattress. Then she pushed him down, climbing onto the bed to straddle his hips.

Baldwin kept his arms around her torso, holding her against him as they explored each other's mouths. The thin fabric of his flannel pants did nothing to hide his body's response, and she felt his hard length between her legs. He released his grip on her waist to tug up the hem of her shirt, and she obliged by slipping it off. But before he could touch her skin, she slid down his legs, hooking her thumbs into the waistband of his pants to draw them down as she moved.

"That was efficient," he said as she pulled the pants free from his ankles. He yanked his shirt over his head, leaving him fully naked now.

Jillian tried not to gape at the sight of his long, lean body draped across her bed. Even her wildest fantasies hadn't come close to matching the reality. He was muscled and hard and broad, and just so overtly masculine that she didn't know where to look first. Should she trace the tattoos on his chest with her tongue, or run her fingertips along the ridges of his stomach? Should she lick his nipples, or wrap her hand around his length? So many choices, and none of them bad...

Apparently, Baldwin wasn't in the mood to pose. "Hey," he said, reaching for her. "You're still wearing pants."

Jillian looked down to discover he was right. She was mildly surprised to find they hadn't melted off her at the sight of him. He tried to draw her close, but she evaded his touch. If he got his hands on her, she'd be totally at his mercy. And she wasn't ready for that. Not yet.

"Is everything okay?" Concern danced across his features, and Jillian realized she was giving him the wrong impression. The last thing she wanted was for him to think she was having second thoughts when she wasn't.

"Oh, yes," she said, smiling as she stepped between his legs. "Everything is definitely okay."

She placed her hands on his chest and lightly raked her fingernails across his skin, moving down his stomach to his hips. Baldwin shuddered out a sigh of pleasure, then sucked in a breath as she bent her head and licked along his length.

"Jillian." His voice sounded broken as she used her hands and lips and tongue to take control of the situation. His muscles tensed, building with leashed power as she pleasured him. The knowledge that she affected this strong, solid man filled her with a sense of feminine satisfaction. She hummed as she moved, enjoying his response to her every touch.

A thin sheen of sweat glistened against his skin and he seemed to grow hotter against her. His scent intensified, taking on a new, slightly darker note that heightened her own arousal. His hips began to move in small, almost restless thrusts that told her he was getting close.

One minute, Jillian was gripping Baldwin, focused entirely on him. The next thing she knew, he pulled her up his body and rolled so that she was flat on her back. She blinked up at him, startled by the look of intensity on his face.

"You need to catch up." His voice was practically a growl as he bent his head to give her a fierce, possessive kiss. Then in one smooth motion, he pulled her pants and panties down her legs. She dimly heard the thump of the fabric as it hit the floor and felt a rush of cool air against her skin, but suddenly Baldwin was there, his hands and mouth radiating heat. The stubble on his chin rasped against her inner thighs, setting off sparks of sensation throughout her body. She threaded her fingers through his hair, wishing the strands were longer. Tension built, her muscles feeling like tightly coiled ropes.

"Baldwin." Jillian moved against him in an instinctive rhythm, seeking release. He had to stop teasing her—she couldn't stand this buildup much longer.

"Hmm?" The lazy sound made her groan in frustration. The man was torturing her on purpose.

Her body demanded she beg, though her pride wouldn't allow it. So she tugged lightly on his hair and said his name again.

He began to work his way up her stomach, pausing to cup and fondle her breasts before lightly dragging his teeth along the length of her neck. She stretched an arm toward the bedside table and he followed the motion.

"Condoms?" he asked.

Jillian nodded, and he breathed out a sigh of relief. "Thank God. Mine are all the way in the other room."

She laughed as he retrieved a foil square from the drawer. "Afraid I wouldn't wait for you?"

Baldwin shook his head as he donned protection. "I'd hate to keep you waiting."

"You might be worth it," she teased as he settled over her again.

"Only *might*?" he whispered. She gasped as he slipped inside, stretching and filling her in the best ways.

Jillian wrapped her legs around his hips as he began to move. "I take it back," she gasped as he settled into a rhythm that made her eyes roll back in her head. "You're definitely worth it."

Chapter 11

Baldwin woke slowly, finding his way to the surface of consciousness like a man driving through dense fog. It wasn't yet morning, but he could tell by the hint of light coming in through the window that it would be soon.

He turned his head to look at Jillian, lying next to him. She slept on her stomach, her face turned toward him and her hand resting flat on his chest, right over his heart. It was as though she didn't want to lose their connection, even for a moment. A sense of tenderness filled him as he watched her breathe, and wondered what she might be dreaming about.

Last night had been…incredible. *Amazing* was too small of a word to encompass what had happened between them. It wasn't just the sex, though that had been among the best he'd ever had. No, it was the connection they'd made that had shocked him. Baldwin was used to enjoying himself in bed, and he made sure the women he was with had fun, too. But the pleasure had always been physical. He'd never made an emotional link with someone, and in truth, had never really wanted to.

Jillian had changed all that. He didn't fully understand it and couldn't really articulate what was happening between them. But he wanted her. His desire...no, his need for her went beyond sexual. He cared about her in a way that went beyond friendship.

When had that happened? How had she become so important to him, so quickly? He'd come here to do a job and bring in his brother. He wasn't looking for a relationship of any kind. It was a distraction he didn't need.

And yet here he was, smiling like a lovesick fool as he watched Jillian sleep next to him.

What was it about this woman that had gotten under his skin?

There was something about her mix of qualities—she was beautiful, approachably intelligent, tough but vulnerable—that pulled him in. Some strange alchemy between them was at play, and Baldwin was helpless to understand it or fight it. He'd have better luck arguing with a thunderstorm.

So what was he going to do about it?

That was the crux of the issue, the question that was going to plague him for the foreseeable future.

This link he felt to Jillian was special—he knew that. He just wasn't sure where to go from here.

For years, Baldwin had been focused on his career. After everything he'd experienced in the military—the good and the bad—he'd decided the safest thing to do was to invest in himself. He was sick of witnessing loss and suffering, tired of the paralyzing bureaucratic red tape that permeated every facet of an organization. By becoming his own boss, he could do what he wanted, when he wanted, on his own terms.

And if the nights got a little lonely? Well, at least he didn't have to contend with a broken heart.

Even in his hazy plans for the future, those "maybe someday thoughts" he had from time to time, he hadn't considered a relationship. Given his lifestyle, it had never seemed like a realistic possibility. He had a few close friends, a few friends with benefits and complete control over his life. The thought of adding a partner to the mix had seemed…unappealing.

Now, though? Maybe it wouldn't be so bad after all.

Except… Grave Gulch *was* his past. He'd left years ago, and apart from the occasional, awkward visit to his parents, he hadn't been back. But Jillian's whole family was here, along with her job and friends. He couldn't imagine she would want to go anywhere else.

He frowned at the direction of his thoughts. Why was he even worrying about this stuff? Who said Jillian even wanted to be with him in the first place? Sure, they'd slept together. But they were both adults. Sex didn't have to mean promises of forever. It was foolish of him to spend time thinking about a future with her, when he didn't even know how she was going to react when she woke and found him still in her bed.

On that note, his stomach began to rumble. As much as he would rather spend the day naked with Jillian, he was going to have to get up eventually.

Moving carefully, he put his marine training to good use and rose stealthily from the bed. Then he slipped out the door and walked down the hall to the guest room.

A few minutes later, he stood in the kitchen making coffee. Maybe he was taking the coward's way out, crawling out of bed before Jillian got up. He could have returned to her after a quick trip to the bathroom. But he thought it was best to give her a little space, a bit of privacy to process what had happened between them. At least this way if she regretted last night, he didn't have to see the look of disappointment cross her face.

He was checking out the contents of the fridge when he heard the shower turn on. Omelets, he decided. Quick, easy to prepare and, most important of all, he had the necessary ingredients.

He pulled out the eggs and butter, then grabbed the mushrooms and cheese. A quick search of the pantry turned up a can of diced tomatoes. Baldwin set to work, humming tunelessly to himself as he chopped the mushrooms and grated cheese.

Twenty minutes later, Jillian walked in as he folded the omelets in the pan. She stopped, eyes widening as she watched him expertly flip their breakfast. "Wow," she said, sounding impressed. "This is a nice surprise."

He shot her a grin, pleased by her reaction. "Good morning."

"Good morning to you, too," she said, heading for the coffeepot. He watched her from the corner of his eyes, searching for any indication as to what she was thinking. Was she happy about the development between them? Or did she wish they'd kept things professional?

Baldwin mentally shook his head. Since when did he get so twisted up about the morning after?

Since you care about her, came the immediate answer.

It was the truth. Baldwin always felt affection for the women he slept with, but Jillian was different. He was attached to her now and no matter what happened between them, she'd always have a space in his heart. He sat with that realization for a moment, expecting to feel nervous or uncomfortable. But instead it just seemed right.

Jillian walked over to stand next to him as he plated their food. "I should have guessed I'd find you here."

He glanced at her, but since she was watching his hands he couldn't see her face. "Did you think I'd run away?"

She lifted her uninjured shoulder in a shrug, still not looking at him. "I did wonder for a second," she said softly.

"No way," he said firmly. He placed the empty

pan in the sink and turned to face her, then put his finger under her chin to tilt her head up slightly. A flash of insecurity danced across her face, making his heart squeeze hard. "You're not getting rid of me that easily."

She smiled faintly at that, warmth entering her gaze. "Good," she said, pushing herself onto her tiptoes. "Because I'm not done with you yet." She brushed her lips across his as her hands landed on his shoulders.

He knew she'd meant to keep the kiss light, but the second their mouths touched, sparks seemed to arc through his body. He pulled her in until her breasts flattened against his chest and he slid one hand down to the small of her back, anchoring her in place. She moaned as he teased her lips apart with his tongue, delving inside to taste her. Would he ever get enough of her unique flavor?

Jillian ran her hands up his neck, threading them through his hair. Wanting to change the angle between them, he locked his hands on her hips and lifted her onto the counter, then stepped between her legs. He grabbed the hem of her shirt and started tugging upward.

"What about breakfast?" she asked between kisses, a hint of laughter in her voice.

"Later," he said, nipping gently at her bottom lip. "We have more important things to do right now."

The food had long gone cold by the time they turned their attention to breakfast. Baldwin offered to make fresh omelets, but Jillian insisted a quick spin in the microwave would make them edible again. They weren't the greatest, but he'd certainly had worse.

They were just finishing up the dishes when the doorbell rang. Jillian frowned as she hung the dish towel on the refrigerator door.

"Expecting anyone?" Baldwin asked.

"No," she said, shaking her head. She started for the door but he put his hand on her arm to stop her.

"Let me get it." It was probably nothing—maybe a neighbor, or one of her relatives checking in. But after the events of the last couple of days, he didn't want to take any chances.

Jillian hung back in the hallway as he approached the door.

"Who is it?" he called loudly. She really needed a peephole; he made a mental note to get one installed.

"Greg's Locks," a voice on the other side of the door said. "You made an appointment to change the locks?"

Jillian came up alongside him and nodded. "I scheduled it two days ago," she said. "After the meeting with my attorney."

"Okay." Baldwin opened the door to reveal a thin young man wearing a blue work shirt and a baseball cap with the company name embroidered on the fabric. He held a large canvas duffel bag and a clipboard.

His eyes went wide when he saw Baldwin cross his arms. "Uh, hi. I'm here to change the locks?"

Jillian moved around him and the young man visibly relaxed. "Yes, that's right. Come on in."

Baldwin took a step back to give them room, but he kept his guard up. Jillian explained what she needed and pulled Baldwin down the hall to the living room.

"You don't have to glare at him the whole time," she muttered.

"I'm not glaring," he protested. "Just keeping a watchful eye. He's a stranger."

"He's a kid doing his job," Jillian said. "Not one of your brother's henchmen."

"We hope," he said darkly. Randall generally had too much contempt for other people to want to work with them, but he might be getting desperate. Still, the idea that he'd somehow recruited a random employee from the locksmith on the off chance Jillian would get her locks changed was a bit far-fetched…

"What made you call them?" he asked, curious about the timing of it all. "Randall broke in the night before last, but you'd already set up the appointment."

"I knew someone had been in my home," she replied. "I wasn't certain who had planted the evidence, but someone had broken in to set me up. I figured changing the locks was a good idea, and if they'd come out sooner, it might have stopped Randall from getting in the other night."

"If it makes you feel any better, I don't think he had a key," Baldwin said. "When we were kids, Randall used to enjoy cracking safes and picking locks. I'm almost positive that's how he got inside."

"Let's hope this new lock will put up more of a fight," she said, a shadow crossing her face.

"We won't be caught off guard again," Baldwin

said softly, drawing Jillian into his arms. He hated that she felt afraid in her own home. Hated more the fact that they were on the defensive, waiting for his brother to make another move. There had to be something he could do to knock Randall off his game. His brother was smart, but he wasn't a fighter. Baldwin needed to surprise Randall. If he could shake up his brother's world, it would give him the upper hand.

But how, exactly, to do it?

Jillian's phone rang and she stepped back. "That's probably my attorney," she said. "He was supposed to call this morning."

"Good," Baldwin replied. The fact that Randall had been caught in the act of breaking into her place to steal additional sources of fingerprints strengthened the case for Jillian's innocence in the robberies. Now that the police had concrete proof Randall was targeting Jillian, he hoped the DA would drop the charges against her.

He listened with half an ear as the locksmith worked, his mind churning as he planned and dismissed various scenarios to find Randall. But no matter what he imagined, he kept circling back to one conclusion:

He was going to have to talk to his parents.

Chapter 12

"I don't understand." Jillian paced the length of the kitchen, frustration building as she listened to her attorney talk. "The man broke into my home and shot me! What more evidence does the DA need to accept that he's framing me and I didn't commit the robberies?"

"I know it's hard," Rodney said soothingly. "But it's not as bad as it sounds."

"Are you sure about that?"

"I am," he said, sounding more confident than she felt. "The DA doesn't disagree that you're a victim here. But until we can conclusively link Bowe to the robberies, there's still the matter of your fingerprints at the last crime scene."

"So nothing has changed," Jillian said flatly. She

wanted to scream at the unfairness of it all. It seemed that unless Randall put out a billboard confessing to the jewel thefts, she was still going to be blamed for them.

"Actually, this has been a positive development." Rodney sounded almost gleeful. "I am sorry you got shot, of course," he hastily added. "But I have to say, this will make you incredibly sympathetic to a jury. Remember, we don't have to prove you're innocent. We just have to create reasonable doubt in the minds of the jurors. Randall's recent actions certainly help with that."

"I suppose," Jillian grumbled. It didn't seem right that she'd had to get shot to make a jury believe she wasn't a thief, but there was nothing to be done about it now.

"Try not to get discouraged," Rodney said. "I know things are stressful now. Just keep your chin up and let me do my job."

"Thank you," Jillian replied. She did trust the man, even if her faith in the system was being tested.

An incoming call beeped, so she said goodbye to Rodney and switched over.

"Jillian? It's Grace. How are you doing?"

Her mood brightened at the sound of her cousin's voice. "I'm hanging in there," she said honestly.

"I heard about the shooting," Grace said, her voice full of concern. "I'm so sorry I didn't come to the hospital. I was working a double shift and couldn't get away."

"It's okay," Jillian assured her. "You didn't miss

much. Besides, with Mom and Wes and Bryce and Madison and Baldwin all there, the place was pretty crowded."

"Baldwin was there?"

Jillian didn't miss the note of curiosity in her cousin's seemingly innocent question. "Yeah," she said, warmth rising in her chest as she recalled how he'd spent the night by her side, despite the uncomfortable conditions for him. "He was there the whole time."

"Wow." Grace sounded impressed. "I'm glad you weren't alone."

"No chance," Jillian confirmed.

They chatted for a few minutes and then Grace said, "Listen, I don't know if this makes you feel any better, but Ian is working almost around the clock trying to find some evidence that Randall was at those robbery scenes."

"He is?" Jillian was surprised to hear that. Ian Elward was one of her coworkers in the lab. They had a decent working relationship, but he wasn't what she'd consider a friend. Ian was a nice enough guy, but he was a bit of a know-it-all and came across as arrogant at times. He wasn't very personable and didn't go in for friendly chitchat, which she knew through the grapevine rubbed some people the wrong way.

"Yeah," Grace confirmed. "He told me that he felt bad about the way he'd treated you when Randall was still there. Something about how he'd thought you were bad at your job, but he now realizes that was all Randall's doing. I guess he's trying to make up for his assumptions?"

"I'm glad to hear it," Jillian said. She and Ian had argued from time to time, and she'd occasionally gotten the impression he didn't think she knew what she was doing. It was nice to know Ian realized she'd been targeted by Randall. She was even more impressed that he seemed to be doing something about it.

"I was shocked," Grace said. "He's normally so standoffish I couldn't believe he was talking to me, much less admitting he'd been wrong about you."

"I have to confess I don't know what to think anymore," Jillian said. "With everything that's been going on, it feels like my life has turned upside down and I don't know what normal is anymore."

"I know," Grace said sympathetically. "Things are definitely unsettled right now, but everyone here is rooting for you. Chief Shea has even brought in an outside CSI team to examine all the evidence and search for any links to Randall."

"Wow," Jillian said. The knowledge that the department really did have her back brought tears to her eyes and made her feel a little less alone. "I don't know what to say."

"You don't have to say anything," Grace responded. "We all know how devious Randall is. We're not going to stand by while he targets you."

"Just don't put your own jobs at risk," Jillian said. "I don't want anyone to get in trouble with IAB on my behalf."

"Not to worry," Grace said confidently. "Things have cooled off on that front, especially since Randall broke into your condo and attacked you."

"My attorney said it helped my case," Jillian said. "I guess it's good to know I didn't get shot for nothing."

"Gotta find that silver lining," Grace teased. "Look, I'm going to spend the rest of my day catching up on paperwork, but I'm off tomorrow, too. Want to grab a bite?"

"That would be great," Jillian said. "Are you sure Camden won't mind being left out?"

"Of course not! He knows I need my regular dose of girl-time. It won't bother him at all. The real question," Grace said, a sly note entering her voice, "is will Baldwin mind?"

At the mention of his name, Jillian automatically glanced across the room to where he was sitting in one of the recliners. He was faced toward the locksmith, but she could tell by the look on his face that he was lost in thought. "Why would he mind?" Jillian said, trying to sound nonchalant.

Grace simply laughed. "Oh, my," she said. "It's more serious than I thought."

"What do you mean—?"

"I'll text you later," Grace interrupted. "We'll figure out a time and a place for tomorrow. 'Bye!"

Her cousin hung up before Jillian could reply. She shook her head and pocketed the phone, then walked over to Baldwin.

"Everything okay in here?"

He nodded absently, making her wonder if he'd even heard her question.

"I was thinking we could hop on a plane and get out of town," she said, testing him.

"Sounds good," he replied.

"But first you should sell your truck."

"Uh-huh."

"And adopt a dog."

"Yep. Wait, what?" He turned to look at her, eyebrows drawn together in confusion.

"Hi, there," she said, smiling down at him. "I take it you're back now?"

"Back from where?"

"You were clearly lost in thought," she informed him. "I'm just giving you a hard time."

"Sorry about that," he said, reaching for her. She let him pull her into his lap, enjoying the contact. Every time he touched her, a spark of energy traveled through her body. It was probably because this thing between them—however they were going to define it—was so new.

But would it last? They hadn't had a chance to talk about the physical turn their relationship had taken. Baldwin had been clear from the start that he had no plans to stay in Grave Gulch. Jillian doubted one night together had changed his mind, but a small part of her heart hoped that maybe he was having second thoughts about leaving. He clearly liked her, and based on his actions before they'd slept together, she was fairly confident his attraction to her went beyond sex. She was probably jumping the gun to even wonder at his future plans and her potential place in them. But Grace wasn't the only one who was curious to know what was going on between them.

"What did your lawyer have to say?"

His question pulled her from her wandering thoughts. She filled him in on the conversation with Rodney, mentioning his positive outlook on the situation. "I just wish I shared his optimism," she sighed.

Baldwin pushed a strand of hair behind her ear. "I know it's not easy," he said softly. "But we will bring Randall to justice."

Jillian leaned down until their foreheads touched. "I believe you," she said simply.

His eyes warmed and he smiled. "Good," he replied.

"I just wish I knew why Randall was so fixated on me." She leaned back and shook her head. "I mean, he's targeted people before. But it seems like he has a vendetta against me or something."

Baldwin frowned. "I noticed that, as well. I've been reviewing some of the cases he tampered with, to see if you have anything in common with the people affected."

Jillian sat up straight. "That's a good idea." She didn't try to hide the admiration in her voice.

Baldwin rolled his eyes. "I may not be a forensic scientist, but I can hold my own in an investigation."

She ran her fingers through his short hair, mussing up the strands as much as possible. "I never doubted you."

"Uh-huh," he said doubtfully. "Anyway, from what I can tell, Randall is obsessed with cheaters. It seems like every case he mishandled had something to do with cheating of some kind, be it in a romantic or business relationship."

"Hmm." Baldwin's observation made something stir in the back of her mind, but she wasn't sure what it was yet…

"Did he ever accuse you of misconduct at work?"

Jillian started to shake her head, then stopped with a gasp as a memory pushed to the front of her mind.

"I take it that's a yes?"

She turned to Baldwin, her eyes wide as she nodded. "Once. Not long after I started working in the lab. He asked me if I wanted to grab a bite to eat with him after work one day. I wasn't sure if he was asking me on a date, or just wanted some company while he ate. Either way, I turned him down." The idea of spending more time with Randall had made her want to gag. "I told him I had a boyfriend and he'd get upset if we went out together just the two of us."

"And did you?" Baldwin asked, his eyes steady on her face.

"Did I what?"

"Have a boyfriend?"

Jillian shook her head. "That's what you want to focus on here?" When he merely arched one eyebrow, she sighed. "No, okay? I wasn't seeing anyone at the time. But Randall didn't know that. He made a big deal of the fact that I was being faithful to my boyfriend. Said I was doing the right thing, stuff like that. I found out later he was married, so I don't even know why he asked me to dinner in the first place."

"She cheated on him," Baldwin said.

Jillian felt her mouth drop open. "She did?"

Baldwin nodded. "Yeah. I'm not supposed to know about it, but our mom let it slip once."

"No wonder he's been going after the cheaters." It all made a sick kind of sense now. But that still didn't explain why he was focused on her. Jillian had never been unfaithful in a relationship.

"Why me, though?" she asked. "I'm more confused now than I was before."

"So am I, to be honest," Baldwin said. "I don't know why Randall is trying to hurt you. Maybe he's lost his grip on reality and for some reason sees you as a threat. After all, you're part of the team who uncovered his crimes."

"I'm not the only one, though," Jillian pointed out. "Several people work in the lab with me. He's not going after Ian or any of the other techs."

"You're special," Baldwin said with a lopsided smile.

"Thanks," Jillian said dryly. "That's very reassuring."

Baldwin kissed the tip of her nose. "Listen, I've been thinking."

Jillian straightened. "I noticed," she said. "You were miles away earlier. Are you going to fill me in now?"

Baldwin nodded. "I'm tired of waiting for Randall to come to us. I think he got spooked the other night, and there's no telling when he'll make another move."

"That makes sense," Jillian said. "He's probably

going to lay low for a while, until he comes up with another plan."

"Exactly," Baldwin said. "I don't want to give him the chance to regroup. I want to go after him, put him on the defensive for a change."

"Okay. How are we going to do that?"

"Well, that's the thing." Baldwin glanced away and shifted a bit, looking uncomfortable. "I think we're going to have to talk to the people who know him best."

Jillian frowned. "I don't think your brother has any friends," she said. "And his wife insists she doesn't know where he is."

"I'm not talking about his wife," Baldwin said, sounding resigned. "I think it's time we visited my parents."

"Are you sure you want to do this?"

Baldwin put the truck in Park and glanced over to find Jillian looking at him with an expression of concern on her face. He reached over and placed his hand on top of hers. "I'm fine," he told her.

"We don't have to go inside."

"What makes you think I don't want to go inside?"

She flipped her hand over to lace her fingers through his. "Because the closer we got to the house, the less you spoke and the more tense your shoulders became."

Baldwin deliberately relaxed his muscles and took a deep breath. She was too perceptive for her own good. "I'm fine," he repeated. "We need to talk to my parents. They might know something that will lead me to Randall."

"Don't you think they would have gone to the police?"

Baldwin considered the question. His parents weren't bad people, but they had always been protective of Randall. "I think if they knew something obvious, they would share it with the police. But I'm wondering if they might have insight into where Randall could be hiding and just not realize it."

Jillian studied him for a moment, her gaze warm. "I don't want you to hurt yourself for my sake," she said quietly. "I want to get your brother as much as anyone, but not if it means causing you pain."

Baldwin clenched his jaw to push back the sudden sting of tears. What had he done in this life to deserve Jillian's concern? His brother had spent the better part of a year psychologically torturing her, he'd broken into her home and shot her and Baldwin himself had started out their time together acting like a jerk. And yet she still cared about him and worried at how he would be affected by seeing his parents.

"Jillian," he said, his voice rough. "I would crawl through broken glass if it meant putting an end to this nightmare for you."

Her eyes widened and she sucked in a breath. "Baldwin—"

"Let's go," he interrupted. He didn't want her gratitude, didn't want to hear her thank him for doing the bare minimum. He had promised her he would keep her safe and find his brother. It was time he did just that.

He climbed out of the truck and walked to the passenger side to help her down. She took his hand and gave it a squeeze in a silent gesture of support.

His parents' home was at the end of a quiet, tree-lined street. The lawn was trimmed and although the front flower beds were currently bare, he had no doubt his mother planted something pretty every spring.

It wasn't the house he'd grown up in; he had no memories of riding his bike down the sidewalk or playing hide-and-seek with the neighbor kids. In fact, he'd only been here a handful of times over the years, always for short, painfully awkward visits that he'd completed more out of a sense of obligation than any real desire to see the people inside.

Jillian's shoulder brushed against his arm as they stood on the porch. In some ways, he was glad to have her with him. She was certainly the first woman he'd ever brought home to Mom and Dad. It was the kind of thing couples did when they were getting serious about each other, and not for the first time, he wished he had a normal family.

But maybe this was for the best. He certainly didn't know what was going to happen between them, and at least Jillian wouldn't mistake meeting his parents as a sign of his intentions for their relationship.

The door opened to reveal his father, who blinked in surprise.

"Baldwin," Dave Bowe said, clearly taken aback. "We weren't expecting you."

"Sorry about that," Baldwin replied. "I'll call next time."

His dad nodded, then turned his attention to Jillian. "And who is this?" The question was more of an accusation, as though he couldn't believe Baldwin had showed up without warning and dared to bring a stranger with him.

"This is Jillian Colton."

"Nice to meet you." Jillian extended her hand, but his father didn't shake it.

"Is she pregnant?" his father asked bluntly.

Baldwin's temper went from zero to full boil in the space between heartbeats. He opened his mouth to reply, but before he could tell his father to go to hell, Jillian laughed.

"You're right, he is funny," she said, clapping a hand on Baldwin's shoulder. She turned to the older man and offered him a tight smile. "Baldwin and I work together. I'm going to assume he got his charm from his mother."

Baldwin's father had the grace to look contrite. "Dave Bowe," he said gruffly. "Please come in."

Baldwin placed his hand on Jillian's lower back as they walked into the house together. "I am so sorry," he murmured.

Jillian shook her head. "Don't worry," she whispered back. "I've dealt with worse."

His father led them into the living room and gestured to the sofa against the wall. "Have a seat," he said. "I'll tell your mother you're here." He walked away, leaving them alone.

Baldwin turned to Jillian. Before he could say anything, she held up a hand. "I'm fine," she assured him. "Let's just get this over with."

"My thoughts exactly."

After a moment his father returned, his mother trailing behind. "Oh!" she exclaimed. "We weren't expecting you!"

Jillian slid him a look of disbelief. "I'm sorry, Mom," Baldwin replied dutifully. "I didn't have a chance to let you know we were coming."

"Lost your phone?" his father grumbled.

His mother brushed aside his apology. "Well, that's all right. You're here now." She made no move to hug him, and Baldwin didn't try to force any affection on her. Linda Bowe turned to look at Jillian. "And who is this?" she asked, echoing his father's earlier question.

"I'm Jillian Colton." This time, Jillian's attempted handshake was accepted.

"Nice to meet you," his mother replied. "I'm Linda. Please, have a seat. Can I get you something to drink?"

"No, thank you." He and Jillian spoke at the same time, and he smiled mentally. Neither one of them wanted to stay any longer than necessary.

They sank onto the sofa while his parents took the chairs seated across the coffee table. The fabric of the couch was stiff and the cushions well-stuffed. It was clear no one sat on this furniture regularly, and a small part of Baldwin was insulted that his father had left them in the formal living room rather than the den, where his parents spent most of their time. It further underscored the distance between them and drove home the point that they considered him a guest and not family.

"Well, what brings you out here?" his mother said. "We haven't seen you in ages, Baldwin."

"Work has been keeping me busy," he replied.

"That's good," Dave interjected. "Keeps you out of trouble."

Baldwin ignored the jab and focused on his mother. "I'm actually here because of a job."

"Oh," Linda replied. She glanced at Jillian. "Are you his client?"

Jillian shook her head. "No. I'm more of a co-worker."

His mother frowned faintly. "I see," she said, though it was clear from her tone she didn't.

"My case is connected to Randall," Baldwin said.

His father raised his hands above his head in a gesture of irritation. "Oh, here we go!" he exclaimed. "I knew there had to be some reason for you to come here. There's no way he's here to visit, I told myself. Of course it has something to do with your brother." He fixed Baldwin with an angry, almost challenging stare, as if daring Baldwin to argue with him.

Linda pursed her lips and shook her head. "I'm afraid we can't help you. We spoke with the police a few months ago and told them everything we know, which isn't much." She studied him for a few seconds, a look of disappointment crossing her face. "Did you really have to take a case involving your own family?"

Baldwin took a deep breath to tamp down his rising temper. "Randall has hurt a lot of people. He needs to answer for what he's done."

His mother looked away. "Randall has always been…complicated," she said. "If he truly did those things, I'm sure he had his reasons."

Baldwin felt Jillian's body go tense beside him and he reached over to take her hand. "I'm not here to argue about Randall's motivations, or to debate the question of his guilt with you."

"Then why did you come?" his father asked angrily.

Baldwin leveled his gaze on the older man. "Everyone is searching for Randall. The police, the FBI. Even me. At some point, we're going to find him. It's not a matter of *if*, it's a matter of *when*. Do you want some trigger-happy rookie looking to make a name for himself to be the one to bring him in?"

His mother looked away, biting her lower lip. His father's anger receded somewhat. "No," he said quietly. "Whatever your brother has done, he doesn't deserve to die for it."

Depends on who you ask, Baldwin thought wryly. His client would happily choke the life out of Randall and not blink an eye. And now that his brother had shot Jillian, Baldwin shared that sentiment.

"Who are you working for?" his father asked.

For a split second, Baldwin debated lying to them. They still clearly thought Randall hung the moon, and they likely felt the whole investigation was an overreaction to what they believed were some honest mistakes their golden child had made at work.

But they needed to hear the truth. They needed to know how Randall had ruined lives, even if they refused to accept it.

"My client's name isn't important," Baldwin said. "But because of Randall's deliberate mishandling of evidence, that man's son was falsely imprisoned. When his son refused to join one of the prison gangs it was treated as a sign of disrespect and he was murdered."

The color drained from his mother's face, and his father squeezed his eyes shut.

"Two nights ago, Randall broke into Jillian's condo and shot her," Baldwin continued, keeping his voice even. "Randall and Jillian used to work together at the police department. He's now framing her for a series of robberies."

Tears began to track down Linda's cheeks, but Baldwin felt no sympathy for her. She needed to understand that Randall was not the good guy. He wasn't some misunderstood genius, or a man who was being unfairly persecuted. He was deliberately and methodically hurting people, and he had to be stopped.

"Why are you here?" His father's voice was quiet, but Baldwin heard the anguish in his tone.

"I want to know where you think Randall might be hiding. What are some places he might think to go? Places that are specific to our family, maybe?" Baldwin had been wracking his brain trying to come up with a list, but he hadn't had much luck. They'd never gone camping as kids, never really had a favorite place to stay nearby. The police had already checked all the hotels and motels in the surrounding area and were doing regular spot-checks of nearby campgrounds. Everyone knew he had to be close, but where?

His mother was shaking her head. "We don't know anything!" she insisted. She was openly crying now, her voice thick with emotion. "We haven't spoken to your brother in months, ever since all of this started. I've been worried sick about him, thinking of him alone and scared, wondering if he's okay."

Baldwin felt a surge of disgust at her words. Even after learning about the horrible things his brother had done, his mother was still more concerned for Randall than his victims.

"If we knew something we would tell the police," his father chimed in.

Baldwin looked at the carpet and shook his head. "See, that's the thing," he said, almost to himself. "I'm not so sure you would."

His mother gasped but Baldwin didn't acknowledge her reaction. He stood, tugging gently on Jillian's hand to bring her to her feet. "This was a waste of time," he declared. He started for the door, Jillian trailing behind him.

"Now you wait just a minute," his father yelled after them. But Baldwin didn't stop. This wasn't a both-sides issue, where he could understand how he and his parents might think differently. Randall had blood on his hands. And while he knew that his parents would always love their son, they also needed to accept that Randall had done some bad things and deserved to face consequences for his actions.

But if their reactions today signified anything, it was that his family was never going to embrace the reality that their perfect son was guilty.

Baldwin walked out the door and headed directly to his truck, not wanting to give his father a chance to catch up to them. This was it, the last straw. He couldn't even pretend that his parents cared about him anymore. They hadn't been happy to see him at all, had been more annoyed that he hadn't warned them ahead of time that he was coming. And the way his dad had treated Jillian? Even if she had been just a coworker and not the woman he was falling in love with, his father's actions had been inexcusable.

Love? Did that word really apply here? He glanced down at Jillian as she walked alongside him. Despite his anger and frustration, her presence made him feel grounded. Like she was the eye of the storm swirling inside his heart.

He could fight it. Try to deny the truth. But what would be the point? He was falling in love with Jillian Colton. It was a heck of a time to realize it, but since when had he ever taken the conventional path?

He unlocked the doors and helped Jillian inside, then rounded the hood and climbed behind the wheel. He glanced up as he put the engine in Reverse to see Dave Bowe standing on the porch, arms crossed as he watched them with a frown.

Probably wants to make sure I leave, Baldwin thought bitterly. Well, the older man needn't worry. Baldwin was going, all right. And he was going to stay gone.

Jillian waited until they were on the main road before speaking. "Are you…?" She trailed off, then tried again. "How are you?"

"Fine," Baldwin muttered, ignoring the ache in his chest. "Just fine."

He'd been such a fool to think that a visit to his parents might have been helpful! The distance between them had only grown larger over the years, and now the gap was insurmountable. He wasn't surprised, but part of him was still hurt to know that he would never have a meaningful relationship with his parents. He'd long ago given up on Randall, but he'd still held out a small glimmer of hope that things with his parents might improve.

Now he knew better. Apparently, in their minds, Randall's sins paled in comparison to Baldwin's desire to live his life on his own terms.

Jillian didn't say anything. She was smart enough to know he wasn't capable of talking right now. But after a moment, he felt her hand on his leg.

It was a simple gesture. Just a light touch, one that he could either acknowledge or pretend to ignore. A reassurance that she was here if he needed her.

As it turned out, he did.

Baldwin had spent most of his adult life alone. Not physically speaking; he was always around people, especially in the military. That wasn't the same as forming real connections with others, though. He mostly kept to himself, content with his own thoughts. An island in the great sea of humanity.

Except now that he'd met Jillian, he didn't want to be an island anymore.

He took one hand off the steering wheel and placed it over hers. He still felt too raw to try to talk about anything, but there were other ways to tell her that he needed her.

"I have an idea," she said quietly.

"What's that?"

"I'd like to take you somewhere, if you're willing."

Baldwin didn't hesitate. "Sure." He didn't know where Jillian wanted to go, but it didn't matter. As long as she was with him, he didn't care.

She gave him directions and he nodded. "The forest?" It was an unexpected destination, but Jillian must have something in mind. "Isn't that where Len Davison was killed?"

He glanced over as she shook her head. "It's a different place. You'll see."

Chapter 13

"It's just a little farther."

Baldwin grunted but didn't say anything. Jillian trudged along the snow-dusted path, grateful she'd chosen to wear sneakers today. She hadn't imagined they would go hiking, but after the visit with Baldwin's parents, she'd sensed he needed to get away for a bit.

The forest was quiet this time of year; it was the off-season for tourists, and most of the campgrounds were closed until the spring thaw. Fortunately, they hadn't had much snow yet, so the trail was still passable.

Jillian led Baldwin another fifty yards, taking one more curve that led them out of the trees. They stepped up to the shoreline of a small lake, a hidden gem tucked away in the forest. Usually during the summer it was filled with hikers and swimmers and campers. But right now, the water was so still, it looked like a mirror reflecting the gray sky overhead.

She took Baldwin's hand and together they walked to a large log set several feet from the water's edge. The gravel crunched under their feet as they walked and overhead she saw a hawk riding the thermal drafts in search of its next meal.

The log was cold when she sat on it, but the view was worth the chill. Baldwin sank down next to her with a small sigh and stared out across the expanse of water. "I had no idea this was here," he said finally.

"It used to be a bit of a secret," she told him. "But as the years have gone by, more and more people have discovered it."

"It can't be more than what, a hundred and fifty yards across?"

"Two hundred," she corrected.

Baldwin glanced at her. "You seem very certain of that."

Jillian shrugged. "I may have swum across it on a dare before."

He chuckled. "Is it deep?"

"Deep enough," she confirmed. She'd never been an especially strong swimmer, but one summer Bryce had taunted her so much that she'd jumped in the water just to shut him up. She'd made it a quarter of the way across before realizing she'd made a mistake, but her pride wouldn't let her turn around. So she'd pushed ahead, barely making it to the other side. She could still recall the rubbery feel of her limbs when she'd crawled out of the water on the opposite shore. Bryce had been there waiting for her, his face as white as a ghost. They'd gone home without another word, and to this day, neither one of them had told their mother about her stunt.

"It's beautiful," he said quietly. He turned his head up to the sky and watched the hawk circle for a few minutes. Jillian reached for his hand, squeezing gently. There were so many things she wanted to say, so many questions she wanted to ask. But she knew that in this moment, he needed silence. If she tried to talk to him, it would only drive him further into his shell.

After a while, he spoke. "They weren't always like that."

Jillian didn't need to ask who he was talking about. "Were you ever close?"

"I don't know." He laughed, but there was no humor in it. "I know that's a strange thing to say. Things weren't as bad as they are now. I guess if you'd asked me a few days ago if we used to be close, I would have said yes. But after seeing the way your family is around each other, I realize that we've never had something like that."

"Every family is different."

He tilted his head to the side. "Yeah, but you and your siblings and your parents seem to have this unspoken connection that ties you together. You might annoy each other sometimes, but I don't think you've ever really doubted that you guys love each other."

Jillian nodded. It was true—despite any differences they may have had over the years, she'd never worried that she'd lose the love of her relatives. And even though her father had been gone for most of her life to date, they were still strengthening their bond with every passing day.

"With us," he continued, "it was like we tiptoed around each other. My parents made no secret of the fact they thought Randall walked on water. He was the smart one, the clever one, the one destined for success. Whereas I..." He trailed off, shaking his head. "My interests were more pedestrian. More middle-class."

Jillian frowned. "Your parents didn't strike me as being snobby about wealth." Their home had been nice, but not overly so. If they had money, they certainly hadn't spent it on furnishings or decor.

"They're not," Baldwin replied. "But my dad was a college professor, which he thought made him the smartest person in any room. He and my mother still think of themselves as part of an intellectual upper class. Randall fit in nicely with their idea of success. I did not."

"You told me a bit about that before," she said, recalling what he'd said about their reactions to his joining the marines after high school.

"I embarrassed them when I chose the military instead of college. Then, when I got out, I embarrassed them again when I went into bounty hunting rather than use my GI bill to pursue higher education."

"But you don't need a college degree to be successful," Jillian protested. "Lots of people do very well for themselves without one. It's not a measure of intelligence."

Baldwin smiled faintly. "It is in my father's eyes," he said quietly.

"Well, he's wrong," she said firmly.

Baldwin smiled at her this time, a hint of warmth entering his eyes. "I'd almost like to see you go toe-to-toe with him over that subject," he said. "He'll never change his mind, but it would be entertaining as hell to watch you smack him down."

"Take me there," Jillian said. "I'll do it right now." Anything to chase the sadness from Baldwin's gaze.

"It doesn't matter," he said. "I realized today that they're never going to accept me. They'd rather make excuses for Randall than believe the truth about him, and despite everything he's done, they'd rather claim him as a son than me."

Jillian scooted closer to him, until their hips were touching. "That's their loss," she said, putting an arm around his back to hug him. "You are an amazing man. The fact that they choose not to see it means there's something wrong with them, not you."

Baldwin didn't reply. He simply stared at the water, his mind clearly a million miles away. Jillian didn't speak. She wanted to give him time to process what she'd said. Because it was the truth. And she needed him to believe it.

His parents were fools to toss him away. And even though Baldwin was putting on a brave face, she knew he was hurting inside. It broke her heart to see this strong, confident man questioning his worth after spending a few moments with the people who were supposed to love him unconditionally. There was no excuse for their behavior; no justification for the way they'd treated him.

They sat in silence for several minutes. The wind started to pick up and the clouds took on a darker hue, but they didn't move. The truck wasn't too far away, and a little rain never hurt anyone.

Jillian wasn't sure how much time passed. She was content to sit next to Baldwin, her arm around his back, holding him as best as she could.

"Why here?"

She took a deep breath. "I wanted to bring you somewhere different. Some place you maybe hadn't been before. One that wasn't at all connected to your parents or your brother."

"Why?"

She leaned her head against his biceps. "I thought it might be easier for you to work through everything if we went somewhere that didn't have any past associations for you."

"A blank slate," he said quietly.

"Yeah," she replied.

He turned and kissed the top of her head. "You really are amazing, you know?"

Jillian smiled, warmed by his compliment. "What makes you say that?" She leaned back to see him look down at their feet.

"You're the only person in my life who cares enough about my feelings to do something like this."

He gestured to the log and the lake before them. "If one of my friends had been with me during that visit, they would have asked if I was okay and then left me alone when I lied and said yes. But you..." He shook his head. "You brought me here so I could think in peace, and then you didn't pester me to talk."

"Would that have worked?"

"Nope," he confirmed. "It would have annoyed me."

"So you're saying I made the right choice," she teased. "Sounds like I know you pretty well."

"You do." There was a somber note in his tone that made her glance up, and she found him watching her, his expression serious. "You see me. Probably better than anyone ever has. I know we haven't known each other very long, but you seem to get me." He paused, swallowing hard. "I... I think I..." He shook his head, unable to continue.

Jillian's heart beat so hard in her chest, it was a wonder it didn't break through her rib cage and fly away. Was he saying what she thought he was saying? Was Baldwin Bowe professing his feelings for her?

"I know," she said, reaching up to cup his cheek with her hand. "I feel it, too," she assured him.

It was the damnedest thing. A few days ago, she'd thought him heartless. Now she realized the depth of his emotions and wanted to pull him close to help ease the ache of his parents' rejection. There hadn't been a magic moment when she'd suddenly realized Baldwin cared more than he tried to let on. But somewhere along the way, he'd gotten under her skin and Jillian knew she'd never be the same.

The only question was, where did they go from here? After Randall was no longer a threat, Baldwin would have to move on to the next case, wherever that might take him. Her job was here, in Grave Gulch. So were her family and the few friends she had. Did they even have a chance of making it work between them? Or was this destined to be a short-term connection, one that she'd remember for the rest of her life?

It was on the tip of her tongue to ask, but she didn't want to add to Baldwin's stress. He was already tied up in knots about finding his brother, and the meeting with his parents had only added to his burden. If Jillian was to press him about where they stood, he'd probably run away and never look back.

As much as she might like to plan for the future, she was going to have to live in the present. That meant enjoying the time they had now, for as long as they had it.

Baldwin turned his face into her palm and kissed her hand. Then he leaned down and brushed his lips against hers.

The heat of his mouth chased away the chill of the wind. Jillian leaned against him, determined to set aside all her questions and worries. She turned down the volume in her mind and focused on savoring the taste of Baldwin, the delicate pressure he put on her lips and the feel of his hand on her back.

There was something different about this kiss. Before, she'd felt the need driving him, the energy he was containing lest he lose control. But this was soft, tender. It wasn't about desire or sex. It was a connection, a communion between them.

It was love.

Jillian wasn't going to say it. To acknowledge it aloud would only further complicate an already complex situation.

But her heart knew the truth. And later, when things settled down, she could figure out what it all meant.

Baldwin drew back and rested his forehead against hers. Then he chuckled softly. "Your nose is like an ice cube," he said.

"Really?" She hadn't noticed. She'd been too caught up in the moment to register anything else, but now that he'd mentioned it, she realized how cold she was.

"Come on," he said. He stood and tugged her up, as well. "We need to get you someplace warm."

They set off down the path together, walking arm in arm. "Thank you for showing me this," he said.

"You're welcome." Jillian smiled up at him. "We used to ride our bikes here a lot as kids during the summer. Our house was pretty small and Mom worked all the time, so we were on our own for entertainment."

"I bet you had fun," Baldwin said.

"Oh, yeah," Jillian confirmed. "Did you do anything like that as a kid? Go off exploring?"

Baldwin shook his head. "Not really. Closest we ever got was my aunt's house the next town over. She had a big backyard that jutted up to a creek. We'd go there a few times a year and I loved catching tadpoles and stuff. Not Randall, though. He always stayed inside to read."

Suddenly, Baldwin stopped walking. The muscles under her hand tensed, as though an electrical current was passing through his arm. Jillian glanced up, worried.

His eyes were wide, his mouth slightly agape. He looked like he'd just been hit over the head with a log, and Jillian glanced around to see if he'd walked into a tree branch. But the path around his head was clear.

"Baldwin? What's going on?"

He sucked in a breath as a gleam entered his eyes. "I think I know where my brother is hiding."

He drove like a man possessed.

Baldwin kept his foot on the accelerator and one hand on the wheel as he talked to Carter, his buddy from the marines who had since started a private security company. Carter had been the one to watch Jillian's apartment that night she'd been shot, and he trusted him completely. Jillian sat quietly in the passenger seat, her curiosity so intense he could practically feel it.

"No, I don't need you to come with me," he said. "You've got to stake out the condo in case Randall doubles back."

"You shouldn't go alone," Carter protested. "You know that goes against all our training."

"I'll be fine," Baldwin said shortly. Carter had

a point, but there wasn't anyone Baldwin trusted enough to accompany him.

"Look, man—"

"Will you do this for me?" Baldwin interrupted. He had additional arrangements to make and didn't want to spend more time than necessary on the phone.

Carter sighed, his displeasure coming through loud and clear. "Yeah, I will. But I'm about two hours away."

"That's fine," Baldwin replied. "Just get here as soon as you can."

He ended the call before Carter could argue further. A small part of him recognized he was being rude, but now was not the time to worry about manners.

"Is it my turn to talk now?" Jillian asked quietly.

The tires screeched in protest as he took a turn a little faster than advisable. "Yeah," he said. "I'm sorry."

"Where do you think Randall is hiding?"

"My aunt's house," he said. "She lived on the outskirts of Lakeside on a big plot of land that backed up to a creek."

"Would she help Randall?"

Baldwin shook his head. "She died about five years ago. She never had children of her own, so her house and everything in it was left to my parents. They decided to rent the home." He turned into the parking lot of Jillian's building and pulled into a spot near the entrance.

"As far as I know, the house is still being rented.

But there was a large shed at the edge of the property, almost like a barn, and my parents used it to store some of her things. They kept it locked so the tenants couldn't access it."

"But Randall has a key?"

"I'm guessing so. Even if he doesn't, it wouldn't be hard for him to pick the lock."

They walked into the building together and headed for the elevator. He was so full of adrenaline that he could have happily raced up the stairs, but Jillian looked tired and she was still recovering from her injury.

Why had it taken so long for him to think of Aunt Ginny's house? The old shed was the perfect place for Randall to lay low and was close enough that his brother would still be aware of everything going on in Grave Gulch.

Jillian unlocked her door and they walked inside. "So what's your plan?" she asked, tossing her keys on the kitchen counter. "I'm assuming that you're going after him?"

"Absolutely," Baldwin said. No way was he going to let Randall spend another night as a free man.

Jillian spun around and leaned against the counter, then crossed her arms. "Alone?" There was a strange note in her voice that he'd never heard before, one that made the fine hairs on the back of his neck stand on end.

"Yes," he said carefully. He could tell she was tense, though he wasn't yet certain why. Was the thought of apprehending Randall making her emotional?

"You're an idiot," she said flatly.

Baldwin reared back slightly. Of all the things she could have said, he hadn't expected that.

"Excuse me?"

"You heard me." Now he recognized her tone—she was angry. Furious, even.

"Jillian, I—"

"Going off after your brother alone is not smart," she interrupted. "You should call the police, call your friend, take someone with you."

"I can't."

"You won't," she stormed. "You're determined to be the one to take down your brother. Your ego won't let you ask for help, because you want all the credit."

"That's not true," Baldwin said, his temper starting to build. This had nothing to do with his pride and everything to do with trying to keep Jillian safe. Why couldn't she see that!

"The sooner I bring him in, the sooner your life can go back to normal. Isn't that what you want?" She glanced away, so he pressed on. "Besides," he said, stepping closer, "I can't risk the chance that if someone goes with me, they'll end up hurt or worse. He's already shot you—I won't put someone else in danger."

"The police are trained to arrest people!"

Baldwin shook his head. "And if he resists? What then? They'll just shoot him?" He couldn't let that happen. "I know he's a bastard, but I want him to stay alive so he can answer for what he's done. He deserves to rot in prison."

"But what about you?" Tears brimmed in her eyes and her voice wavered. "What if he hurts you? Or..." She trailed off, shaking her head. "If something happens to you, Randall isn't going to stop to help you. He'll leave you there, all by yourself."

Baldwin took another step closer, touched by her concern. "Nothing is going to happen," he said quietly.

"How can you be so certain?" She looked so vulnerable, staring up at him. He wanted to pull her close and hold her, to promise her that he would come back whole and unharmed.

But he couldn't say that for sure. No matter how confident he was, no matter the fact that he had experience and training for this kind of situation, there was always an element of chance that couldn't be discounted.

Still, it would be easy to lie to her. To play up his past as a marine, to emphasize his medals and awards, as if they were some kind of proof that he was untouchable. At one point in his life, he *had* felt bulletproof. It wouldn't be hard for him to pretend that he truly was.

Except...now he had something to lose. He had no idea what the future would look like for the two of them, but he couldn't deny he cared about Jillian. If he was being truly honest, he was falling in love with her. If the worst happened, he didn't want to lie to her in their last moments together. Better to leave her with the truth, no matter how unpleasant.

"Nothing is ever certain," he began. "But I have experience on my side. Not to mention the element of surprise. Randall doesn't know I'm coming. I'm betting he's gotten comfortable, having spent so much time out there with no one ever thinking to check the storage shed. The police have been looking for him for most of the year with no luck—you know from the messages he's sent people that he's getting even cockier, if that's possible."

She was quiet a moment, clearly thinking. "I get that you don't want anyone to hurt your brother. And I know you're a big, bad ex-soldier."

"Marine," he interrupted with a smile.

She rolled her eyes. "Ex-marine," she corrected. "But didn't you always have at least one partner when you went on a mission?"

Her words echoed Carter's earlier objections. Baldwin recognized they both had a point, but he couldn't afford to waste time. If he called in the cops, they'd insist on taking control of the situation and he wouldn't be able to act. Despite everything, he still held a sliver of hope that he could talk Randall into coming in peacefully. Surely his brother was smart enough to know when he'd been beaten? But if Baldwin turned up with the Grave Gulch Police Department, Randall would panic.

Panicked people got themselves killed.

"Maybe I should come with you," she suggested. "I can wait in the truck. Just in case—"

"Absolutely not." Baldwin started speaking before she even finished. "There is no way I'm bringing you close to Randall. If it was up to me, you'd never see him again."

The ghost of a smile flitted across her face. "Am I not allowed to worry about you?"

He hooked a finger through one of her belt loops and tugged her close, until they were only a couple of inches apart. She hesitated a few seconds, then leaned against his chest.

Baldwin wrapped his arms around her, dipping his head until his nose touched her hair. He took a deep breath, drawing in the scent of her.

"I won't be gone long," he said. "I'll be back before you know it."

Her arms came around him as she rested her cheek against his sternum. "Am I just supposed to sit here twiddling my thumbs until that happens?"

"No." He rubbed a hand down her back, hoping she would agree to this next part without much fuss. "You're going to call your brother and hang out with him."

She tensed in his arms. "Why would I do that?"

"I'm just being cautious."

Jillian leaned back to look up at him. "You can't have it both ways," she said. "You can't tell me this is going to be a walk in the park, and then insist that I spend the evening with my brother while you're gone."

He should have known she would argue. Nothing about this woman was ever simple.

"If it's safe for you to go after Randall by yourself, then it should be safe for me to stay here alone. Besides, didn't you call your friend? Charles, is that his name?"

"Carter," Baldwin grumbled.

"Yeah, him," she continued. "You asked him to do something for you. Is he coming back to watch my place again?"

"He is," Baldwin admitted.

Jillian nodded. "Right. So even though everything is perfectly fine, you've asked someone to guard my condo while you're gone."

Baldwin closed his eyes. "Please don't make this harder for me," he said.

"Oh, yes," she said, dropping her arms to end their connection. "Wouldn't want to inconvenience *you*."

"Jillian—" This wasn't how things were supposed to go. Why couldn't she understand he had to do this alone? That he couldn't handle it if his brother hurt anyone else?

"You should go," she said shortly. "I know how important your job is to you. Don't let me hold you back."

There were so many things he wanted to say to her. It was clear he hadn't explained his strategy very well, and he hated that Jillian was upset. But she was too angry to talk to at this point. Even if he tried to tell her that she wasn't holding him back—that she was more important to him than his job—she wouldn't believe him.

He sighed, a sense of resignation creeping over

him. This conversation was effectively over, at least for the moment. Hopefully, once he returned from successfully capturing Randall, she'd be so happy that the threat from his brother was gone that her anger would disappear and they could move forward.

"I'll wait until Bryce gets here," he said quietly. "I don't want you to be alone."

"I'm not calling him," she said. "If he knows what you're doing, he'll insist on going along. And since he's already been shot once..."

"Who, then?" Baldwin asked, ignoring the jab. "I don't want you here alone. Carter is two hours away."

"Grace," Jillian replied. "Maybe she can come over."

Baldwin nodded. "Will you call her, please?"

Jillian stared at him a moment, emotions swirling in her eyes. Then she nodded once and stepped away with her phone.

It was on the tip of his tongue to call after her, to warn her not to tell her cousin about his plans. But he knew if he said anything, her simmering temper would likely boil over. He was already on shaky ground here; he didn't want to make things worse between them.

After a few minutes, Jillian returned. "She'll be here in ten," she said, her tone flat.

"That's good," Baldwin said quietly. "Thank you."

She nodded, but didn't look at him. "Go on," she said. "Wouldn't want you to miss your shot."

Baldwin was torn. On the one hand, she was right; the longer he stayed here, the greater the chance he'd miss finding Randall. He was fairly certain his brother was at their aunt's old storage shed, but what if he wasn't? Better to find out quickly so he could come up with another plan if needed.

But on the other hand…he didn't want to leave Jillian. Not just because it was risky to leave her alone. Because he cared about her and enjoyed spending time with her. She made him laugh, and she lightened his mood. And when things were stressful, like now, her presence helped keep him grounded. Even though she was angry with him, he still didn't want to walk away from her. Part of him was worried that if they didn't resolve this issue before he left, they might never be able to do it. It made him feel unsettled, as though he was walking blindfolded through a field of land mines. One wrong step, and things between them would explode, never to be repaired.

It was clear Jillian was upset. She'd told him to leave twice already; he wasn't going to make her ask a third time. Despite his worries, it was probably best to give her some space. They could talk about this later, when they were both calmer.

"I'll go," he said. He walked over to where she was standing and leaned down to kiss her forehead. He would have liked to have kissed her lips instead, but he wasn't going to press his luck. "I'll be back later. And then we can finish talking."

Jillian looked up at him, her expression worried. "You'd better come back," she muttered. "If you wind up hurt, I'll kill you myself."

He chuckled, happy to see she seemed to be moving from anger to irritation. "Yes, ma'am." He turned and took a step toward the door, then stopped as Jillian grabbed his arm and tugged hard.

She spun him back around and in one fluid motion she stood on her toes, cupped his face in her hands and pulled him down for a kiss. Baldwin started to put his arms around her, but she stepped back, evading his touch.

"You'll get the rest when you return," she said, touching her fingertips to her mouth as if to prolong the feel of his lips against hers.

Baldwin smiled, desire flickering to life inside his chest. "Then you'd better wait up for me."

Chapter 14

At Baldwin's insistence, Jillian followed him to the exit. He waited until he heard the lock click into place before walking away. She turned and leaned against the door, listening to the fading sound of his footsteps and trying not to cry.

Stubborn, infuriating man!

Why was she surprised? Baldwin was bound and determined to catch his brother. She should have known there was no way he would entertain the possibility of waiting for help, not once he'd figured out Randall's likely hiding place. The man was like a dog with a bone, refusing to give up his precious, hastily put together plan. No amount of talking was going to change his mind; she would've had better luck trying to argue with a brick wall.

Not even her worry for him had mattered. Baldwin was so convinced of his tactical skill that he hadn't stopped to think about the fact that what his brother lacked in physicality, he made up for in deviousness. Randall was no match for Baldwin in a fair fight, but since when had Randall ever fought fair? But Baldwin didn't appear to consider the possibility that he might be outmaneuvered. His ego wouldn't allow him to acknowledge it. In that way, the two brothers were alike—both supremely confident of their own abilities.

So why was she sitting here, almost crying over a man who had made it clear he didn't need her tears?

"You idiot," she muttered, not sure if she was talking to herself or to Baldwin. Things had been so much easier when he'd just been the jerk who was using her to get to his brother. If they'd stayed impersonal, she could have waved him off without a second thought. But now that she'd gone and fallen for him, it was different. All she saw were the risks he was taking, all she could think about were the ways he might get hurt, or maybe even killed. Her chest grew tight as her mind worked, as if someone was cinching a belt around her rib cage. She'd never forgive him if he died. She'd spend the rest of her life angry with him for leaving before they knew what was going on between them.

"Stop it," she told herself. This line of thinking was only making things worse. Baldwin was a decorated marine veteran—he didn't get that way by sitting in the barracks while everyone else went out to fight. He knew what he was doing, and she had to trust that he wouldn't take any unnecessary risks. He'd practically promised her he was going to come back. She should believe him—after all, he'd never lied to her before.

Jillian pushed off the door and wiped her eyes. Grace would be here in a few minutes, and Jillian didn't want her to think anything was wrong. She'd told her cousin that Baldwin was meeting with some friends in the area to see if they had any leads on Randall's whereabouts. She felt a little guilty about the white lie, but Baldwin had been insistent that he didn't want the police involved. Even though she wanted him to have backup, she understood his desire to do this alone. Baldwin had a lot of complicated feelings about his family and she knew he'd never forgive himself if Randall was killed, even though his brother was guilty of so many crimes.

She walked to the bathroom and splashed cold water on her face, then went back to the kitchen and poured herself a glass of iced tea. Part of her was glad Grace would be joining her shortly—she would be a good distraction. If left to her own devices, Jillian would spend the evening pacing the condo and clutching her phone, desperate for some kind of update from Baldwin. At least if Grace was here she'd have company, should the news be bad.

A knock on the door interrupted her maudlin thoughts. "It's me," Grace called from the other side.

Jillian opened the door and tried to smile, but it must not have worked very well. "Oh, no," Grace said. "What's wrong?"

"It's nothing," Jillian said, waving her cousin inside. "I'm fine."

Grace gave her a doubtful look. "Uh-huh. I can see that." She lifted one hand to emphasize the bottle she held. "Good thing I brought this. Now let's get some glasses and you can tell me what's going on."

Jillian led her to the kitchen, debating what to say. She had to tell Grace something, but she didn't want to betray Baldwin. How to thread this needle?

"Baldwin and I had an argument," she said finally. It was the truth…mostly. She retrieved two wineglasses and set them on the counter.

Grace had already found the corkscrew and was busy peeling the label off the top of the bottle. "I see. What were you fighting about?"

"He thinks he needs to go after Randall alone," Jillian said carefully, keeping her eyes on Grace's hands. "I told him he should have backup, in case something goes wrong."

Grace nodded as she twisted the corkscrew. "That's the smart thing to do," she said. A *thunk* punctuated her words as she pulled the cork free from the bottle.

"Yeah, well, he's worried that Randall's actions have made things personal between him and a lot of people on the force. He thinks Randall might provoke someone into shooting him, so that he wouldn't be taken alive."

"Suicide by cop?" Grace poured wine into each glass, then set the bottle on the counter. "It's possible," she said. "It definitely happens sometimes.

And with Randall's outsized ego, he might try that approach."

"What do you mean?" Jillian picked up her glass and took a small sip. The red wine had a woodsy flavor that burned a little going down.

Grace shrugged. "I'm just saying, Randall prides himself on his intellect. He thinks he's outsmarted us all. Can you imagine what it would do to him to be arrested and forced to answer for what he's done? He thinks he's above normal people. It wouldn't surprise me at all if he'd rather die than be judged by us."

A chill skittered down Jillian's spine as she realized Grace was likely correct. She hadn't thought of it like that before, but it made a lot of sense. No wonder Baldwin didn't want the cops involved.

But...what if Randall tried to get Baldwin to kill him? It was the ultimate act of revenge between the two siblings, as Randall had to know his brother would carry the guilt for the rest of his life. Baldwin wouldn't hurt anyone except to defend himself. What if Randall didn't give him a choice?

Was Baldwin even now walking into a trap?

Jillian's heart jumped into her throat and she fought the urge to run out the door to try to find him. *Don't be silly*, she told herself. Not only was she clueless as to the location of the storage shed, but she was also almost certain Baldwin had thought of this exact possibility.

Right?

"Are you okay?" Grace eyed her over the rim of her wineglass. "You look like you've seen a ghost."

Jillian forced herself to take a deep breath. "Just hungry," she said. "Should we order a pizza?"

"O-o-oh, yes please," Grace said. "That sounds delicious."

"Any preference?"

"Veggie supreme with sausage, please," Grace said. She walked into the living room and glanced around. "You don't seem to be in the winter spirit."

"Can you blame me?" Jillian picked up her wineglass and followed her cousin. "I haven't exactly been thinking about cocoa or ice skating, what with everything else going on."

"Maybe putting up some cozy decor would help cheer you up?" Grace asked. "Should we give it a try?"

Jillian considered the suggestion. She didn't automatically hate it, which meant it was probably worth doing. "Yeah," she mused. "I think we should." At the very least, that would help keep her mind off Baldwin and the risks he was taking. "I'll call in for the pizza and then start pulling stuff out of the closet."

"Perfect!" Grace walked over to the television and picked up the remote. "I'll find us a cheesy movie to watch while we work."

Jillian dialed the number for Paola's Pizza and placed their order. A few minutes later she hung up and joined Grace on the couch. "They said it'll be about an hour."

"They must be busy tonight," Grace remarked. "That just gives us more time to get stuff done. Let's get started!"

Grace's enthusiasm was infectious, and soon Jillian found herself smiling and even laughing as they worked to retrieve her wintry decorations from the depths of her closet. In no time at all, they had everything spread out in the living room.

"Where did you get all of this?" Grace asked.

Jillian shrugged. "Some of it I bought because it caught my eye. I always have big decorating plans, but they never seem to materialize because I get so busy with other things. A lot of it came from my mom—she's always buying me little things, and eventually, it adds up to this." She lifted her arms to encompass the room. "We definitely don't need to put everything out."

"I don't think we could even if you wanted to," Grace remarked. "You still need to live here, after all."

"That's true."

"What's in this box?" Grace gestured to the corner of the room."

"Fairy lights," Jillian said. "I put some up last year but haven't gotten around to it yet."

"We'll start there," Grace decided. "Once we get the lights up and some of the other wintry decorations out, we can figure out what the rest of the room needs."

Jillian was happy to let her cousin take the lead. Normally, she enjoyed decorating her space with the changing seasons. But there was nothing normal about this year.

Together, they maneuvered the tangled ball of lights out of the box.

Grace stood back and eyed it critically. "This looks complicated."

"It'll just take a bit of time," Jillian said. "At least we'll have something to do while we wait for our dinner."

Grace shook her head. "I can see I'm going to need to help you take everything down later."

"What makes you say that?"

Her cousin sighed. "Your storage strategy leaves a lot to be desired. For someone who is so organized in her job, I'm surprised you don't apply a similar philosophy at home."

"Not everything can be perfect," Jillian said absently as she worked to untangle the strands of lights.

It took a few minutes, but soon she and Grace were hanging the lights between sips of wine, the light from the television screen adding a warm glow to the room.

He's okay, Jillian told herself for what had to be the millionth time. Baldwin would be back soon, filled with triumph over finally catching his brother. They'd spend the rest of the night holding each other, celebrating the fact that Randall was finally going to face justice. And, most importantly, Baldwin would be safe and whole and in her arms.

It was a nice thought, one she was going to cling to until Baldwin walked through her door again.

It's going to be fine. It's all going to work out.

Maybe if she said it enough times, it would turn out to be true.

The alternative was too upsetting to contemplate.

Baldwin spent the drive to his aunt's place thinking about Jillian, worried about how he'd left things. She'd seemed okay when he'd walked out the door, but what if she was only pretending? What if that kiss was her way of telling him goodbye, and he'd been too distracted to notice? So many questions, but no obvious answers.

As he pulled into his aunt's old neighborhood, he forced his mind to focus on the job at hand. If he allowed himself to be distracted, he'd make a mistake. Possibly the last one of his life.

Aunt Ginny's house was set about twenty feet off the street, shaded by two large oak trees that had been there since his youth. They were much bigger now, obscuring most of the front of the house. This area was mostly ranchettes, so the nearest neighbor was at least fifty yards away. Hopefully the distance meant he wouldn't have to deal with any bystanders.

Baldwin coasted to a stop about ten yards up the road and cut the engine. He sat in the dark for several minutes, studying the house and the surrounding area. The windows were dark, betraying no hint of light within the home. That was good; if he was lucky, the renters wouldn't be home to catch him prowling around the backyard.

Satisfied that no one was around, Baldwin reached into the glove compartment and retrieved a flashlight and his gun. The textured grip of the Glock was a familiar extension of his hand, but he felt a flicker of reluctance as he held the weapon. Randall had surprised him in Jillian's condo. He couldn't let that happen again.

Even if that meant shooting his own brother.

Baldwin quietly shut the door of the truck and walked toward the house, sticking to the shadows as much as possible. He crept along the side until he came to the gate that led to the large backyard. Fortunately, the gate was partially open and he was able to squeeze through the gap without making any noise. Once inside the yard, he paused, listening hard for the sound of a dog, or any indication someone was aware of his presence. But all he heard was the hum of the heater as it kicked on inside the house.

Moving carefully, he approached the large storage shed in the far corner of the yard. There were no lights back here, and at this distance, it was unlikely anyone would see him from the house. Still, he didn't rush. If Randall was inside, Baldwin didn't want to give him any warning of what was about to go down.

The mini barn loomed up before him, still solid and strong after all these years. Baldwin crept cautiously around the perimeter of the structure, looking for any signs of life within. No light escaped the cracks around the windows and the night was still and calm. He sniffed quietly, hoping to detect some hint of cologne or food that would give away his brother's presence. But the cold air held no clues for him.

Time to go inside.

Baldwin approached the door and flicked on his flashlight, angling his body to hide the light from the house as much as possible. The silver handle was dull where the plate joined to the door, but the knob itself was shiny, indicating recent use. A latch was bolted to the door a few inches above the handle, and a padlock hung open through the hook.

Baldwin's heart sank. Since the padlock was there, Randall couldn't be inside. There was no way for him to enter the shed, close the door behind him and replace the lock. So where was he?

His thoughts immediately turned to Jillian, and he was tempted to run back to the truck and head to her place. But he forced himself to stay put. She wasn't alone; Grace was with her, and Carter would be watching the condo soon. Much as he hated to be away from her with Randall at large, he needed to see this through to the end. Maybe there were clues inside the building. If Randall had been hiding here all along, he must have left something behind. Baldwin might even be able to figure out what his brother was going to do next. Spending a little more time here might yield big dividends in this case.

He holstered his gun in the waistband of his pants and used his now free hand to carefully remove the lock from the latch, pocketing it so he could put it back when he was done. Then he pulled the flat metal piece away and placed his hand on the doorknob.

Just before he turned the knob, a thought occurred to him. What if his brother had set up booby traps? It was the kind of thing he'd do, to ensure anyone looking for him would receive a nasty surprise. A quick glance around the frame of the door betrayed no wires or signs of explosives, and Baldwin didn't see any tape or other markers commonly used to determine if a site had been disturbed. Still, he didn't trust Randall. His brother was too clever by half, and Baldwin wasn't about to walk into one of his snares.

Instead of standing in front of the door, Baldwin changed position so he was pressed against the wall of the barn, with only his hand on the knob. His body was no longer in the line of fire, decreasing his chances of being the victim of a booby trap. He turned off his flashlight, then slowly turned the knob and pushed open the door.

It swung inside the building on silent hinges. Baldwin remained still for a moment, waiting to see if something was going to happen. But nothing did. No sounds came from inside the structure, not even the squeak of a startled mouse.

Interesting.

He angled his head to the side slightly, chancing a quick glance at the door and the dark interior it had revealed. It was pitch-black inside the barn, too dark for even shadows.

Time to go inside.

Baldwin clicked on his flashlight and aimed the beam through the door. It landed on the far wall, which was plastered with what looked like photographs and newspaper clippings. Off to the right side, at the edges of the light, he saw a cot with a pillow and blanket strewn on top.

"Gotcha," he whispered.

He swept the floor with the light but saw no traps. He took a step into the storage shed, and immediately realized his mistake.

A blur of movement came from the left. As Baldwin turned to react, a burst of foul, oily liquid coated his face.

His eyes and mouth began to burn, and his chest constricted as he fought to breathe. Almost instantly, he was back in training, when he'd been forced to stand in line with his fellow marines while they endured pepper spray directly to the face.

Baldwin staggered back, reaching for his gun. But before he could grab it, something hit him hard in the knees and he went down.

"Hello, brother."

He would have known that smug voice anywhere. Randall. But how—?

"The window, you idiot," Randall said, apparently sensing Baldwin's question. "I put the lock back into place and climbed in through the window."

Baldwin coughed, then gagged as he fought to breathe. He couldn't see a thing, but he sensed a light had been turned on in the barn. Randall would want to watch him suffer.

"I figured you were coming," his brother continued. "I've been keeping tabs on you."

"How?" he choked out. He didn't try to get up yet—given the intense pain in his left knee, he didn't think his legs would support his weight.

"Her phone," Randall said, as if it should be obvious. "I noticed it on the counter when I was there the other night. Saved me having to search for it. I installed a little program before you interrupted me. Lets me track where she's going. And as a bonus, I can see who she's calling or texting."

"You've been listening?" He was wheezing now, but he knew from experience it wouldn't last forever. Still, that was cold comfort at the moment.

"No, it's not that good," Randall said ruefully. "It just tells me the number she's contacting."

"Why?" Just the one word triggered a bout of coughing so intense he thought he might break a rib. Tears streamed from his swollen eyes but they did nothing to wash away the acrid, burning chemicals.

"How are Mom and Dad?" Randall asked, ignoring his question. "Were they surprised to see you?"

Baldwin refused to waste a breath answering him.

"Doesn't matter," he said. "I don't have time for this, anyway. I have a date with Jillian."

"No!" Baldwin lunged in the direction of Randall's voice. If he could just get his hands on him, he could overpower his brother…

Randall dodged and laughed. Baldwin felt the air move and then something hit him on the back of the head. He fell, temporarily dazed by the blow.

"I think it's cute you have a crush on her." Randall grunted and Baldwin realized he was being pulled across the floor. "Stand up," Randall instructed. When Baldwin didn't respond right away, Randall pulled the gun from his waist and pushed the muzzle into his side. "Now."

Baldwin managed to get his feet under him and he stood, biting back a scream as his knee protested his weight.

"Good boy," Randall said. He clicked a handcuff around Baldwin's left wrist, then pulled his right arm behind him to finish the job. "You're going to stay here until I get back."

Baldwin moved his arms and felt a tremor as the cuffs made contact with something metallic. It seemed Randall had circled his arms around a pole of some kind.

"That's right," his brother said. "You're stuck here. But don't worry. I won't be gone long. I might even bring Jillian back to join us."

"Leave her alone," Baldwin choked out. "This is between us." Some of his vision was starting to come back now, and he saw Randall's blurry figure standing several feet away.

"It was," Randall agreed. "But the more, the merrier." He moved out of Baldwin's field of view, then returned a second later holding something in his hands. He reached out and Baldwin jerked as he felt his brother's hands on his head.

Randall fit the gag over his mouth, positioning it between Baldwin's teeth. "There, that's better," he said, standing back once more. "You should know the people who rent the house are out of town for the holidays, and the neighbors are too far away to hear you scream. Besides," he said, a note of anticipation entering his voice, "you might want to save your strength for what's to come."

His words sent a chill down Baldwin's spine, but he refused to show any reaction in front of his brother. Truth be told, he wasn't worried for himself. He was terrified of what Randall was going to do to Jillian.

Randall reached for him again, shoving his hand into Baldwin's front pocket and withdrawing his cell phone. He held it in front of Baldwin's face, wiggling it back and forth to taunt him. "You won't be needing this anymore."

Baldwin glared at him. He considered provoking Randall into staying here and attacking him, but under the current circumstances, there was no guarantee he'd be able to get free and overpower his brother. If Randall started beating him, Jillian would be unprotected once his brother was done. As much as he hated to do it, Baldwin had to feign helplessness now so Randall would leave.

"See you soon," Randall called as he walked through the door. A few seconds later Baldwin heard it shut and the latch click into place. Randall cursed when he noticed the lock was missing, but apparently he thought Baldwin was secured enough without it, because he didn't come back inside.

Good. Randall's cockiness was going to be his downfall. He just didn't know it yet.

Baldwin waited until he no longer heard the sound of his brother's footsteps outside. He took the opportunity to try to control his breathing, overriding the intense urge to cough and gasp. His eyes still burned, but they were getting better. His main problem was going to be his knee, which was throbbing in time to the beat of his heart. Still, all things considered, he'd been in worse situations. Granted, he was older now and not quite as fit. But his determination to save Jillian more than made up for any softening of his skills.

Randall had taken his gun. But if he'd done a thorough search of Baldwin's pockets, he would have found the multitool Baldwin always carried. He fumbled for it now, twisting and contorting his body so he could get one of his bound hands into his pocket. It took longer than he liked, but his fingers finally brushed over the metal. Once he extracted the tool from his pocket, it didn't take long to pick the lock of the cuffs. They opened with a click, and Baldwin felt a burst of gratitude toward his younger self for absorbing all the training the marines had offered him. He'd never be an academic like his parents or his brother, but he'd taken his time in the military seriously and had focused his efforts on learning everything he could. The lessons had saved his life on more than one occasion while in the service, and they were still paying off now.

He ripped off the gag and tested his knee, gritting his teeth as a fresh burst of pain radiated up and down his leg. It hurt like hell, but it still supported his weight. As long as he could walk, he'd be fine.

He moved toward the door, his foot hitting something on the floor. Based on the rolling sound it made, he figured it was his flashlight. Baldwin kneeled and managed to find it nearby. The beam wouldn't help his vision much, but he felt better holding the solid, heavy weight. He missed his gun, but he was never truly unarmed.

The journey back to his truck was slow and painful. He wanted to run, his desperation to get to Jillian driving him to go as fast as possible. But there was only so much his knee could take, and if he pushed it now, he wouldn't be able to help her later. So he plodded along until he reached his truck.

The steering wheel was cold against his hands. There was an unopened bottle of water in the passenger seat; he grabbed it and unscrewed the cap, then opened his eyes as wide as he could and poured the water over them. The cool liquid temporarily soothed the still-burning tissues, but the feeling didn't last long enough. His shirt was saturated with both water and pepper spray, so he carefully peeled it off and tossed it in the bed of the truck. Then he reached into the glove compartment and retrieved his backup gun.

"Hold on, Jillian," he muttered as he started the truck and pulled onto the road.

"I'm coming."

Chapter 15

The place didn't look half-bad.

Jillian took a step back and eyed it up and down as she held her wineglass. She and Grace had wrapped the strands around the room, giving it a soft, cozy glow, and now it twinkled in a multicolored display that reminded her of the storefront windows along Grave Gulch Boulevard.

Grace picked up a plaid throw pillow. "Ready to start adding accents?"

Jillian nodded. "Absolutely. That will clear up some space for the pizza."

A new romantic movie was starting on the television. Grace glanced at the screen for a minute, watching the opening scenes. "She's going to get stranded in a small town and fall in love with the local vet. Or maybe the mechanic?"

Jillian chuckled. "Have you seen this one before?"

Grace shook her head. "No. But the signs are there."

"The signs?"

"Yeah. High-powered job, small dog. She's traveling for the holiday but has to take a car. The car is going to break down and because of the storm or the holiday, the part she needs won't be in for a few days. So she'll be stuck in town and she'll start to get to know the locals."

Jillian laughed. "Sounds like you've seen a few of these."

Grace grinned. "Oh, yeah. They're my kryptonite. I watch as many as I can."

"Does Camden like them, too?" Jillian had a hard time imagining the straitlaced Internal Affairs officer curled up on the couch in front of a romantic movie.

"He tolerates them for my sake. Honestly, I think they're growing on him. They can be a little cheesy, but there's something really nice about watching a story that has a happy ending."

"Especially in your line of work," Jillian remarked.

Grace nodded as she glanced around the room. "I think that's why I like them so much. It's like the best version of real life, you know? Even if something bad happens in the movie, you know it will all turn out okay in the end."

"Yeah." Lately, Jillian had been wishing for that kind of guarantee in her own life. Everyone around her seemed so certain that the charges against her would be dropped and Randall would be brought to justice, but unless that happened soon, she was on the hook for these robberies.

Her thoughts circled back to Baldwin and her anxiety ratcheted up another notch. Was he okay? Had he found his brother? Was he even now bringing him to the police station?

Or was he out there alone and injured, subject to Randall's unlikely mercy?

Grace touched her shoulder and she jumped, startled. She glanced over to find Grace standing next to her. When had she moved?

"Do you want to tell me what's really going on now?" her cousin asked quietly.

Jillian's eyes stung as tears built. She should have known she couldn't fool Grace for long. She so badly wanted to talk to her, but Baldwin had insisted on going alone. If she talked to Grace, it would be a betrayal of the trust he'd placed in her.

Except...she didn't know where he was. Not exactly. So even if Grace wanted to call for backup on his behalf, she wouldn't know where to send them. The stubborn man had made sure of that.

"Baldwin has gone after Randall," she said in a rush. It felt good to get the words out, even though it didn't change anything.

Grace's eyes went wide. "Alone? I thought you said he was meeting with friends."

Jillian shook her head. Damn that man, and damn her twisted sense of loyalty to him! It was one thing to support him emotionally and connect with him physically. But there was nothing healthy about keeping a secret that might cost him his life. She should have told Grace from the start.

"He thinks his brother is hiding in a storage barn on his dead aunt's property," she said. "His parents are renting the house but the barn has always been locked. He thinks Randall might be holed up there."

"And so he went to investigate by himself," Grace muttered.

"Yeah," Jillian confirmed. "I told you earlier why he didn't want to take anyone."

"Idiot," Grace said under her breath. She glanced up at Jillian. "Sorry. I know you two have a thing."

Jillian shook her head. "Don't apologize. I agree with you. I would have told you earlier, but I don't know where he's gone."

"We can find out," Grace said. She pulled her phone from her pocket and dialed. "This is Grace Colton," she said. She rattled off her badge number. "I need a records search. We're looking for the address of Randall Bowe's dead aunt." She glanced at Jillian. "Do you know her name?"

Jillian shook her head, feeling powerless to help. "His parents are Dave and Linda Bowe. But I don't know the aunt's name."

Grace relayed the information. "Call me back when you get an address, please," she said. She ended the call, then dialed another number.

"Chief? It's Grace."

Jillian listened to Grace talk, her chest growing

tighter with every passing second. Baldwin would be furious if the police showed up to his aunt's home, but Jillian wouldn't be able to live with herself if something happened to him, knowing she could have acted to stop it.

Her biggest worry now was would they get there in time to help him?

Grace hung up and looked at Jillian. "Okay. As soon as we get an address, he's going to send some officers out there to check things out. Chief Shea is excited about this new information, but he doesn't want to go in guns blazing unless we have more evidence that Randall is really there."

Jillian nodded, biting her bottom lip. "That's understandable." It was a neighborhood, after all. And Baldwin wasn't certain his brother was present.

The doorbell rang, signaling the arrival of their dinner. "I'll grab it," Grace said, still holding her phone. "Why don't you pour us some more wine? You look like you could use it."

Grace headed for the door, and Jillian took the moment alone to pick up her phone. She held it for a few seconds, debating. Should she text Baldwin to check in? Or would that distract him at a crucial moment?

She heard the door open and the sound of Grace's voice as she spoke to the delivery guy. But then Grace screamed her name.

"Jillian!"

There was a dull *thwack*, as if a baseball bat had struck a bag of rice. Then a thud sounded.

Jillian's heart pounded hard as adrenaline flooded her system. Something was terribly wrong.

"Grace?" She started for the hallway to the front door, intent on helping her cousin. Grace might be the trained police officer, but if she was being attacked Jillian wasn't going to stand by and do nothing.

She reached the entrance to the hallway to see Grace curled up on the floor, a man standing over her. He looked up and Jillian caught sight of his face.

Randall.

Her stomach knotted as he smiled at her. "Hi, Jillian. Good to see you again."

She turned and dashed back into the living room, frantically looking for anything she could use as a weapon. Randall was blocking her only exit, but surely she could find something to use to defend herself.

His footsteps grew louder as he approached, his pace measured and deliberate, like every villain in a bad horror movie. It was almost enough to make her laugh, but this was real life. And her cousin was lying unconscious on the floor.

Desperate, she moved to stand by the tree. Before Randall walked into the room, she hid her phone behind her back, careful to stay near the branches so he couldn't see her arm. She located the button on the side of her phone and pressed it five times in rapid succession, activating the safety feature that automatically dialed 911.

Randall stood in the doorway to the room, glancing around. "Getting ready for winter, I see." He sounded so casual, as if he was a friend dropping by for a visit and not a man trying to make her life hell.

A small voice from her phone spoke as the dispatcher answered her call. Jillian began to talk, hoping Randall wouldn't notice.

"What do you want, Randall? Where is Baldwin?"

Randall shrugged as he stepped into the room. He was holding a tire iron, and a wave of nausea swept over her as he lifted it to rest on one shoulder. If he'd hit Grace in the head with that, she might very well be dead.

"Baldwin is fine. He sends his regards." Randall began a slow tour of the room, stopping every few steps to examine her things. Jillian began to move, as well, trying to keep as much distance between them.

"Did you kill Grace Colton?" She spoke loudly, hoping the dispatcher would catch her words.

Randall paused and frowned. "Why did you do that?"

"Do what?"

"Say her full name. Grace Colton. Why not just say Grace?"

Jillian tried to shrug but panic clawed up her throat as she watched Randall connect the dots. "Who are you speaking to, Jillian?" His voice was harsh now, and a dangerous gleam entered his eyes.

"N-no one," she stammered, but Randall began to walk toward her.

Knowing her time was short, Jillian yelled out her address as she tried to dodge him. "Randall Bowe is here!" she screamed. "Officer Grace Colton is down!"

Randall grabbed her arm and pried the phone from her hand, then threw it to the ground and stomped on it. The glass of the screen cracked, and plastic pieces shot out in all directions from under his boot.

He wrenched her arm behind her back in a painful twist, pulling her up against his chest. "That wasn't very nice," he snarled. "I only came here to talk."

"You're lying." Her voice trembled but she held his gaze, refusing to show weakness. "If all you wanted was a conversation, you wouldn't have hurt Grace."

"She was in my way," Randall replied. "I needed her to move."

"So you killed her?" A pang of guilt and grief stabbed her like a knife in the heart. Her cousin was dead, all because she'd asked her to come over tonight.

"She's not dead," Randall said dismissively. "At least, I don't think she is."

"And I'm supposed to trust your assessment?" Jillian shook her head. "No way."

"It doesn't matter." He tugged on her arm, forcing her to take a step or fall. "We're leaving."

"No." Jillian planted her feet, determined not to move. "I'm not going with you."

"I thought you might say that," Randall replied. "But you should know, I have your precious boyfriend bound and gagged and totally at my mercy. If you ever want to see him alive again, you'll come with me now."

Anguish washed over her as her imagination painted a picture from Randall's words. It was possible he was lying to her, preying on her emotions to get her to cooperate with him. That was definitely the kind of thing he would do.

But what if he wasn't? What if he really did have Baldwin tied up somewhere? If she antagonized Randall, she was risking his life. And with Grace already seriously hurt, Jillian didn't want another victim on her conscience.

"Why are you doing this?" she asked. She was trying to buy herself some time, but she also needed to know the truth.

"You know very well why," Randall said, his voice low and tight.

Jillian shook her head. "No, I don't. I've never understood why you targeted me. After your crimes were exposed, I figured you were trying to plant doubt about my abilities so that any irregularities would be dismissed, and if anyone ever suspected you, you could simply point the finger at me. But now that the truth is out and people know what you did, why are you still focused on me?"

She spied a flicker of movement over Randall's shoulder, coming from the direction of the hall to the door. Her breath caught in her throat—was that Grace?

No. It was Baldwin!

Jillian nearly sobbed with relief. He was here! And even though she could tell he'd been hurt, he was still alive.

He lifted his forefinger to his lips, telling her to

keep quiet. Jillian blinked in acknowledgment, resisting the urge to say his name.

Randall noticed her change in expression. He started to turn his head, so Jillian jerked against his grip to hold his attention. "Tell me!" she demanded.

"You lied to me," Randall barked. "I couldn't let you get away with it."

"What are you talking about?" She squirmed, trying to put distance between their bodies. Randall responded by wrenching her right arm up behind her back until she cried out in pain.

"I never lied to you," she spluttered, trying to find a position that would relieve the stress on her arm. If Randall moved it again, her bones would break.

"Yes, you did," he insisted. "I asked you out to dinner once, do you remember?"

He punctuated the question with a squeeze of her wrist. Jillian bit her bottom lip and nodded. "Yes," she said, her voice thick with tears.

"You turned me down."

Another squeeze, and this time he added a little tug to her already strained arm.

"I remember."

"You told me you had a boyfriend and that he was the jealous type. But that wasn't true, was it? You weren't dating anyone." He waited, and Jillian realized he expected her to respond.

"No," she said. "I wasn't."

"You cheated me, Jillian. You cheated me of the opportunity for us to spend time together, to get to know each other."

Jillian saw movement in her peripheral vision, but from this angle, she couldn't tell what was happening. All she knew was that the longer she kept Randall talking, the harder it would be for him to escape the police.

"So you decided to frame me for the robberies?" Since he was in a chatty mood, maybe she could get him to confess. Surely her lawyer could do something with that, even if Baldwin was the only witness.

Randall laughed, his breath hot on her cheek. "You made it so simple," he said. "It wasn't hard to break in here and lift some of your prints. Easier still to return and leave the jewelry. You work all the time, so it's not like you were ever home to catch me."

"So now what?" she asked. "Did you decide the courts weren't moving fast enough for you? Is that why you're here—to punish me for lying to you?"

"Something like that," he said. "Now move."

He swung her roughly around, apparently determined to shove her down the hall and out the door. But as soon as Randall turned around, he froze.

"Let her go."

Baldwin stood just inside the living room, feet planted in a shooter's stance, his gun pointed directly at Randall. Jillian noticed an officer standing a step to the side of him, also aiming a weapon at Randall.

He wrapped his arm around her neck in a loose choke hold, keeping her body between him and the guns. She heard a thud as the tire iron hit the floor, and then something small and hard was pressed into her ribs.

"Let's not be so hasty," Randall said. His muscles trembled against her, betraying his nerves. He was caught, but he wasn't ready to admit it just yet.

"Drop your weapon," the officer commanded.

"You must be new here," Randall sneered. "That's not how a hostage negotiation goes."

"What do you want?" Baldwin asked. His eyes were swollen and his face was red, but Jillian could tell he was looking at her, trying to determine if she was okay.

"I'm going to leave," Randall replied. "And you're going to let me."

He pushed her forward a step, testing them. When no one fired, he pushed her forward again. And again.

She stared at Baldwin as they drew closer, saw the uncertainty on his face. She could see he wanted to act, but he feared doing so would cause her to get hurt. So he waited, clearly hoping to find an opening.

The other officer adjusted his stance as they approached, obviously trying to find a better angle. But Randall maneuvered to keep her body in the line of fire as they haltingly made their way across the room.

Jillian's heart pounded as they walked closer to the hallway. She wasn't going to let Randall take her out of here tonight. If she struggled, he would shoot her, but at this point, she was willing to take her chances.

She just had to time it right.

Her eyes caught on the decorations on one of the end tables. Most of them were too flimsy to use as a weapon, but one candlestick stood tall and proud above the rest. It was solid wood, hand-carved by her great-grandfather on her mother's side and passed down through the generations.

It would have to do.

Jillian held her breath as they got closer to the table. If she moved too soon, Randall would see what she was trying to do and shoot her. If she waited too long, the opportunity would pass. She was only going to get one shot at this.

She stared hard at Baldwin, trying to communicate with him. But his eyes were so bloodshot she wasn't sure he could even see her. Still, she dropped her gaze to the table, then back to him. He nodded almost imperceptibly.

Message received.

They were coming up alongside the table. It was now or never.

Jillian grabbed the candlestick with her left hand, quickly drew it up as high as she could and then brought it down against Randall's knee. He shrieked in pain, temporarily loosening his grip on her neck. She jerked free of him, stumbling forward.

As soon as she was clear, a thunderous boom split the air and Randall screamed again. Jillian turned in time to see him fall to the floor, his hand clutching his shoulder as blood welled around his fingers.

An officer rushed forward to retrieve Randall's gun, then he ran his hands over Randall's body to ensure he wasn't hiding another weapon.

Baldwin stood in place, his gun still pointed at his brother. Jillian walked over to him and put her hand on his arm.

"It's over," she said, watching his face.

A storm of emotions swirled in those pale blue eyes. Pain, disappointment, betrayal. Maybe even a hint of guilt. Baldwin was clearly distraught, but Jillian couldn't help him just yet. She had to check on Grace first.

"Grace?" She stepped into the hallway to find another officer at Grace's side. Her cousin was sitting up, holding her head with her hand and wincing in pain.

"Are you okay?" Jillian dropped to her knees next to the other woman, relief making her want to cry.

"I will be," Grace replied. "I'm sorry he got past me. As soon as I recognized him he hit me with something and I went down."

"Don't apologize," Jillian said. She wrapped her arms around Grace in a gentle hug. "I was so afraid he'd killed you," she whispered, tears stinging her eyes.

"A Colton head is far too hard for that," Grace teased. "Now go to your man," she said. "He needs you."

EMTs and additional police arrived at her door. Jillian stood and walked back to the living room. Baldwin still hadn't moved. She took his arm and led him to the side of the room, making space for the medics and police to do their jobs. She dimly heard someone reciting Randall's rights and felt a huge weight lift off her shoulders as she realized he was being arrested.

It was all over. Randall was in custody.

"Hey." Jillian searched Baldwin's face, looking for some hint of his thoughts.

Baldwin glanced at her. "Are you okay?" His voice was thick with emotion and probably a little shock.

"I'm fine," she assured him. "More importantly, how are you?" He looked terrible, his eyes puffy and red, his lips a little swollen. She looked down the length of him and realized with a small shock that he wasn't wearing a shirt. "Where are your clothes?"

"Pepper spray," he said, as though that explained everything. "Randall ambushed me with it. Had to take off my shirt or it would keep affecting me."

"I see," she said. She didn't ask about what had happened after the pepper spray. There would be time for that later. Right now, all she wanted to do was hold him tightly until she no longer felt like falling apart. But as she studied him, she realized she had to keep it together a little bit longer. Baldwin's body was so tense she thought his muscles might snap. He was clearly on the edge, and it was up to her to bring him back.

"You shot him." It wasn't a question; he'd barely looked away from his brother since Randall had fallen to the floor.

"Had to," he said shortly. His voice was flat, but Jillian heard all the things he wasn't saying. By shooting his brother, he'd effectively ended any hope of a reconciliation with his parents. Baldwin was now a man without a family.

Jillian's heart ached for him, as she realized that he'd made the choice to save her life even though it had cost him dearly. He talked a good game about not needing his family, but she could tell that deep down, he still wished that things could be different between them. After seeing the way his parents had reacted to seeing him, and hearing their defense of Randall, Jillian knew they would never forgive Baldwin for what he'd done.

"You saved my life," she said, touching his shoulder. He didn't respond. Worry began to bubble in her stomach, growing more intense with each passing second. Baldwin was withdrawing before her eyes. If she couldn't reach him now, she'd lose him forever.

"And you saved his, too."

He turned to look at her then, his eyes glassy with unshed tears. "What did you say?" he asked.

"I said you saved your brother's life."

He blinked at her, clearly not believing her. She started speaking before he looked away again.

"You did, Baldwin. Anyone else would have shot Randall when they had the chance. He was armed and had taken me as a hostage. Police are trained to neutralize a threat in that kind of situation. But you pulled the trigger first, before the officer acted. And you made certain not to hit him in a vital area."

He pressed his lips together but didn't deny her words.

"I know you feel guilty about hurting your brother," she said, lowering her voice so that the other people in the room wouldn't overhear their conversation. "But better for you to hurt him than for him to wind up dead."

He looked away then, his eyes finding his brother. The medics had placed him on the gurney now and were preparing to wheel him out of the room. "Maybe," he muttered.

Just then, two uniformed officers approached. "Ms. Colton? Mr. Bowe? We need to take your statements, please."

Jillian went in one direction, Baldwin the other. It took a while, but she described everything that had happened and answered all of the officer's questions. While she talked, her condo slowly drained of people as Grace was loaded up by the medics and the other responding officers wrapped up their business.

Finally, the officer she was talking to finished questioning her. "Thanks for your time," he said, getting to his feet. "I'll be in touch over the next few days with some follow-up questions."

"That's fine," Jillian said automatically. She glanced around the room, expecting to find Baldwin still talking to the other officer.

He wasn't there.

He wasn't in the guest room, either. Or the bathroom, or the kitchen.

She was alone.

One week later

Baldwin pulled into a parking spot along Grave Gulch Boulevard and climbed out of his truck, then started walking across the street. The courthouse loomed large in front of him, the domed structure a tangible symbol of justice and the rule of law.

Today, at least, he knew justice would be served.

Jillian was inside right now, attending a hearing in which the DA was going to formally drop the charges against her. After Randall had been arrested, both Baldwin and the other officers at the scene had given statements about Randall's confession of framing Jillian. With so much evidence pointing at his brother, the case against Jillian had fallen apart. Bryce had called to let Baldwin know that today was the big day.

He found a spot outside the entrance to the courthouse, his stomach aflutter with nerves. Would Jillian be happy to see him? Or would she be angry with him for walking away without saying goodbye first?

He glanced around, taking note of the decorations hanging on the light poles up and down the street. The mayor had scheduled a celebratory parade to tout the hard work of the police department. Hopefully, the move would help restore relations between the GGPD and the community. He'd seen on the news that the protests had stopped after Randall had been brought into custody. With his brother due to stand trial in the New Year, confidence in the police department was at an all-time high.

Part of him felt proud to have been involved in bringing his brother in. Shooting Randall had been one of the hardest things he'd ever done, but at the same time, it was a bit cathartic. In that split second, he'd realized that his family and their issues were all part of his past. They were never going to be close, never going to have a loving, supportive relationship. If Baldwin kept clinging to that misguided hope, it would sink him emotionally. He had to let them go.

He'd pulled the trigger, drawing a line under that part of his life so he could move forward, into the future.

With Jillian.

If she'd still have him.

He shifted, scuffing at the ground with the toe of his boot. He hadn't meant to leave without saying goodbye. But he'd been so twisted up inside he'd had to get away from everyone, get some air. Clear his mind of the shock of the moment and take stock of what he wanted in his life. So he'd laid low for a few days, figuring it all out. He was tired of working underground. His bank balance reflected his client's satisfaction for a job well done, but Baldwin wanted more. He craved legitimacy, to work out in the open again.

To be with Jillian. He knew through the grapevine that she'd been reinstated as a CSI for the Grave Gulch Police Department. Her life was getting back to normal, which was what she'd wanted.

And as for him? He could keep working in the shadows. Maintain his underworld contacts, his growing roster of anonymous clients. But if he did that, he'd be subject to the rules of that lifestyle. In certain circles, he would be a target. Along with anyone he loved.

After everything that had happened here, it wasn't a risk he was willing to take.

Jillian had already been through too much. Baldwin couldn't ask her to be with him if he had painted a target on her back.

The front doors to the courthouse opened, and a small group of people started walking down the steps. He picked her out of the group immediately, his eyes drawn to her as if she was some magnetic force.

She walked alongside an older man—her attorney, most likely. Her sister, brother and parents trailed a few steps behind. They were all smiling, and he could tell even from this distance that a weight had been lifted off their shoulders.

They stopped at the bottom of the steps, and Jillian hugged the older man. He walked away, while she and her family turned and started moving in Baldwin's direction.

He didn't move from his spot by the tree until she'd walked past him.

"Jillian Colton," he called out.

She froze, then slowly turned around to face him. Her family stopped, but when Bryce saw him, he gestured to his sister and parents to keep walking. Baldwin nodded at him in a silent expression of gratitude.

Jillian eyed him up and down. "You came back." Her tone was neutral, betraying no hint of her emotions.

Baldwin's anxiety made his hands shake. He could face down a lethal sniper, lead a squad into battle and perform first aid on a wounded buddy while under heavy fire, but standing in front of this slender woman in broad daylight on a public street was enough to make him crack.

"I shouldn't have left like that."

She tilted her head to the side. "No," she agreed. "I deserved better than that."

It was the truth. He thought about making excuses, wondered how he could explain what had been going through his mind at the time. Instead, he opted for the simpler answer.

"You're right," he said. "I'm so sorry. I had to figure some things out, and I needed to be alone to do it."

"And did you?" she asked, sounding a little curious. "Figure it out, I mean?"

He took a step closer, hoping she'd tolerate his presence. "I think so," he said quietly.

Jillian nodded. "That's good." She looked down and swallowed hard, then glanced back up at him. "What are you doing in Grave Gulch again?"

"I have unfinished business here." He risked another step, wanting so badly to touch her. But, no, he had to earn that privilege again.

"I see." She discreetly swiped at her eye and he realized she was trying hard not to cry. "Then I imagine you'll be off again, going to work for another client in search of a bad guy?"

"No."

Her head jerked up at his response. "What?"

"I said no."

Confusion danced across her face, along with something else: hope.

"I…don't understand," she said slowly. "I thought

you loved your job. Are you taking a break or something?"

"Not exactly," he said, taking another step. "I found another job."

"Really? Doing what?" She was genuinely curious now and he resisted the temptation to smile.

"I'm going to be a private investigator," he said. "I start after the holidays."

Jillian nodded. "Good for you." A quick, sad smile flashed across her face. "I'm glad you're doing something different. I know you were good at being a bounty hunter, but now I don't have to worry about you living in the shadows."

He did smile then, touched by her admission that she worried about him still. "I haven't told you the best part," he said.

She lifted an eyebrow. "Oh? Well, don't keep me in suspense."

Baldwin took the final step, bringing him directly in front of her. They were now only a few inches apart, close enough that he could see the amber flecks in her brown eyes. "I'll be working with the Grave Gulch Police Department."

Jillian sucked in a breath, her eyes going wide. "Are you serious?"

Baldwin nodded. "Have I ever lied to you?"

She shook her head, her gaze warming as she looked at him. "No. You haven't."

His hands itched to touch her but he held himself back. She had to make the first move. He needed to be sure she really wanted this.

Wanted him.

"So that means…" She trailed off.

"I'll be living here. Working here."

"No taking off for parts unknown," she said.

"Not anymore," he replied.

"And that unfinished business?"

"It's you," he said. "It's us."

"So there's an 'us'?" she asked.

The question made his heart skip a beat. This was it, the moment he was going to put it all on the line. He was about to take the biggest risk of his life, with no guarantee of success.

"There is if you want it," he replied quietly.

Jillian studied him for a moment, clearly thinking it over. Just when he thought she'd decided to let him down, she nodded and a smile spread across her face.

"Yes," she said. "I'd like that very much."

She jumped into his arms, wrapping hers around his neck. He dipped his head to kiss her, joy spreading through him as he held her against him once more. He wasn't sure what he'd done to deserve this woman, but now that he had her, he was never going to let her go again.

Epilogue

End of January

"Are you sure you like it? Because we can always exchange it for a different one."

Jillian smiled at Baldwin, then looked down at the ring on her left hand. He'd proposed that morning as they'd sipped coffee together. She'd said yes before he could even finish the question, and they'd spent the morning making love and planning their future.

"Baldwin, it's perfect. I love it and I love you."

It was the truth. He'd chosen a beautiful ring, a square-shaped diamond solitaire channel set in white gold. The ring was smooth all over, with no protruding prongs to catch on her gloves while she worked.

Practical and romantic—a perfect reflection of the man himself.

"You won't hurt my feelings," he continued. "If you have something else in mind—"

She leaned over and kissed him, interrupting his ramblings. "No," she said firmly. "I have no intention of taking this ring off my finger. Now, are you ready to go inside?"

They were parked in the driveway of her mother's house—no, her parents' home, she reminded herself. Wes and her mother had been living together for some time now, but Jillian still slipped on occasion. She was doing better, though. They all were, especially Bryce. His relationship with Wes had deepened over the past few months. They could never regain the time they'd all lost, but at least they could move forward together.

"I'm ready," Baldwin said. "Let's go inside."

Her mother was hosting a family reunion of sorts, a party to celebrate the capture of Randall Bowe, and all the weddings, engagements and pregnancies that had happened over the past year.

She led Baldwin up to the house and walked in without bothering to knock. As soon as the door opened, she was hit with the soft buzz of conversation and the smell of her mother's sugar cookies. Her stomach growled loudly.

Baldwin suppressed a laugh. "No wonder you wanted to come inside," he teased her.

She took his hand. "Come on," she said. "Let's get some food and I'll introduce you to everyone."

It wasn't that simple, of course. As soon as they

were spotted, a cheer of greeting went up in the room. They stopped to talk to everyone on the way to the kitchen, starting with Melissa. She pulled Jillian in for a hug as Baldwin shook hands with Antonio, Melissa's husband.

"I told you it would all work out," Melissa whispered.

"You were right," Jillian said softly. "You always are."

Melissa released her with a smile. "Go get some food and then come back and say that louder so my husband can hear you."

Jillian laughed and moved down the line to greet Grace and Camden. "Doing okay?" she asked as she hugged her cousin.

"Never better," Grace replied. "Looks like I could say the same for you." She touched Jillian's left hand with a smile.

"You're the first one to notice," Jillian said quietly.

"I'll let you break the news," Grace said. "Your mother will be thrilled. She hasn't stopped talking about that nice young man from the hospital since you got shot."

Jillian laughed. "Where is she?" She glanced around but didn't see Verity in the mix.

Grace nodded her head toward the kitchen. "Hard at work, as usual. We've all offered to help, but only Soledad and Olivia are allowed in there right now."

"At least she's letting them assist her," Jillian replied. Verity was infamous for driving everyone out of her kitchen and insisting on preparing everything herself. Apparently, she'd decided the baker and restaurateur of the family were skilled enough to contribute.

She and Baldwin made their way through the room, stopping here and there as they went. She introduced him to the relatives he hadn't met before, and their significant others. He and her cousin Clarke immediately hit it off; no surprise, as Clarke was also a PI working with the GGPD.

She left them talking and slipped away to find her mother. She poked her head into the warm kitchen to find the older woman arranging cookies on a plate while Soledad and Olivia chatted as they placed hors d'oeuvres on a platter.

Verity glanced up as she walked in. "Jillian! You made it!"

She walked over to hug her mother, then greeted the other women. "Sorry we're late."

"Not at all. I'm just happy you're here now." She took Jillian's hands in her own and her eyes widened. "Honey, do I feel a ring?" She lifted Jillian's left hand and let out a whoop. "It is! Oh, my goodness, it's gorgeous! Where is that man?"

She dropped Jillian's hand and barged into the other room, loudly calling Baldwin's name. A hush fell over the group and Jillian stepped into the room to see her mother reach for Baldwin, pulling him down for a hug. He embraced Verity, looking around for her, clearly hoping for some kind of explanation for this rather public display of affection.

Verity released him and wiped her eyes. "I am so happy," she said, reaching up to touch his cheek.

Then she seemed to realize everyone was watching them. She glanced around and laughed. "Jillian, come here, honey."

Jillian walked forward to stand next to Baldwin, slipping her hand into his.

"They're engaged!" Verity announced, beaming with happiness and pride. "Isn't that wonderful! My baby is getting married!"

Everyone let out a cheer, and Wes, Bryce and Madison closed in to congratulate them.

As soon as her siblings stepped away, another round of family approached. The next few minutes were a blur of smiling faces, handshakes and hugs. After they'd spoken to everyone, Jillian took the opportunity to tug Baldwin into a quieter corner of the room.

"Doing okay?" she asked softly.

He nodded, looking a little shell-shocked. "I had no idea your family was this large," he confessed.

"It can be a lot to take in," she said. "Especially now that everyone has a partner. We've grown a lot in the past year."

"I don't know if I remember everyone's name." He sounded worried, as though he feared there might be some kind of test.

Jillian laughed. "Don't sweat it. You have the rest of your life to learn them all."

He leaned down to kiss her softly on the mouth. "I can't wait to get started."

Jillian wrapped her arms around him and rested her cheek against his chest, loving the solid feel of him. She could stand like this forever, holding Baldwin and basking in the glow of her family's happiness. They'd been through some dark times this year, but they'd all come through intact and together. In some ways, they were all better than ever.

She watched Antonio place his hand on Melissa's growing bump, smiled as Danny weaved through the crowd and felt a tug of longing as she saw her cousins Palmer with baby Lyra and Travis holding his newborn daughter.

"Someday," Baldwin said quietly, apparently reading her mind.

She looked up at him, needing to see his face. "Really?"

He nodded. "Yes. I want them. Do you?"

"Yes." Her smile grew until she feared her face would break. She did want to be a mother. But not right now. Still, knowing that she and Baldwin were on the same page gave her a sense of peace and reinforced her belief that they were meant to be together.

The sound of a fork hitting a glass rang through the room. Everyone focused on the center once more, where Wes and Verity stood together.

"Thank you all for coming today," Wes said. "It means a lot to have us all together again."

"We've lost some things over the past year," Verity said. "But as I look around, I see that this family has gained so much."

"Hear! Hear!" Geoff remarked, raising his glass.

Wes nodded at the older man. "With that in mind, we have one more announcement to make."

Verity smiled up at him. "We're going to be gaining another family member," she said. "Wes and I are getting married!"

"About time," shouted Frank, Verity's oldest brother.

Everyone laughed, and a new round of congratulations began.

Jillian and Baldwin were among the last to reach the happy couple. "Congratulations, Mom and Dad."

Wes teared up and pulled her in for a hug. "Thanks, baby," he said softly.

Verity wiped her eyes. "Who's hungry?" she called out. "I think it's time to eat." An affirmative noise rose up from the group and people started making their way into the dining room, where Verity had set up a table full of food.

Jillian and Baldwin hung back, letting the group move ahead. He glanced down at her. "I thought you were hungry?"

"I am," she said, smiling up at him. "But I'd rather be with you."

"You don't have to choose," he said, sliding his arm around her shoulders. "You're stuck with me forever now."

Her heart seemed to swell as they headed for the dining room. She was so happy in this moment it was a wonder she didn't burst with it.

"I'm counting on it," she said, slipping her arm around his waist. "Forever is exactly what I had in mind."

* * * * *

Check out the previous books in the thrilling Coltons of Grave Gulch series:

Colton's Dangerous Liaison *by Regan Black*
Colton's Killer Pursuit *by Tara Taylor Quinn*
Colton's Nursery Hideout *by Dana Nussio*
Colton Bullseye *by Geri Krotow*
Guarding Colton's Child *by Lara Lacombe*
Colton's Covert Witness *by Addison Fox*
Rescued by the Colton Cowboy *by Deborah Fletcher Mello*
Colton K-9 Target *by Justine Davis*
A Colton Internal Affair *by Jennifer D. Bokal*
Uncovering Colton's Family Secret *by Linda O. Johnston*
Agent Colton's Takedown *by Beverly Long*

All available now from Harlequin Romantic Suspense!

COMING NEXT MONTH FROM

HARLEQUIN

ROMANTIC SUSPENSE

#2167 COLTON'S PURSUIT OF JUSTICE

The Coltons of Colorado • by Marie Ferrarella

Caleb Colton has dedicated his life to righting his father's wrongs, but when Nadine Sutherland needs his help proving an oil company took advantage of her father, he wonders if his priorities haven't skewed. Will he be willing to open his heart to Nadine? And will she live long enough to make it matter?

#2168 CONARD COUNTY CONSPIRACY

Conard County: The Next Generation
by Rachel Lee

Widow Grace Hall experiences terrifying incidents at her isolated ranch: murdered sheep, arson, even attempted murder. Her late husband's best friend, Mitch Cantrell, is her greatest hope for protection. But the threat to Grace's life may be even closer than either of them believes...

#2169 UNDERCOVER K-9 COWBOY

Midnight Pass, Texas • by Addison Fox

The instant a rogue FBI agent wants to use Reynolds Station for a stakeout, Arden Reynolds is skeptical of his motives—and his fine physique. She knows attraction is dangerous, but allowing Ryder Durant into her home and her life could prove deadly.

#2170 PRISON BREAK HOSTAGE

Honor Bound • by Anna J. Stewart

When ER doctor Ashley McTavish stops to aid a bus crash, she finds herself taken hostage. Undercover federal agent Slade Palmer's investigation takes a dangerous turn when he vows to keep Ashley alive—even as he finds a new reason to survive himself.

When ER doctor Ashley McTavish stops to aid a bus crash, she finds herself taken hostage. Undercover federal agent Slade Palmer's investigation takes a dangerous turn when he vows to keep Ashley alive—even as he finds a new reason to survive himself.

Read on for a sneak preview of Prison Break Hostage, *the latest in Anna J. Stewart's Honor Bound series!*

"Sawyer?" Her voice sounded hoarse. She sat back on her heels and looked behind her. He was a fair distance away, moving more slowly than she'd have thought. Ashley shoved to her feet, her knees wobbling as she stepped back into the water and shouted for him. "You're almost there! Come on!" But he was gasping for air, and for a horrifying moment, he sank out of sight.

Panic seized her. It was pitch-black. Not even the moon cast light on this side of the shore. No homes nearby, no lights or guideposts. How would she ever find him?

But she would. He would not leave her like this. She would not lose him. Not now. She waded into the water, stumbled, nearly fell face-first, just as he surfaced. He took a moment to wretch, his hand clutching his side as he slowly moved toward her, water cascading from the bag on his hip.

HRSEXP0122A

"What is it?" She'd seen enough injuries to know something was seriously wrong. She wedged herself under his arm and helped him walk the rest of the way to dry land. "Where are you hurt?"

"Doesn't matter," he wheezed as he dropped to the ground. He leaned back, still pressing a hand to his side. Blood soaked through his shirt and onto his fingers. "I'll be fine in a minute. We need to get moving."

She dragged his shirt up, tried to examine the wound. "I can't see anything other than blood."

"I know." He covered her hand with his, squeezed her fingers. "Ashley, listen to me. Valeri left with Mouse and Olena, but he ordered Taras and Javi to stay behind. They're coming after me, Ashley."

"Us. They're coming after us. Let me—"

"No. It's me they want. Which means you're in even more danger than you were before. You need to go on alone. Now. While it's still dark."

"I'm not leaving you." She slung his arm over her shoulders and, with enough effort that her feet sank into the dirt, helped him up. He let out a sound that told her he was trying not to show how hurt he really was.

"You have to."

"Hey." She gave him a hard squeeze. "You aren't in any condition to argue with me. I am not leaving you, Sawyer Paxton. So be quiet and let's move."